Guardian Angel

To My Favorite Ballerina,
Thanks for your Support
Best Wishes
Joseph Pasquarosa 10/23/2021

P.S. Please do not judge me psychologically By the contents of the Novel!
Tubby

JOSEPH PASQUAROSA

First Edition

PAGE PUBLISHING, INC.
New York, NY

First originally published by Page Publishing, Inc. 2019

ISBN 978-1-64544-849-5 (Paperback)
ISBN 978-1-64544-850-1 (Digital)

Printed in the United States of America

CHAPTER 1

It was one o'clock in the morning, Saturday night going into Sunday, Easter Sunday, when plant engineering employee Harry Barker exited Guardian Angel Hospital in Parsippany, New Jersey, and headed for his favorite smoking spot. The hospital enforced a no-smoking policy on any of the grounds. This ban included the sidewalks surrounding the hospital, the parking lot, and even the employee's car in the parking lot. The injustice made Harry so angry, he wanted to smoke.

Harry labored as the boiler room attendant on the third shift, 11:00 p.m. to 7:00 a.m. Harry's routine included checking and logging all gauge readings and water levels, and generally maintaining the boilers. He'd held this position since he left the Navy eighteen years earlier. Plant engineering, he believed, was the department that kept the rest of the hospital operational. It housed the boilers, air handlers, water heaters, and steam makers that ran throughout the complex, protecting patient care and comfort, providing environmental safety, even creating steam for cleaning the different tools and equipment used in the operating rooms and emergency department. Realizing how important his job was in keeping the hospital with plenty of heat, hot water, and steam, Harry did not take his job lightly. A bonus for a veteran like Harry was the plant engineering uniforms. He liked them. Every day he would arrive at work with his dark blue pants and light blue shirt with "Plant Engineering" emblazoned on it

He had boiled his tasks down to a science. He'd perform the same routine daily. Upon arrival he made sure all the gauges were in the green zone indicating all was well: boiler check, 11:10 p.m.; water softener check, 11:50 p.m.; steam pressure check, 12:15 a.m.; air handler check, 12:50 a.m. Next, he'd turn on the faucet that protruded from the boiler and fill a beaker half full of water, then add three drops of a reagent and wait for the color to change. The water in the beaker turned blue: all clear. Had the reagent turned the water red, he would have placed a call to the head engineer to determine how much salt he needed to add to balance of the acidity in the water. He logged all his findings in the daily journal.

Harry often thought about how the hospital had grown, not just in Parsippany but the entire Guardian Angel Hospital System. Parsippany grew from a one-building, four-story hospital, to a four-building, four-stories-each hospital. Furthermore, they had been buying up the smaller, weaker hospitals every year, adding new hospitals to the system. He wondered if this growth would ever end. Right now it appeared the answer was no. None of his business, he thought. Let the suits figure it out.

Harry decided to take a break and go to the alleyway between the new emergency department entrance and plant engineering and have a smoke. The alley was Harry's oasis, quiet and peaceful, away from the loud noises he labored in. The spot was dark and deserted. Moss covered part of the ground and walls. The alley had not been used in years, and when they replaced the sidewalks, they bypassed the path leading to said alley, leaving it as a forgotten relic from a different age, not unlike Harry himself, he mused.

Harry remembered when this area was busy, very busy, bustling with foot traffic from the different departments that used the old entrance as a shortcut to the main hospital elevators. Since the hospital had become so big that all available space had been used for expansion and additions, the room that was left for employee parking got pushed further and further back. In between the employee parking lots and the main entrance that led to the different departments were sterile areas controlled by swipe cards: the emergency department, the operating suites, and trauma center, all off-limits to regular foot traffic. Employee cut-through was forbidden. So workers from every department—environmental, food service, even doctors and nurses—used the former entrance as a shortcut by way of plant engineering rather than walking around the building from the parking lots to the main entrance. For a while.

Harry gazed at the wall at the end of the alley where, in years past, the door led into plant engineering. When they upgraded the equipment with new boilers and air handers, the door fell from use and was nailed, barred, and covered over on the inside with Sheetrock. They sealed the door's exterior with a plain sheet of metal, without any doorknobs or handles. The steel sheet seemed to say, "No entry here, buddy. Keep walking." Others seemed to agree that the effect was too severe, and an order came down to plant forsythia bushes between the hospital building and the sidewalk. They grew high and full and finished concealing the location, especially now as they were blooming into their spring sparkle of golden yellow. For Harry it was the perfect covert spot. With no windows above and no traffic, it was the one place at the hospital where he could now enjoy a well-earned smoke.

Harry took the last drag, stamped out the cigarette on the pavement, and was about to slip the cigarette butt into his shirt pocket—no point in leaving evidence—when he heard the bushes rustle. Great, Harry thought. Now security would report him for smoking on the grounds. The streetlamp provided enough light for navigating to the alley and smoking, but not enough for Harry to see who was approaching him. As the person drew near, Harry realized it wasn't security. No uniform, no badge, just a shadowed figure running straight at him.

He backed up, but the wall stopped him as the stranger plunged a knife into Harry's throat, slicing through cartilage, veins, and arteries. It was done so fast and with such expertise that Harry did not have a chance to utter a word, let alone to call out. Harry felt the cool blade as the attacker drew it back out, and he felt the pavement hit him as he dropped to a sitting position against the wall and fell over on his side. He tried to make words, but all that came out was the gurgling breath escaping from his windpipe. He couldn't make out the intruder's face, but he could see the intruder shining a flashlight where the door had been. The intruder spat something that sounded like a curse, but not one that Harry had heard before. The last thing Harry heard was the slamming of a car door and the engine's roar as the car sped away from the hospital where, Harry thought as his final breath left him, some people get well at hospitals while others aren't so lucky.

CHAPTER 2

It was 3:00 a.m. when Guardian Angel Hospital Security Officer Jim Adamson, assigned to outside patrol and security, finished his tour of the annex buildings across from the hospital. He had driven to the annex, less than a mile from the hospital, turned doorknobs like a neighborhood cop to ensure they were locked properly, and then proceeded around the perimeter, checking that all was clear and secure. He was thinking of taking a coffee break but, looking at his watch, realized it was time to make the rounds of the main hospital, checking there to ensure all doors were locked and secured and that no one was causing any mischief. He left the patrol vehicle in the parking lot, swiped his ID card, then walked inside through the unmarked door and followed the hall, checking doors and scanning the grounds as he went: maternity, cardiac, emergency department, and plant engineering—all secure. He then walked outside and walked between the bushes and shined his flashlight down the alley. He spotted a shadowed figure lying on the pavement against the wall. Adamson figured it was a homeless person and walked down to wake him up. It happened occasionally; they would find this secluded spot to sleep until they were chased. When Adamson reached the body he nudged the homeless guy's leg.

"Come on, buddy, you can't sleep here. Get up and go to the mission shelter. The beds are clean and softer than the ground you're sleeping on."

He realized the guy was wearing a uniform. Maintenance? Plant engineering? Adamson shined his flashlight at the guy's face. He saw the blood both on the neck and all over the ground. Was the guy breathing? Adamson yelled into his radio, "I need help and a trauma team to the alley outside the old plant engineering door, stat! Victim is on the ground and bleeding badly." Then he dropped to his knees and tried to stop the bleeding when he realized it had stopped already.

"Oh, buddy," Adamson heard himself say. "I'm so sorry."

Minutes later, two patrol cars from the Parsippany Police joined the three officers from security and the trauma team in blue scrubs that had already responded to Adamson's request. Adamson observed them looking at the victim's identification badge and verifying the face matched the photo.

"Harry Barker, engineering," one of the cops read aloud, then scanned the faces. "Any of you know him?"

Shaking heads and shrugs. Who notices the guy from engineering?

Adamson heard one of the cops ask, "So, what's the official cause of death?" To Adamson, it seemed obvious.

One of the doctors responded, "Laceration to the neck. Looks like they missed the carotid, so he probably bled out. But the body will be brought to the morgue for a complete official autopsy."

Adamson stepped away and called in. "Three-eight-five to Security Command."

"Go ahead, Adamson."

"Pre…prelim cause of death is homicide."

"Aw, man! I'll wake him up. He'll tear my head off."

"I…" Adamson trailed off.

"Shit," Adamson heard the operator mutter, followed by the punching in of a phone number, ringing, and the raspy midnight voice of Security Director Thomas Shane.

"What?"

"Homicide at the old plant entrance, sir. Someone stabbed a guy from engineering."

"Goddamn it!" Shane muttered a few more things Adamson missed, then, "Call Nick Moore and have him meet me at security. Now!"

CHAPTER 3

Investigator Nick Moore tried to find the quickest route possible, jumping on Route 287 south, where the exit placed him one block from the hospital. He made a left, traveling east, and pulled into the hospital parking lot. He arrived at the hospital at 4:45 a.m. and wondered what had happened for the director to already beat him to the hospital and to have security call him in. Nick had a flashback to the phone ringing and waking Jen and him up, then hearing security tell him to meet the director at the hospital now and Jen starting to complain that it was Easter and they had plans. Nick remembered he promised to be home on time for their plans.

Nick ached for coffee. He'd thought these early emergency calls were over when he retired as a narcotics detective from the Essex County Sheriff's Office. Now that he was a corporate investigator for the Guardian Angel Hospital System, he didn't think anything would ever happen that was so important to have him come in immediately. Nick recalled that in his eight years as an investigator for the hospital this was the first time he was called in early by the director. Guardian Angel was the essence of corporate control, the flagship hospital, now, of a five-hospital system, and the state's largest trauma center. What could happen that they couldn't handle without him?

Director Shane's office was located in the security department on level B. The hospital was set up so that the ground floor was the first floor and all floors above the first floor were numbered. All levels below the first floor were lettered so that level A was directly below the first floor and level B was two levels down, then level C. Level D was the last level below the hospital, four levels below the first. Besides field offices for the director and Nick, the commander, captain, and lieutenant, level B was also the command center for security. The command center, with all the monitors, computers, and alarms, was enclosed in bulletproof glass on the top half of the walls and sat at the front of security department. The glass was used so the officer in the command center could see in any on the three possible directions of approach in the event of a hostile attack. The only way into the security department was with a swipe ID card that would unlock the door or to be buzzed in by the officer in the center. From the command center, the officer could stay in contact with the more than two dozen security officers on any given shift, also receive transmission from all the radios, computers, television cameras, and alarms, both fire and panic alarms as well as the "newborn" alarms in maternity, to prevent any kidnappings. Babies were an easy target. Two security officers and a lieutenant manned the command center, with a shift commander supervising every shift, making sure the helm was covered twenty-four hours a day, seven days a week, forever and ever, amen.

Nick was running down the stairs to level B when he heard the overhead paging system call for the hazardous material team to contact Security Director Thomas Shane. He swiped into security and saw it was a beehive of activity for this hour of the morning. Parsippany Police was reviewing reports, the phone was ringing constantly, and security was attempting to run the shift. Nick walked into Director Shane's office, who was on the phone. Shane yelled, "Well, fucking find out!" into the phone and slammed it down.

Shane, looking up at Nick's arrival, handed Nick the preliminary report and said, "It happened outside the hospital, near the old plant engineering door. His name was Harry Barker, he worked in the engineering department for the last eighteen years, and he was never a problem to anyone. Here's what doing your job gets you."

Nick perused the photos: throat lacerated, body drenched with thick crimson.

Nick knew Harry Barker and liked him. Humble and committed, Harry lived by the clock. He had to have been killed on break, which would be logged in his journal. Harry would never sneak out when he was supposed to be working.

Shane went on. "Parsippany Police were here and have already begun their investigation, I'd like you to work with them and see if you can come up with any answers on who would want to kill this man."

Nick scanned the preliminary report, then looked around the office and finally at Director Shane, dressed this early morning in jeans and a red Rutgers University sweatshirt. Nick thought how much older the director looked when dressed this way—the youthful informality highlighting his heavy, sagging frame and his thinning white hair—as though the suits he wore somehow concealed his age. Nick wondered how he didn't notice that before or that the director's office was drab and confined and, for obvious reasons, windowless. He knew this was the director's "field office," but it was a far cry from his posh wood-paneled office at corporate headquarters where Nick and the other investigators' offices were located. But this was where the action happened. There was a field office here for investigators' use, and this week it would be Nick's.

"Listen," Shane said. "There'll be people watching us, reporters, hospital administrators, board members. You don't have to tell them anything, but for God's sake, be polite. And if you have to be on camera, wear a tie. Can you manage that? They pay our salaries."

"You have six other guys who can glad-hand the trustees better than I can."

"Yeah," Shane said, grabbing his keys. "But I want answers."

Nick and Shane found Officer Jim Adamson, who had found the body. He was in the locker room on level B. He'd just come from the shower, his sandy hair dripping wet. He was sitting at the end of the bench that ran along a row of lockers, his back against a gray cinder block wall. He'd managed to pull on a pair of gray civilian slacks, but he was barefoot, shirtless, and staring into the distance.

Nick sat in front of him, breaking Adamson's stare. Adamson seemed to have trouble focusing on Nick's face. Normally Nick addressed officers by their last names. Anything else seemed disrespectful. But there was nothing normal here.

"Jim," Nick began. "I'm Nick."

"Investigator Moore!" Adamson said, consciousness breaking through the clouds.

"Yes. I want you to tell me what happened earlier."

Adamson sat up straight, almost at attention. He was checked out emotionally. Nick had seen it before. But mentally, he was hanging on.

He began, "I was performing my regular check at the far side of the hospital, and everything…everything was normal. Then I checked the old alley. See, the homeless tend to sleep there. I can't blame them. It's hidden since they planted the bushes in front of it. It's a safe spot." A vision jolted him. "Safe until tonight. Oh my God! Nick, sir, it was terrible. I thought I was waking up a homeless man, but when I shined the flashlight—I never saw that much blood." Adamson pulled himself together for a moment. "I called it in. Then I kneeled by him and attempted to admin—" He stopped short, braced himself and went on. "Administer first aid. I applied direct pressure. That's when I realized the bleeding had stopped." Whatever was holding Adamson together gave out. "His neck stopped bleeding, but the blood was all over him, the wall, the pavement. A dark red puddle shined as the light hit it. I administered CPR. I called for help while I was trying to help him. But it was too late! It was too late!"

Since the alley was at the other end of the hospital, Nick asked Adamson to drive him and the director around. "Can you do that?"

Adamson, in civilian clothes, drove Nick and Shane around the hospital. Nick was thinking how deceptive things could be. All seemed to be peaceful and quiet, yet a homicide had taken place not two hours ago. If Adamson hadn't scoped the alley, no one would have been the wiser except for poor Harry who was now dead.

They arrived at the back of the hospital. Nick, Adamson, and Shane went into the alley, now crowded with the Morris County Prosecutor's Office homicide squad along with two detectives of the Parsippany Police. One, Bill Ricks, spotted Nick and nodded almost imperceptibly. They were on separate teams, and anything that looked like friendship, or even trust, could make their own teams suspicious. The men broke huddle and loaded the body onto a gurney. The hazardous material team arrived, soaking up what blood they could with a composition similar to kitty litter, then power washing the area to ensure it was clean. By statute, they would all be required to share their results with Nick, but they'd leave out what they could.

Nick began to wonder what Harry Barker was doing back there. It was getting light out, and Nick noticed a cigarette butt, white and filterless, stamped with a tiny circle around the words "Great Smoke," on the pavement near where Harry's hand had been. It wasn't burning, nor had it been stamped out. Nick wondered why the cigarette butt was ignored and turned to one of the investigators, pointing to the butt, asked, "Are you gonna take that?"

Almost as an afterthought, the investigator picked it up and placed it in an envelope, then turned to Nick and sneered, "Thanks." Nick just shook his head, then looked at the old sealed door.

Nick asked Adamson to take him to the inside of the old entrance and show him where Harry worked.

"Call me later," Shane said, lumbering across the blacktop.

Adamson and Nick arrived in plant engineering. This was the heart of the services for the hospital. As far as the eye could see there were machines whizzing and whirling to make the hospital run. Nick could see by the shape of the wall where the door had been. There was a raised framework that stuck out from the wall, and it was layered with Sheetrock and shelves.

Nick said, "Take me to Harry's desk."

They found Harry's desk, a gray steel number, the quality used by men who don't spend much time at their desks, men like building superintendents and auto mechanics. Three photos in gold leaf frames all showed the same woman in different poses: standing in a field, holding a flower, smiling at the camera. Nick could imagine Harry sitting there, loving her, checking the clock to see when he could go home.

The city cops would be waking her about now.

Nick saw an unopened pack of Great Smoke filterless on the desk, the same brand as the cigarette butt he saw in the alley. Now Nick knew why Harry was out there; he was hiding out from the smoking ban, which didn't explain who had slit Harry's throat, or why.

Nick turned to Adamson, "The report said they found Harry with all his possessions on him. You were there. Is that right?"

"Yes, sir. Wallet. Security keys, private keys. ID badge. It wasn't a robbery. At least there's nothing to indicate that."

Nick went through the desk. Old reports. Nondairy creamer. Change. But didn't find any clues as to why someone would kill him. Nick found his nightly log: time check for the boiler check, 11:10 p.m.; water softener check, 11:50 p.m.; steam pressure check, 12:15 a.m.; air handler check, 12:50 a.m.; break, 1:00 a.m.

Nick stated, "Well, now we know he was on his break, having a cigarette since his meticulous record keeping says he took his break at one o'clock. I'll hang on to this and make a copy for the police. Can you run this back later?"

Adamson stated, "No problem, sir."

"Thanks."

Adamson's shock was settling into stern quietness. As they were driving back around the complex, Nick asked, "Did you know him?"

Adamson replied, "I saw him around, in the hallways, cafeteria. But no, I really didn't know him."

"How long have you been on the job?"

"Four years," Adamson replied. "No, this isn't my first corpse. First one that—"

Adamson stopped short of saying "died in my arms."

Adamson pulled the car up to the front entrance and shifted into park. Nick stepped out of the car and turned back. "You didn't do this, Adamson. You just witnessed it."

"Yes, sir." But Nick could tell Adamson was traumatized. Whether he'd get past it or not remained to be seen.

Nick went down to security and waved at the two officers and the lieutenant inside the command center. He walked over to the wall containing all the mailboxes for everyone in security. In his mailbox was a copy of Harry's human resources report. He stepped into the bunker that was the investigators' field office—four desks, chairs, phones, computers—and sat down to read the file.

Harry was never a problem. No disciplinary issues. High marks on all his reviews. The report stopped just short of saying "Loved by all who knew him." Nick grabbed the phone and dialed.

An operator answered. "Parsippany Police?"

"Nick Moore for Detective Bill Ricks."

He held for a fraction of a second before he heard the familiar voice answer, "Ricks!"

"Hello, Bill. Nick Moore here."

"Nick. Holy Christ, are you seeing this?"

"That's what I'm saying. Here we have a guy, well-liked, squeaky-clean, not a robbery, no motive, and yet here he is on a slab in our morgue."

Bill Ricks replied, "I know what you're saying. This makes no sense."

Nick said, "I found the victim's log. I'll make a copy for you. He was a detailed guy. Very precise. His log stated he went on break at one o'clock, and from the cigarettes found on his desk that matched the one at the scene. It's a good bet he was taking a smoke break."

Ricks responded, "Makes sense. We don't have much on this end yet. His wife says he didn't drink, do drugs, or gamble, and she didn't know anyone who wanted to hurt him. Maybe she's right. As far as she knew he didn't screw around. He was always home when he should be and never gave her any concern to be suspicious. We'll subpoena his phone records and any social media he may have used. Beyond that, they don't have any children, and neither he nor his wife has any siblings. Had. I'll let you know if we come up with anything."

Nick replied, "I'll let you know if we find anything on this end."

Nick hung up, flipped on the computer, logged in, and watched as each camera's title and location came on the screen: ambulatory care—no, B-level corridor—no, cafeteria—no, emergency room—no, emergency room entrance—*yes.* He clicked on the camera and knew instantly this was one of the cameras that might have recorded the incident. Nick marked down ER entrance, camera 2. He returned to the main menu and began to scroll: endo suite—no, engineering storeroom—no, engineering perimeter—*yes*. Nick clicked on the camera. He pressed the past segment button, filled in the date and time to 12:01 a.m. to 2:30 a.m., set which camera, ER entrance, camera 2, and waited until the system stated it was ready. There was only one problem with the system: there was no option to scroll segments in a controlled fast-forward. It was either total fast-forward or watch in real time. Nick figured he would try fast-forward, beginning from midnight.

A figure buzzed past the camera. Nick rewound it back halfway. Again, he started the video, and again, the figure buzzed by. He started the segment at midnight and watched it in real time. He had just begun when he spotted a truck in the driveway that led to the location. Nick watched a man exit the truck and approach the emergency entrance. He began to write down the time, counter number, and was about to call the director when he realized it was the newspaperman dropping off a bundle of newspapers. Still, he made a note to contact the driver to determine if he saw anything.

Nick wondered if he could do more at the corporate office. The director was instrumental in having the corporate offices at another location for a logical reason: if there ever was a problem at the hospital like a fire or flood, the major departments could continue to run unaffected from the off-site location. Every department that was needed in the event of a crisis had an office at the hospital and one at the corporate building. The hospital accommodations were spartan but functional. Nick's office at corporate sat on ground level with windows, carpeting, televisions, monitors, computers, and Etta, the administrative assistant. Nick and his colleague Al Stokes each had their own offices, a reward for years of hard work in cramped quarters in the pre-corporate days.

Nick called the *Daily Gazette* newspaper and asked for the dispatcher. A minute later a husky voice said, "Dispatch, can I help you?"

Nick replied, "Yes I work security at Guardian Angel Hospital, and I wanted to speak to the driver that delivers there, can you have him call Nick Moore?"

The dispatcher replied, "That would be Miguel. He should be back shortly from his route. What's the number?"

Nick gave him his cell number and thanked him. Five minutes later Miguel called.

Nick asked, "When you made your delivery to the back of the hospital today, did you see anything?"

Miguel replied, "No, there's nothing around at that time, just the occasional ambulance, but today, no, nothing."

Nick said, "Okay, thanks for calling back."

Al Stokes strode into the field office, an athletic man the same age as Nick. They shared a military and law enforcement background, but there the similarities ended. Al was a product of the projects in Orange, New Jersey, and was a perfect example of a black male setting goals to achieve the success and following through. He dressed smart, while Nick wore almost identical gray suits one day to the next, grateful for a dress code that didn't make him think about clothes. Al had a quick wit, while Nick seldom joked. Nick stood five-ten, solidly built in spite of midlife thickening. Al, at six feet two, was strong and agile. In spite of his years, anyone would find him a formidable adversary. Clean-shaven with close-cropped hair, he had the weathered good looks that women enjoyed. Nick always meant to be jealous of Al, but he never got around to it. In Nick's mind, Al was a street cop who rose through the ranks on merit and nothing but, and came to Guardian Angel Hospital System right after retirement. Al was from a big city like Nick and possessed the certain survival quality the other detectives from smaller cities didn't seem to possess. Furthermore, and probably most important to Nick, Al did not relive his career by telling old-time war stories of his days on the street.

Nick and Al hit it off from the first time they met and often consulted each other for an opinion about a job or help each other if needed.

"What did I miss?" Al asked.

Nick filled him in.

Al asked, "Who's investigating?"

Nick replied, "Bill Ricks is handling the case for Parsippany PD, and I'm reviewing video from two security cameras to see if they caught anything. Wanna help?"

Al sat on the desk next to Nick's and chimed on. Al fast-forwarded, saw something, rewound, slowed down, and saw it was an ambulance dropping off a patient. He hit fast-forward again and saw something flash by in the corner of the screen. He played it back and saw a dark-colored boxy car arrive, maybe an older model Honda or Toyota.

Al said, "I've got a dark-colored car entering the complex."

Nick looked at the screen and copied down the time: 1:15 a.m. "Let's see what was going on in the alley just then. Well, well. What's this?"

On Nick's screen they watched one blurry, shadowed image exit the car and head for the alley, while the driver remained in the car. Less than two minutes later, the individual from the alley jumped into the car and they left the area.

Nick said, "Call the IT department. Let's see if they can clean up this image, get us a better look at those faces."

Ten minutes later, Nick and Al were standing in the IT department feeling useless, as Lionel Carter—a computer technician and part-time photographer—manipulated the image with little success.

"The lighting sucks out there," he said.

Al said, "Next time we'll ask them to come in the afternoon."

"That's as good as I can get it. If I make it any bigger, the image falls apart. How many copies you need?"

Nick looked at the picture. The image was so grainy, it was hard to tell if the man in it was white or possibly Hispanic. Also, he appeared to have facial hair, but Nick was uncertain whether it was a beard or just shadows from the lighting. Looking at the car, Nick couldn't determine if the color was dark blue or black, but it appeared to be a Honda, late model.

Nick replied, "Better let me have ten and send me that segment of video."

Carter replied, "No problem. Be back in five."

Nick called Security Director Shane and told him what the camera revealed, and what it didn't. "A man, possibly Hispanic, exits a vehicle, an older model Honda, enters the alley and remains there for less than two minutes, reenters the car, and it speeds away."

Director Shane said, "Send me the segment and get it to Parsippany Police. Go home and have a nice Easter."

"No, I'm okay—"

"That's an order," Shane said. "I've presided over one too many divorces. Harry Barker's dead. We'll call you if anything comes up."

Al said, "Nick, go home. Happy Easter. I'll wait for the photos."

Nick headed up toward the exit, with the familiar feeling that he was forgetting something.

Chapter 4

Easter had fallen late this year. The sun was shining bright, the trees were beginning to bloom, and even to a retired police detective turned corporate investigator like Nick Moore, life seemed good. When Nick arrived at his sister's house at two thirty in the afternoon, his wife and kids were already there. When Nick's kids heard him arrive, they ran up to him yelling, "Happy Easter!" Nick Junior, fifteen, was telling him something about a ball game while Lilly, thirteen, tried to give him a hug, which Nick returned in a half-hearted way. Not because he didn't love his kids or wasn't happy to see them, it was that he kept on going over the case in his head trying to sort things out and seeing if he was remembering everything.

Nick's sister, Marlena, planned on dinner at three. As was usual for the holidays, Nick's wife Jen brought most of the food. Jen prepared a veritable Italian feast. Already on the table was a vast assortment of antipasti, both hot and cold, different dishes of hot and sweet peppers, egg frittatas with meat or without, and of course, baskets piled high with Italian bread. Jen was an Italian-American who still followed old world traditions and ideals and imparted these customs on all the people she came in contact with. This was Nick's second marriage. Nick's first wife Felicia, an operating room nurse, was killed in a traffic accident on the New Jersey Turnpike driving home from work. Both worked long hours, and they never had children. From the outside, it was as if the marriage had never happened. He bore the devastation in silence.

Jen was almost fifteen years younger than Nick. Jen stood five feet, two inches tall, slim, with a great figure, brown hair, and blue eyes. Blue eyes was a trait in her family. Her mother, father, and grandparents had blue eyes. Yet both their kids had brown eyes like Nick, something Jen never let him forget.

Jen was the head chef at this feast, giving orders and tasting everyone's contribution, in spite of the fact that the event wasn't happening under Jen's roof. The table burst with the first of what was to be four courses: ravioli and gravy meat, salad, then roast turkey and ham with all the trimmings, and roasted chestnuts, fruit, and Italian pastries.

Nick couldn't help but spy on his own kids, Nick Junior and Lilly, as they interacted with the explosion of aunts and cousins. The kids were well-adjusted, anyone could see that. They mixed well, did well in school, and in their social lives. Nick took no credit for this. He attributed it to Jen who, through most of the children's lives, was both the mother and father figure while Nick worked long hours, many weekends, and some holidays. He had promised things would be different when he retired from the force. They were different, all right. Nick puttered around the house, got antsy, and grumbly, and it wasn't long before a consensus developed that he should get a job.

Jen liked being a stay-at-home mom. She was conservative in every aspect of her life, including, to Nick's ongoing dismay, in the bedroom. Nick kept thinking of different ways to spice things up, but Jen would always say no or tell him he was perverted. One thing Nick did know was that Jen, without doubt, was the best possible mother for his children. For this reason he adjusted to her and in his own way loved her. Jen never wanted to know about Nick's work or why he was sometimes so emotionally drained. Nick would have liked nothing better than to tell her of the dangers he faced, the day's stresses and traumas. But Jen got too nervous for such conversations. No one could listen to the confessions of a cop, except another cop. Still they'd been dating since about a year after Felicia's death. For better or worse, they both knew they were in for the long haul. Nick could have done far worse.

Marlena called the family in for dinner, saying with a slight touch of exasperation, "Now look for your name tag on the plate as Jen has graciously made them for us."

The entire family sat down at the dinner table, and Nick's cell phone began to ring. Caller ID read "Director Shane."

Jen didn't plead, didn't reprimand. She just said his name, "Nick," as if to remind him who he was.

"I'm sorry," he said, stepping away from the table's sudden silence. "Yeah."

Shane said, "Sorry to get you on Easter Sunday."

"It's fine," Nick lied.

"There were two suspicious people attempting to gain entry to the hospital. They gave security the slip. They could still be in the hospital for all we know. Stokes is at Parsippany PD attempting to chase down that Honda. So…"

Nick had the option of passing this off. But since it was Easter he decided he would go. It would have been petty to send some underling.

"I'll be there in ten," he said. Then he walked back into the dining room, sat, and tentatively reached for the ravioli.

Jen dropped her fork. "Go," she said. "Just go."

He said, "I'm sorry, everyone. I'll try to make it back before dessert."

Jen was always trying to keep her anger in check in moments like this. She wanted him to have a job, but a *normal* job, one where he didn't get called in at midnight or on holidays. For Nick, there was no normal job.

But she knew the risks. Anytime they said goodbye could be the last. And she wouldn't let their last moment be one of anger. Jen grabbed his hand. "Be careful."

With his stomach hurting from hunger he grabbed a piece of bread and walked. His sister caught up with him at the door.

"You know what happens to married men your age when they suddenly become single," she said, "when they get widowed or, you know, divorced?"

"What?"

"They die," she said. "They just drop dead."

He found his car and drove to the hospital.

Nick began thinking, as he was driving, that when he started the job eight years back, he learned fast that Guardian Angel Hospital prided itself on being the "friendly hospital," with all departments touting customer satisfaction along with quality care that a patient would receive. In order to accomplish this, patients were encouraged to visit the hospital before their procedure—whether it was delivering a baby, replacing a heart valve, or inserting a stent—to see where they would be staying. A concierge showed off the newly remodeled suites. Furthermore, visiting hours extended from eight o'clock in the morning to ten o'clock in the evening. And, as with any large business, Guardian Angel Hospital boasted four billion dollars in reserve funds, and relied on good press, social media, and word of mouth for attracting patients to their facilities. The maternity department, for one, was always conducting tours and classes for expectant mothers and their significant others. You couldn't assume the significant other was a husband anymore. Nick thought, and just as fast realized he was thinking like an old person ("Why, in my day..."). The new approaches were motivated by more than sensitivity. Since the hospital built the new neonatal intensive care unit that attached to maternity, accounting saw a 39 percent increase in deliveries at the hospital. This was, by far, the largest percentage increase in the hospital's business and made maternity the busiest department.

Good PR was good business. And in his own way, Nick was part of that.

As he approached the entrance to the hospital parking lot, Nick recalled that on Mondays and Wednesdays, the maternity department assembled groups of five couples—five pregnant moms and five nervous "others"—and conducted tours of the department every hour from 9:00 a.m. to 4:00 p.m. The coordinators of the different units would explain every facet of the labor and delivery process to the expectant parents, everything they'd experience from arrival at the hospital to departure a scant two days later with their new baby. This was always an educational experience for the couples who attend and very comforting. If a couple couldn't make the scheduled tour, arrangements would be made for an off-hour tour. Though the hospital flexed to accommodate a new patient, no one would be allowed a special tour upon arriving at the hospital without previous arrangements being made.

This policy was a contribution from Nick's department. The hospital went to great lengths to ensure no intruders breach the security in place. Yet today a suspicious couple had done just that.

Chapter 5

Nick parked in the patient pickup area and ran up the stairs, still hoping to put this event to bed and return to the family dinner before it was over. As he approached the security desk, Security Officer Jacob York jumped up from his chair, saying, "Investigator Moore, can I help you?"

Nick replied, "York, is Adamson here today?"

"Yes, sir. I was just here relieving him. We're shorthanded as usual for the holiday."

Nick spotted Adamson walking toward them. He had shaved and put on a clean uniform, but Nick guessed the man hadn't slept. Nick said, "Adamson, don't you ever go home?"

Adamson answered, "I could say the same for you, Sir."

"Fill me in."

"A couple came in and told the duty guard they wanted to tour the maternity department. I was standing right here. They said they had an appointment. They looked kind of…"

"Go ahead," Nick said.

"I don't want to profile."

"Profile?" Nick asked.

"They looked kind of…Middle Eastern."

Nick respected the integrity behind the kid's hesitance. "Middle Eastern could mean Israeli."

"Okay," Adamson said. "Middle Eastern, *not* Israeli. Swarthy?"

"Got it," Nick said.

Adamson went on, "I knew something was wrong. I told the couple to have a seat in the lobby and I would call the appropriate department."

The lobby to the right of the security desk was furnished with plush couches and chairs and glass tables. It looked more like someone's living room than a hospital lobby.

Adamson stated, "I radioed security command and asked for a supervisor who notified Director Shane and the nurse administrator. Then I approached the couple and stated that someone would be with them shortly. No one would schedule a tour on a Sunday, let alone on Easter Sunday late in the afternoon."

It was highly suspicious, Nick thought. Like attacking Israel on Yom Kippur.

Adamson went on, "As I walked back to the desk, I decided to stand a few feet away from my chair in order to observe the couple until the supervisor arrived. Then, as I turned back to face the couple, I saw they were gone."

Adamson continued, "I ran outside, but they'd vanished. There must have been a car waiting for them. I radioed the command center that they'd left."

Nick thanked Adamson and ran down the steps to security on the B level where he was briefed again by the shift commander. Nick asked, "Has anyone reviewed the security video?"

The shift commander said, "We were just about to."

Nick suggested, "While we're at it, security should be tightened at maternity."

The shift commander agreed then said to the lieutenant, "Double up at maternity. Furthermore, all officers at the hospital exits as of now are on high alert and must report in immediately if they spot the couple."

The lieutenant left to deploy the officers.

Nick sat down at the desk and rewound the tape to the point where the couple approached the desk. They were swarthy, all right. Both around forty. And if she was still having babies, they didn't seem like the kind of couple to tour a hospital first, or necessarily even see a doctor. Nick hit play. Everyone in the command center watched intently as the couple went to sit down. Now in plain view of the camera, now out of view. Nick switched cameras and again hit rewind to the time that corresponded to the other video. At this point, Nick watched the couple go into the lobby and sit. Then Adamson approached them for a very brief conversation. Nick saw that as Adamson walked away, the couple got up and began to move. As another camera was reviewed, the male could be seen leading the female behind a cardboard advertisement that was as large as a room divider. Once behind the display, the couple virtually circled Officer Adamson out of his view and then headed for the stairway. Nick then switched cameras in order to bring up the lab camera, and the covert closet camera, on a split screen in real time.

Nick, getting impatient not spotting the couple on film, got up and spoke to the shift commander, stating, "If anybody spots this couple, retain them. Assume them to be armed and dangerous."

Nick had just about finished talking when the desk officer who was scanning all cameras yelled, "Look, I found them."

Everyone saw the couple was now at the lab taking photos of the entire floor, where the elevators and stairs were located, and the exit nearest to the lab. As the commander barked out orders for security to respond to the lab, Nick was already on his way. He removed his .38 Colt Detective Special five-shot revolver from his ankle holster and ran down the corridor. It infuriated Nick, but hospital policy only approved ankle holsters so the patients and public could not observe firearms on the investigators. It was another case of diplomacy trumping safety.

Nick was not going to the lab. Instead, weapon in hand, he headed for the exit he thought they would use, the employee exit by the boiler room. As Nick rounded the last corridor before the exit, he spotted them. By the time Nick reached the exit they were gone, out the door, and into a black older model Honda that was waiting for them outside the door. The same Honda. As they sped away, Nick began to chase after the car in a futile attempt to catch up to it. There were cars everywhere, and people walking through the lot. He couldn't get a clean shot. His heart pounded. He tried to make out the license plate, but didn't see it. Something was happening, he wasn't sure what, but he knew that a sinister plan was afoot and that two terrorists in the black Honda got away and he couldn't even get the license plate. He stopped, winded, near the parking lot exit. He leaned his hands on his knees and tried to catch his breath. They had taken photos and got away with it, photos that could facilitate an attack and this despite all the cameras, security officers, investigators, and police.

When he got his wind, Nick called the shift commander on his cell. "Call Parsippany police," he wheezed, on the slim chance of apprehending the vehicle. "It was a dark gray Honda, I think a Civic. Midnineties." Nick slowly turned and headed back to the blood lab, realizing again how hungry he was, and that he'd barely eaten the entire day. Nick then got a flashback of the car he saw on the tape Friday night when employee Harry Barker was killed. Nick thought it may have been the same car. He couldn't be sure. But it didn't feel like a coincidence.

Nick returned to security and met up with Al Stokes and Director Shane, as they sat in the director's field office and began discussing what had transpired.

The director was the first to speak, "Okay, so we got a couple that comes in on Easter Sunday and states they have made an appointment for a tour."

Al Stokes said, "Then, knowing they would be found out, gives security the slip and heads to the lab where they take photos."

Nick then responds, "When they are done, they head to an employee exit, jump in a car, and make a clean getaway."

Al asked, "Why the lab? What are they interested in there? You think it has to do with Harry's death?"

Nick replied, "Don't know. It doesn't feel right, but there's a connection. I think Al and I should head down there and talk to the manager and the employees to see if they saw or heard anything."

Shane spoke in a whisper almost to himself. "Is it possible? Could they know what's down there?"

Chapter 6

On their way to the lab where they last saw the couple, Al said, "Nick, I don't see this as part of the Harry Barker investigation. What is there to gain by a couple heading to the lab? Are they stealing specimens?"

Nick replied, "I agree. I can't think of any possible motive for the killer or his henchmen to return to the hospital."

Al questioned, "Any ideas?"

Nick answered, "If someone sent that couple to take photos, it could only be a scouting party surveying the structure and security for resistance. This had to be a small part of plans getting ready to be implemented. What the plans are, we don't know."

Al asked, "What the hell is so special about this place? Why take out a place full of sick people?"

Nick was about to answer, "Beats me!" but the corridor was busy with hospital personnel and visitors. When they turned the next corridor it was much less crowded and the logical answer came to him. "Fuck."

"What?" Al asked. Nick didn't answer right away. "What?!"

Nick answered, "For the sheer terror of it. They hit the hospital along with a target, and now there's nowhere to take the injured. Or the dead."

Nick realized, as the words came out of his mouth, that this was way bigger than a single random killing.

When Nick and Al arrived at the lab they walked through an unlocked door in the override position that was always supposed to be secured. Guardian Angel Hospital System spent an enormous amount of money to install and maintain self-locking doors that require proper identification cards in order to access the room. These locks were not intended to be in the override position so as to give access to anyone and defeating the whole purpose. Nick and Al silently made their way through another door and into the room with a radiation warning and a "Keep Out" sign. There was no immediate threat of radiation as the isotopes were encased in a protective shell; however, only authorized personnel should be in the room who are trained if an emergency occurred and the door automatically locked. During the walk through the lab, Nick counted twenty-two workers in the two rooms who neither questioned them nor looked at them. Nick and Al then went to meet with Lab Manager Linda Patel. They knocked and entered.

Nick showed her the photo. "This couple penetrated the security of the hospital, and were taking photographs of the lab. When we attempted to stop them, they exited the hospital and got away. They penetrated the room that contains the 'Keep Out' sign because the card-reader doors were in the override position. Furthermore, we just walked through two rooms and the 'Keep Out' room, counted twenty-two of your employees, and not one stopped us, questioned us, or even looked up at us." Nick continued, "We want to interview all the workers. We will start with the individuals in this room, then continue with the employees in the second room. I want to find out if they heard or saw something that will lead me to their motive for this incident."

Al said, "All the more reason for the doors to be secured at all times and the personnel to report to security anything that seems out of the ordinary."

Al added, "This is for their safety as well as the safety of the hospital. Tell them to be selfish, look out for themselves."

Nick said, "Let's begin the interviews."

Nick and Al sat at opposite ends of the conference room table. It looked like a dozen other conference rooms he used throughout the hospital—a twenty-foot-long table, chairs, television, and hookups for various electronic equipment. Moments later, the first employee timidly walked in and, at Nick's prompting, sat down. Asian female, short, stout, approximately forty-five years old, with dark black hair. She considered the layout of the room, Nick and Al each at one end of the table, and sat in the middle, swinging her focus from end to end, as if afraid to take her eyes off either of them.

Nick said, "Hi, I'm Nick Moore from corporate investigations, and we're here to ask the employees working in the lab some questions."

The woman stated, "I'm Rose Chow."

Nick began, "Rose, today we had intruders in the hospital, who entered under false pretenses, breached security, and were eventually spotted taking photos in and around this lab. This would be highly suspicious under any circumstances. But the way they appeared really raised security's concern and brought us here. Do you understand?"

Rose replied, "Yes."

Nick responded, "Good, then I want to ask you, did you see anyone in or around the lab that looked like this?" Nick produced a still photo of the couple, printed from the video segment of the incident.

Rose took the photo in her hand, studied it, returned it to Nick, and replied, "No, I did not see this couple before."

Nick said, "They walked through the lab, past you. Did you hear them say anything?"

Rose stated, "I told you, I didn't see them. I didn't hear anything."

Nick replied, "Okay, thank you, Rose. Please keep your eyes and ears open and report to security anything that you see out of the ordinary."

Rose got up and left without answering or saying goodbye.

"Very helpful," Al said. "And not at all suspicious."

The next person to arrive for Nick was employee Derick Smith.

Nick asked, "Derick, did you see a couple walk through the lab or hear anything?"

Smith replied, "No, sir. I didn't see anything. You know we're very busy down here in the lab."

Nick replied, "Yes, I know. Please keep your eyes and ears open and let us know if you see anything."

He then handed Derick his card as the man got up and left the room.

As Nick and Al interviewed the remainder of the workers, they saw a pattern developing in their answers that Nick and Al didn't like. They all claimed they were too busy and never saw anyone enter or leave the lab. Further, most told Nick they sit in a cubicle with their eyes looking into a microscope and not into the hallways.

Al went to find Patel in the lab and brought her to the conference room.

Nick said, "Ms. Patel, we finished our interviews, and believe it or not, twenty-two employees in the two labs saw or heard nothing. I know it's a busy place, and all the other departments, operating rooms, and emergency are all looking for results ASAP, but I find it difficult to believe that not one person saw anything."

Patel answered, "We all have our jobs to do. Ours is running the lab, and security's job is to look out for couples that shouldn't be here."

Nick didn't get angry at Ms. Patel. In fact, it was a sad feeling that overcame him. A feeling of doom that something was going to happen and no one cared. Nick now understood how the couple was not reported to security. No one noticed or stopped them. No one felt it was their job. Everyone thought that another person would do it. Or they figured someone knew better than they did. Why make waves?

Back at the security command center, Nick began to question the shift commander about overriding the doors with swipe cards. Detective Ricks had arrived and joined them.

Ricks asked, "Is it easy to override the swipe card doors so the employees can leave the door open?"

Nick replied, "It's not so easy. Every manager is provided a code that allows them to override the system in the event of repairs, painting, cleaning, and so forth where there would be a lot of traffic that are not assigned to the unit. However, they are required to report this to security before doing so. If the manager did not override the system, the crew would have to be buzzed in each time they came to the door. With the override on they can come and go, bring equipment, or take out old equipment, without the need of bothering anyone."

Ricks asked, "If a door is placed in the override position, does a report generate in security?"

The shift commander replied, "No, it doesn't, but that would be a terrific way to keep track of all the doors and which have been overridden."

Ricks asked, "If a call is placed to security reporting an override, what happens?"

Nick responded, "The security officer is required to both log it into the shift logbook and then note it on the electronic report they make each shift."

"Has there been any reports for the lab door to be placed in the override position?" Nick asked.

After looking in the logbook then checking the electronic computer log the shift commander replied, "No, no door has been reported in override for the past seventy-two hours."

Nick thanked him, then he, Detective Ricks, and Al went to report their findings to Director Shane, knowing the deficiencies in security he reported would be corrected immediately by the director, and the suggestion for a new override report would be implemented. When they arrived, the director was examining blueprints of the hospital.

He turned to them, saying, "Look at this. The couple entered the main entrance, circumvented our security, took these stairs, and arrived on D level. Then they navigated the entire floor to arrive at the lab situated at the other end of the hospital."

Nick couldn't comprehend how they did it. Looking at the blueprints was confusing enough, and yet they know how to transverse the floors. He kept wondering about this but couldn't think of an answer. Nick brought up the security deficiencies regarding the lab and swipe doors, and the director wrote everything down.

Detective Ricks said, "Let's walk down to the lab, so I can see what we're all talking about."

When they arrived at the lab, all the doors were locked and Manager Patel came out to greet them. Nick introduced Detective

Ricks, who asked, "Why would a couple go through this much trouble to take pictures of a lab?" Manager Patel answered, "If you are looking for the reason that couple was taking pictures down here I can tell you. It's because the 'Keep Out' room houses the blood irradiator."

Ricks asked, "What is a blood irradiator?"

Patel said, "The blood irradiator is the size of a freestanding copy machine. The purpose of the machine was to cleanse the blood of patients who were diagnosed with different pathogens in their blood. The blood would be hooked up to the machine, and it cleansed it as it passed through the chamber containing a radioactive core. The core is highly radioactive made of compressed cesium 137 chloride powder contained in a doubled stainless-steel container. Whether these blood pathogens were viral, biological, or living organisms, the irradiator would purify the blood by destroying them so that it could then be replaced in the patient now pathogen free and radioactive free. This nuclear material can produce enough radiation to cause extensive damage if it was uncontained."

"So, I can get clean blood without risking a transfusion," Al suggested.

Patel said, "That's one consideration, yes."

Nick asked, "How much radioactive material are we talking about?"

Patel said, "It's only the size of an adult thumb but has enough radiation to damage the entire hospital and surrounding area if exposed. The Nuclear Regulatory Commission has very strict rules on how it is to be stored in its own room with alarms, motion sensors, and video camera surveillance."

Patel continued, "The irradiator was just recently moved when the lab was completely reorganized, and the problems it caused between the alarm company, the motion-sensor company, and the new steel walls that encased the device was just a pain for all."

This knowledge was not readily accessible to employees, let alone the general public or possibly potential terrorists, Nick thought.

Things were starting to click in Nick's mind.

Nick left the hospital and returned to his car. Glancing at the dashboard clock, he noticed it was 9:00 p.m. It was too late to return to his sister Marlena's house, so he went home. On the stove, as she'd done a thousand times before, Jen had left his dinner wrapped in aluminum foil. Nick realized he was no longer hungry. He put the food in the refrigerator, walked into the living room where Jennifer was watching television, kissed her, and said he was going downstairs. She didn't give him a look.

His man cave was nothing more than a television room in the basement. No one used it but Nick, who furnished it himself: portable stocked bar, two leather reclining chairs, and a television. The walls were decorated with all the awards, commendations, and honors Nick received throughout his career. He only displayed the important ones, which took all the area, and left the rest of the numerous awards in the cardboard box.

Nick poured himself two fingers of twelve-year-old Scotch, settled into the leather chair, sipped his drink, and pondered what had transpired. First, someone killed an employee, who, by the looks of it, didn't have an enemy in the world. Then, a couple gained entry to the hospital by subverting the security officer. Next, they gained entry to the lab and took photos of the irradiator, exits, hallways, and elevators. Finally, they exited through a door they had no business of knowing even existed and made their getaway in a car that was waiting for them, on the other side of the building from where they entered. Furthermore, Nick was almost sure it was the same car as the one he saw on the tape from Friday when employee Harry Barker was killed. He finished his drink, turned off the light, and headed upstairs.

While washing his face, Nick had a terrifying idea. The intruders had to have inside information! Someone on the inside was helping them. The couple moved too fast as if secure in the knowledge of where they were going. The hospital was a big behemoth that kept changing on a monthly basis. There was no guarantee that where the lab was last month was where it would be this month. As the hospital continued to grow, different departments were moved to aid the health-care workers for the ease in accessing the department that they used the most. Nick slipped into bed and curled next to Jen. Nick remembered that Patel told him the irradiator was just recently moved when the lab was completely reorganized, and the problems it caused between the alarm company, the motion-sensor company, and the new steel walls that encased the device, which was all confidential information. Nick knew he had to tell Shane. He could call Shane now, but he was so tired. He felt himself drifting off to sleep.

CHAPTER 7

It was barely seven thirty the next morning when Nick arrived at the hospital. He met Al Stokes in the hallway, and together they went to security. Director Shane wasn't in yet, so Nick had time before the eight o'clock meeting. He and Al grabbed coffee from the break room. Nick swallowed it as fast as he could. Nick was the first to admit that no security system was impenetrable. The system at Guardian Angel was better than most. It consisted of 480 cameras throughout the hospital, 257 doors to sensitive areas that could not be accessed without an identification card, and panic alarms throughout the hospital wherever money or drugs were present as well as the emergency department and behavioral health. Playbacks could be accessed by an authorized security employee's computer or the command center. And yet the hospital was being penetrated and navigated as if there were no security presence at all.

As he and Al exited the stairway on B level where the security department was located, Nick realized his suspicions were correct. He himself had to pass a security officer, swipe in for the secure hallway, then punch in a code to unlock another door. An intruder or intruders could only manage to navigate the labyrinth of corridors so successfully with inside help. Employees who walked the hallways every day often got lost, sometimes walking into a dead end, and at other times seemed to go in circles. When Nick first began working at the hospital he compared the maze of hallways as confusing as trying to navigate the streets of Venice, Italy, on foot. Nick and Jen had honeymooned there. In Venice, walkways just dead-ended at canals, and you had to keep retracing your steps. The hospital was the same way, with corridors blocked off by walls that were constructed seemingly overnight. Nick realized that someone was giving the intruders information, specific information they were trying and testing. Whoever was giving the information, it appeared to Nick that the receivers of it were then testing the information for accuracy. The security breaches Nick found himself investigating were happening with more frequency—the couple entering the hospital and taking photos of sensitive areas, and poor Harry getting killed. Nick didn't know how, but he was ready to bet they were linked.

Shane's secretary waved Nick and Al past her, and Nick stepped through the door, stopping short when he saw two people—a man and a woman—talking with the director.

"Sorry," Nick said. "We'll wait in the hall."

He was about to walk out when the director said, "Guys, come in. I want to introduce you to CIA agents John Smallwood and Phyllis Grazie."

Nick reached out his hand as Smallwood did, introduced himself, and noticed the handshake was strong. Nick noticed that Smallwood was maybe ten years Nick's junior, slim and athletic as though he spent all his free time jogging. Nick then turned to shake the woman's hand and, for some reason that he could not understand, did not want to let it go. Nick was not the type to be flirtatious and usually would rather draw back during an introduction, so this was completely out of character. As Nick looked her over he found her to be attractive, young—he guessed thirty-three—with long brown hair, but it was her captivating big blue eyes that he found himself lost in. He let go of her hand and felt himself turn red as he took a seat. Al shook their hands. Agent Grazie gave a smile. Had Grazie paid attention, she would have noticed the look on Agent John Smallwood's face. His square jaw and tiny eyes seemed to dominate his face. While Nick was captivated by Grazie, Agent Smallwood was seething, his face flushed with jealousy and anger directed at the attention Nick was paying to her. Nick noticed this reaction and quickly took a seat.

Smallwood had seen right through him.

Director Shane began, "Early Saturday morning, one of our employees was murdered on the grounds of the hospital in a most gruesome fashion, with his throat slashed from ear to ear. Then a couple arrived on Easter Sunday wanting a tour of the maternity department claiming they had an appointment. When the security officer called for a supervisor to talk to them, the couple disappeared. Later, we find them taking photos of the nuclear blood irradiator. Then, when Nick raced down to the lab to confront them, they disappear through an employee-only exit and get away in an older model dark car which we've now identified as a 1994 Honda Civic LX, charcoal gray, four doors. We haven't seen the license plates, but Nick glimpsed the mounting bracket indicating the plates were missing. The same type of car the murderer escaped in the night before. Nick, please give your thoughts concerning these incidents."

Nick surveyed the office, the oaken desk, the paneled walls, the curtains where there were no windows, the comically large flat-screen TV opposite the director. All geared to make one forget, while visiting the director in the hospital's subbasement, that they wouldn't be here unless something had already gone horribly wrong.

The director, seeing that Nick was not comfortable talking in front of the agents, stated, "Nick, John is a longtime friend. He is here because we have mutual interests in what he has discovered, and we think it is directly related to these incidents. I want you to speak freely in front of them."

Nick started by recounting Sunday's events, stating, "While I was in active pursuit mode I could not focus on something that was bothering me. As a matter of fact, I did not realize what that was until later in the evening when I had a chance to process the events."

Nick continued, "As I started playing the events back in my head, I realized the couple was always one step ahead of security, be it the uniform division or the investigative division. I put it all together when they used the employee exit to make their getaway. The exit is not easily accessible and is off the main corridor where there is an exit that is clearly marked at the end of the hall. Instead, they made a right and went into plant engineering to emerge out the employee door. That's when it hit me, they must have someone giving them inside information. That's how they were always one step ahead. The inside information allowed them to navigate the hallways as though they were veteran employees. Secondly, I am almost sure the car that was waiting for them is the same car used by the assailant that killed one of our employees the night before. How they're tied together, I don't know. But I feel they are."

The director nodded.

Agent Smallwood then said, "Nick, that is exactly why we're here. Based on the transcriptions of notes and books found in Pakistan, I came to the same conclusion."

Nick sputtered. "Pakistan?"

Smallwood said, "Take a look at this. These are just some of the notes describing items in your hospital and other hospitals."

Nick looked at the papers while Agent Smallwood spoke. "These notes and CDs describe the covert closets and blood irradiators' locations in trauma centers throughout the United States. However, this hospital had the most complete details of everything, from labs and closets to exits and stairwells. Agent Grazie and I are going to be working on this, and the director would like you to handle your end of the investigation and give whatever supporting help we need until we catch this evil bastard that is supplying the information."

Nick nodded. "Yeah. Sure. I'll support you."

Smallwood said, "I didn't mean it like that. We'll support each other."

Agent John Smallwood started explaining what he had discovered.

He said, "When the US forces finally caught up with and killed Osama bin Laden at his compound in Pakistan, they retrieved compact discs and handwritten notebooks describing various terrorist attacks bin Laden approved or was about to approve. The books were eventually decrypted and translated and turned over to us."

"To you and Agent Grazie?" Nick asked.

"To us and others like us," Smallwood said, not easily distracted by heckling. He went on. "One book in particular caught my eye. When I read it, I was amazed and frightened at how simple yet devastating the attack would be. I realized they knew about the covert closet containing supplies of reagents or tests to determine the threat, such as smallpox, anthrax, and ricin antidotes and other vaccines stored at various medical centers in the metropolitan area and throughout the country."

The director asked, "John, was our hospital singled out by name or location, or was it all trauma centers in general that were storing the stockpiles?"

Agent Smallwood answered, "Your hospital was singled out, and that's why we're here. Through the CDs and notes and some confidential informants, the agency learned that some kind of biological or chemical attack was being planned. The location and target was unknown. However, based on their previous attacks, a large urban area was the best bet. Therefore, at the approval of President George W. Bush, and right after 9/11, a top secret plan was developed by the Department of Homeland Security to store millions of vials of vaccine, antidotes, syringes, and needles in various hospitals. The locations of these hospitals were not known to anyone except the president, secretary of Homeland Security, superintendent of the state police, and security officials at the hospital for whichever state that had this storage, normally a major trauma center. Without public knowledge, these stockpiles were being prepared to combat what the White House took as a viable and imminent threat. As time passed, with no terrorist strike, and different people hired and fired in the health system, various individuals who knew about the covert storerooms told their coworkers, wives, husbands, and significant others. The secret was out, but to a greater extent than everyone realized. Everyone except me."

Smallwood went on. "I analyzed the confiscated notes and CDs. I observed that Al-Qaeda knew almost all of these locations stretching across the country, with greater knowledge and detail concerning the hospitals on the East Coast, specifically in the New York / New Jersey metropolitan area. I found some of the information to be extremely precise, in some instances listing the floor the closets were on and what they contained such as the antidotes and reagents."

Smallwood said, "What I wanted to know was how they had gotten this information. I realized the only way I was going to get the answers I was looking for was to have an agent or confidential informant infiltrate one of the radical mosques in the United States and find out."

"A mosque is a house of worship," Nick said.

Smallwood answered, "Yes, and some are more than that. Our intelligence showed that some of the more radical sheikhs and clerics in the US were teaching on the East Coast. I asked for permission to continue the investigation in an undercover or covert capacity."

Al said, "You were gonna go undercover until you got a look in the mirror and realized you were the whitest guy in the world."

A laugh burst from Agent Grazie. She hid her face.

Smallwood flushed but went on, "When permission was granted, I began a search for a Muslim agent or agents of Arabic descent. As I had surmised, all agents were tied up in investigations in other parts of the country and overseas, and my request would take months to complete, months I knew we didn't have. So, I posted a request on the agency's confidential bulletin board, and Agent Grazie e-mailed me."

Nick said, "And you've been together ever since."

"Nick," Shane snapped. "A word?"

Nick, Al, and Shane stepped outside the office, and Shane closed the door. Shane said, "What the hell is wrong with you?"

"What?"

"You want to get into a pissing match with this guy? Now?"

Nick shook himself as if he were a wet dog. "No. I don't know what's wrong with me. Let's go in."

Agent Smallwood said, "There is more that you need to know, Nick. On the tapes and CDs, there is information from many hospitals, especially on the East Coast, but it is all in bits and pieces. However, the most revealing and complete information is specific to Guardian Angel Hospital."

Smallwood squeezed a remote, and the TV screen lit up.

Smallwood began, "This photo presentation is the transcribed files that were retrieved from both the caves in Afghanistan and the compound of Osama bin Laden in Pakistan."

Nick felt his jaw drop with each passing picture. The photos began with the Guardian Angel Hospital entrance, then each successive one was taken as though the person was on a walking tour on Patriots Path in Boston, Massachusetts, which, when followed by a tourist, would bring them to a historic site. Except in this case it brought the terrorists that would follow it to all the important and extremely sensitive areas of the Guardian Angel Hospital: the covert closet of antidotes, the lab, and the Emergency Medical Unit. Nick was in awe of how detailed the photos were and the quality looked almost professional. On each photo was added whether the individual had to walk right or left while looking at the hospital.

Nick said, "If you had this information why did you wait until now to show it to me?"

Agent Grazie answered, "After we looked at the information at the photos, we needed to have the Arabic transcribed, decrypted, and translated. Then to ensure that the interpretation was correct we had it done again and compared the two for the most accurate transcription possible. This all takes an exorbitant amount of time." Agent Grazie continued, "It was not a deliberate delay, but one that was necessary to ensure accuracy. We were still working on it when Director Shane contacted us about yesterday's incident."

Nick tried not to sound irritated. "All right," he said.

What could he say? They were CIA and he was hospital security. But he wasn't about to click his heels and keep his mouth shut.

While watching the presentation, the first clue Nick noticed was the notes on the photos were originally written in English probably by the inside non-Arabic person who took them, then translated to Arabic, indicating the traitor was possibly American.

Nick explained what he had observed.

As the photo tour continued, the first close-ups were of the entrances, the card readers, and the cameras. The tour then went to the outside gas storage tanks. Every hospital stored these massive tanks outside and away from the hospital for safety reasons. They were usually fenced off, out of sight of the general public and highly alarmed with cameras and motion sensors on the outside perimeters. Continuing around the building the next frame was of the garbage dumpster exit and the medical waste exit, followed by the morgue entrance to the immediate right. The next photo revealed the auxiliary building to the north of the hospital that contained a state-of-the-art Emergency Medical Unit with computer workstations for forty people and two large monitors in the front. Nick remembered some of the specifications from when it was built. The room could be sealed if needed, and communications to the rest of the hospital could be conducted in no less than four different ways: electronically to every computer, by telephone to every station by bypassing the telecommunications department, via text messaging, and by fax. Thus, if there were a pandemic or other such catastrophe, the Emergency Medical Unit would be utilized calling in individuals from each department who had been training for months on different scenarios: medical emergencies, natural catastrophes, and terrorist attacks. The Emergency Medical Unit would be calling the shots, without fear of contamination or attack after the doors were sealed and their own water and oxygen implemented.

The Emergency Medical Unit was a state-of-the-art complex, built with federal funds courtesy of the United States government through the Office of Homeland Security. It was built in the old nursing school dormitory, a freestanding structure just two hundred yards from the hospital. In the event of an emergency, natural or man-made, this would become the "brains" of the hospital, where the director would be calling the shots and making the decisions. The center was built to withstand any conventional explosives and was rated to withstand a small nuclear explosion. If there were a terrorist attack on the hospital itself, plans were made to set up a temporary hospital at the Morris County Arena, an ice-skating rink situated approximately 1.5 miles from Guardian Angel Hospital. Once mobilized, the arena would be transformed into a mobile hospital that could triage patients, with a full mobile emergency room, operating room, and care for the wounded with up to a thousand portable beds that were stored at that location. Based on the MASH units utilized during the Korean War, the mobile hospital would be fully functional, self-contained, and in communication with the Emergency Medical Unit.

Again, in great detail, the photos Agent Smallwood was displaying disclosed entrances, exits, and emergency exits, and camera locations as well as electric and cable hookups. The photos continued both outside and inside the hospital, with special attention focused on the blood irradiator and the hallway and corridors of the covert vault.

The second clue Nick noticed while watching the presentation was the photographer took a photo of an underground hatch near the exit of plant engineering that led to the boiler rooms.

Nick asked, "What is that in the corner of the photo on the bottom right? Is that a woman's shoe?"

The photographer inadvertently photobombed the front of a woman's shoe. Not that much was visible— just enough to notice the shoe was leopard spotted with a gold tip and with enough of the top of the foot showing to determine the woman had fair skin.

Agent Grazie answered, "It certainly is, and a very expensive shoe."

Nick continued, "So, from the angle of the shot, isn't it apparent the photographer was the owner of the shoe?"

"Yes."

The presentation continued, and there were not many surprises or shots that caught Nick's interest, that is, until the presentation was nearly ended.

The third clue Nick observed was the final shots of the security department. This, in and of itself, would not be that big a deal, but for one exception: the photos were taken in the secured unit, behind a card reader or electronic bypass door without an apparent break in time according to the camera's internal overlay and time stamp. Nick began to explain this to the group and said, "The photographer had entered with a security officer in what is known as 'piggybacking' on someone's entry before. If you look in the background of the photo, a hand was holding the door for the photographer. However, this also indicated the person was known and allowed in the secured area and was not questioned for the piggyback entry. A piggyback entry is made when an intruder waits near a secure entrance for an authorized person to gain entry, then when the door is open, slips in on the same entry as the legitimate person. Had the person used their ID card for entry, a report could have been generated, cross-checked with the time on the camera, and the identity of the individual would have been revealed."

Grazie asked, "Can't you just look at the videotapes for that day?"

Director Shane sighed.

Nick replied, "I could if you showed it to me a little sooner. The internal closed-circuit television system held approximately thirty days of data from the recorded footage. After the thirty days, the cameras simply records over the previous data for another thirty days. The process keeps repeating itself with rerecordings unless or until someone needs information on the recorder. The operator would simply put in the date and time and retrieve the requested data, providing it was not recorded over."

Shane chimed in. "Nick suggested years ago that we increase recording capacity to sixty or ninety days. But to increase recording time would involve buying new recorders which were expensive—"

Grazie finished his sentence, "And out of reach for the security department's budget."

Nick said, "This photo is not of a sensitive location, but you will notice, this is a great shot of the camera location in the lobby." Nick asked, "Can I have copies of these photos? Maybe I can see what else we missed."

Agent John Smallwood answered, "Of course."

Neither agent mentioned they observed any clues by themselves. Quite possibly they did not notice any, or they were, for some reason, withholding the information.

The screen went dark with the photo presentation over. Agent Smallwood continued, "Following the death of Saddam Hussein, Al-Qaeda continued to carry out attacks. Some plots were already underway in Europe, Indonesia, and Africa while others were in the formative and planning stage. And some were right here in the United States."

One of these locations, Nick observed, was right in his old backyard. Plans, drawings, surveillance photos, and blueprints for one of

America's largest insurance companies were found in the Afghanistan caves. The Newark Insurance Building in downtown Newark, New Jersey, was one of the targets for the next terror strikes. Coincidently, Nick had worked there part-time in the last three years of his previous career. He was stationed at the front of the building as security, in uniform, and escorted the women who worked there. He would walk them to the different parking lots where their cars were parked in order to ensure their safety. Nick had been reassigned to the civil warrant squad in the last three years with the sheriff's office, with the hope of his superiors that this step-down would help him acclimate back into regular society.

During his career Nick led a life that was far from normal, dealing with drug dealers, wise guys, outlaws, and other dregs of society. When he was about to retire his superiors felt he needed time in a different squad to decompress. They felt delivering civil summons and complaints to businesses in the suburbs would be just what he needed. This new assignment led to different part-time jobs Nick could now take advantage. His superiors hoped to take the "jungle" out of Nick so that he could retire without the reactions and actions that he lived by on the streets.

No such luck.

Smallwood continued, "In conjunction with hospitals being targeted for their contents such as the irradiator and antidotes, hospitals were also targets themselves."

Grazie asked, "Why target hospitals?"

Smallwood said, "So as to take them down and render them useless before the next terrorist strike. Think about it, after a terrorist strike where would the wounded be taken?"

They were silent for a moment as the realization of the two-part strike settle over them. Smallwood said, "The emergency responders would not have anywhere to take the injured when the terrorists hit another target. This, of course, would bring up the number of fatalities and the amount of worldwide press. On the tapes were childcare centers, schools, and malls considered to be soft targets since there would be no resistance to an attack. All were under surveillance by the terrorists as targets. Attacks on places like these would strike fear into the American public and show them that no one was safe. The jihadists could strike anywhere. Remember, the key to terrorism is fear and disruption of the populations' normal routines and way of life. The key to terrorism is terror."

He continued to explain that attacks were to be simultaneously carried out in large cities such as Newark, suburbs like Parsippany, and the rural areas of the Midwest. "The preferred choice of attack would be suicide bombers and death squads. This was never publicized. The media instead were given reports on the Middle Eastern men attempting to register for flying lessons in order to fly crop dusters containing chemical or biological agents they hoped to spray on an unsuspecting public. Though this was also listed a possibility, there were no immediate plans to carry out the crop-dusting plan since the jihadists could not figure out how to deliver the poison at the height and speed a plane would have to travel. The wind would likely blow the toxins away rather than down at that velocity as the substance was too light for a lethal concentration to fall and do harm."

Smallwood explained, "The federal agencies—CIA, FBI, and others—would neither confirm nor deny whether the more spectacular targets listed on the disc were true. These targets were leaked to the media and broadcast nationally. The public would never know if the Statue of Liberty, the footings of the George Washington Bridge, gassing of subway trains, the blowing up of the Hoover Dam in Nevada, or nuclear dirty bombs set off in a major metropolitan area were ever actually in the works or planning stages. A regular nuclear bomb is a long shot since nuclear material is hard to come by even with the collapse of the former Soviet Union and other rogue nations with nuclear capabilities. A dirty bomb, on the other hand, would be composed of a large amount of regular explosives with nuclear material attached in order to have both the explosive effect along with the radiation from some type of nuclear material, such as waste from a nuclear generator, medical nuclear components, or other nonmilitary sources."

Smallwood said, "Considerable effort, money, and time were placed in tightening up security where the nuclear waste materials would likely be shipped. That included rail yards, the seaports on the

New Jersey coast, and the known trucking terminals that were regulated to carry the waste across the country to the National Nuclear Storage Facility in Nevada. Extra fences, cameras, alarms, and personnel were utilized in order to protect the waste from falling into terrorists' hands. Now, with ever-improving technology, unmanned drones are being utilized at these locations and facilities almost on a daily basis. The new technology that is now available can be attached to drones to detect radiation. Private firms are being contracted to operate the drones with multiple cameras attached and radiation detection that report back in real time any intruders or security breaches that appear on the screen. Then, armed security personnel are dispatched to the site in a matter of minutes. The security company has both drones and personnel stationed at each target area so that personnel can be deployed as quickly as possible. Equipped with night vision cameras, and motion sensors, these drones are deployed day and night, giving the security team an edge it did not have only a few short years ago." Agent Smallwood handed his remote over to Agent Phyllis Grazie.

Agent Grazie began by stating, "Many of the terrorist plans were interrupted and thwarted by the FBI and CIA working in conjunction with state, local authorities and private security personnel. A vehicle was stopped trying to cross the Canadian border into Washington State packed with enough explosives to do major damage to an unspecified target, quite possibly Hoover Dam. Thanks to an alert street vendor in New York City, a disaster was averted when he observed an illegally parked vehicle with what appeared to be a smoldering fire in the interior. It was discovered the vehicle had enough explosives and shrapnel that if exploded could have done immeasurable damage. Still, at other times, without enough information, the authorities have not been as successful in stopping the attacks beforehand. Think of the Boston Marathon bombing and the shootings at Fort Hood, Texas.

"American allies," she continued, "similarly suffered acts of terrorism. Consider Italy, Spain, France, England, and Israel. Though plans were recovered and Internet and communications chatter were up substantially, there just was not enough information to thwart these terrorist strikes beforehand, resulting in the loss of life and substantial other damage. Enough damage and carnage was done to swing public opinion in those countries, and accomplish what the terrorists planned all along: the breakup of the United States coalition that was fighting in Iraq and Afghanistan. Then, as members of the coalition pulled their troops, America was left to fight in Iraq and Afghanistan, fighting alone. The political climate in the United States changed, and there was more and more clamor by the public and politicians to withdraw. Barack Obama won the election in part by promising to bring the troops home, despite the fact that military personnel, both active and retired, predicted a vacuum would be formed once we pulled out that would be worse than the problems caused by Al-Qaeda. This prediction came true in the form of the radical Islamic group called Islamic State in Iraq and Syria, which you know as ISIS. Furthermore, as predicted by military intelligence, ISIS will be more ruthless and more difficult to contain once they spread across these two countries, Iraq and Syria, spreading ideology to hurt America and Americans both overseas and in the United States."

Al chimed in. "So Obama created ISIS."

"I'm not saying that," Grazie began.

Al said, "Do you blame him for starting a war with no viable exit strategy?"

Shane said, "Let's just deal with the problem we have now."

Agent Grazie continued, "My confidential informant has been cited in many affidavits for wiretaps and search warrants that have been granted and have proven fruitful. Fortunately for us, there are Muslims who hate these radicals as much as the rest of the civilized world does. The radicals interpret the Koran in the way they can recruit and justify what they do in the name of Allah, including killing innocent people not of their faith, rape, and plundering entire villages. To this extent I have the privilege of working with a confidential informant who has proven trustworthy and reliable in the past and has provided information that made it possible to prevent large-scale terrorist attacks both here in the United States and abroad."

Grazie continued, "After 9/11 when the country was still reeling from the terror attacks, both Congress and the President wasted no time in passing the Patriot Act, which gave federal investigators the power to use surveillance against crimes of terror, and made it easier to obtain wiretaps. The Patriot Act expanded the use of surveillance to allow agents to follow terrorists trained to evade detection, by using roving wiretaps and to follow lone wolves or individuals suspected of terrorism but not hooked up with a particular organization. This allowed the agents to follow and wiretap the instrument the person was using and not just one particular phone. Furthermore, a single individual could be placed under surveillance when they are suspected of terrorism but not linked to a known terrorist organization. Next, it allowed federal agents to conduct investigations and delayed notification. The act also allows federal agents to ask the court to obtain business records in terrorism cases. Before the Patriot Act, obtaining any information had to be done through grand jury subpoenas. The Patriot Act contains other provisions to aid the federal investigators and increases punishment for those convicted."

Nick suspected that Agent Grazie was laying out options allowed by the Patriot Act for a reason. The reason, the CIA planned to utilize everything at their disposal to prevent this new terror threat from happening

Shane said, "Nick and Al, you keep chasing down that leak."

Grazie said, "I'll be meeting with my informant." She handed him a manila folder fat with eight-by-ten color photos of some of the images they'd seen on the screen. "We'll speak again soon."

As they left the office, Nick turned to Agent Grazie and was going to ask her if she would like to go to lunch. Then seeing the wedding band on her finger and remembering he was married also, he decided to forgo the invite.

Grazie said, "Nice to meet you, I'll see you in the next few days."

Nick replied, "Looking forward to it."

Nick couldn't stop looking at her as she walked away, then noticing, she turned and gave him a smile. He couldn't understand what came over him as he never reacted to a woman this way, that is, except for his wife Jen. And he hadn't reacted this way to Jen in a while.

Nick put all that out of his head as he and Al left the building for his office at the corporate building. He was thinking of the different events, the agents' arrival, and the presentation they made. While he was driving, Nick was trying to think of what piece was missing. The puzzle was laid out before him, and now he had to arrange the pieces into a coherent investigation. What, Nick wondered, was the reason for all this to start occurring now? Was it because they had a spy or spies on the inside providing them with information that they never had before? Or was this a subplot of some greater plan they were hatching? Nick knew he had more questions than answers, but as with any investigation he was going to develop a plan of action to answer the questions, sooner than later.

Nick arrived at his office with the photos from Agent Smallwood where he wanted to discuss with Al what had transpired and look at the photo presentation again more closely. Though the corporate investigators at Guardian Angel Hospital work independently from each other and conduct their own investigations, he and Al got along well and understood the real dangers America faced every day. Not the local crime or corporate violations, but the very real knowledge that something was imminent.

Nick and Al studied the photos. As they did Nick pointed out the clues that he observed in the photos. They decided to examine each photo with a magnifying glass to make sure they did not miss even the smallest clue. Next, Nick poured over Harry's human resources folder, making sure he did not miss anything in the documents that may give him another lead.

"Al," Nick said. "Get the records of anyone who worked on the day imprinted on the photo taken by the unknown photographer and compare them to the records for the door access." It was a long shot, but as Nick had discovered, you never know what you might find. He next went to see police Detective Ricks at Parsippany PD.

Nick asked, "Did you see the vehicle that the suspect was driven off in?"

Detective Ricks answered, "Yes I did. We enhanced the photo. It's a black 2009 Honda Civic. With that information, limited as it is, we put out an all-points bulletin. We don't have that much, but you never know. We're doing a motor vehicle search for all registered like models. We met with Harry Barker's widow and went through his personal belongings, and I tell you, Nick, it just doesn't make any sense why anyone would want to kill him."

As he was leaving the office, Nick turned and replied, "I know, he seems to have been a quiet, working man. Hopefully we will be able to crack this case soon before someone else is murdered."

CHAPTER 8

"Guardian Angel Hospital has gone through many metamorphoses in its history. The hospital began as a parsonage and was utilized as an ad hoc hospital by General George Washington during the Revolutionary War. Later, the building was again utilized as a facility to treat Union soldiers injured, maimed, blinded, or otherwise disabled in the numerous battles of the Civil War. Always the center for commerce and trade, Parsippany played an intricate part in the battle for independence. The Continental Army camped not far from Parsippany several times during the Revolutionary War for its resources, roads, and location."

Max, if that was his name, which it wasn't, chivalrously led his wife along to the next stop on the hospital tour, a hand gently guiding her lower back as if they were waltzing. If she was his wife. Which she wasn't.

"Parsippany had railroad service in 1836 and the Morris Canal shortly thereafter, which stretched from the coal mines of Pennsylvania to the iron mines of Mine Hill and foundries of Morris County. The Morris Canal furthermore stretched to the large cities on the East Coast, including Newark and Jersey City. The coal mines in Pennsylvania were an imperative part of the manufacturing process along with the iron excavated in Morris County, just west of Parsippany. These resources were used in the making of guns, cannons, ammunition, railroad tracks, ships, and many other products that were necessary in the Civil War."

What she was, was blonde and buxom and stupid. All she knew was to smile and nod, and no one would question either of them. All he had to do was videotape the hospital tour.

"The expansion of train travel was directly responsible for the commercial boom, not only in manufacturing but also for the farmers who could now get their produce, meats, and dairy products to market in a timely manner. During the Civil War especially, the transportation systems proved invaluable for feeding and clothing the Union soldiers. Just as important was bringing the wounded troops home. Foreseeing a problem as to where to treat the soldiers before returning them home, the parsonage was again turned into an impromptu hospital. After this period, Guardian Angel Hospital greatly expanded. Through the bequest of many benefactors and the formation of a Ladies Auxiliary, funds were raised, and the hospital officially opened in 1893."

She was a prostitute, of course. He hadn't met her before, considered it unlikely he'd see her again. She just had to wear the clothes, the wife clothes he'd brought for her. She just had to wear the clothes and be blonde and stacked. Who would question them?

"Guardian Angel Hospital from its inception to the present day has continued to grow and expand. Furthermore, each wing that was constructed contains a different medical specialty such as a cancer center, heart center, and this, the children's hospital. As the hospital continued to grow and became nationally renowned in different fields of expertise, the population of the patients, visitors, and staff expanded at an extraordinary rate. Parking garages, satellite offices, ambulance fleets, storage warehouses all began to spring up along the hospital's periphery. New corporate offices were needed to house the ever-growing directors, billing, finance, central purchasing, human resources, information technology, and corporate security to name but a few of the different departments conducting the day-to-day business of this health-care system. Hospitals were bought in different cities adding to the system, as were medical helicopters and ambulances to transport the patients to different facilities for specialized treatment. Along the way, it was determined that the Guardian Angel Hospital's boilers, water pressure, steam, and air-condition-ing needed to be replaced and enlarged to accommodate all the new wings."

Thank you, Guardian Angel, thought Max, who was not named Max, holding his wife who was not his wife. Thank you for welcoming us. Thank you for all the helpful information.

Nick drove home, and as he thought of the advancements of security he marveled at the changes over the years, including the changes in hospital security. In years past, there was no need for high-tech security at a hospital. A hospital was a place where a mother delivered her baby, dad got treated for an injured hip, and a kid got his tonsils out. Crimes of opportunity always occurred. A patient's missing wallet or money were the usual reports to the security department. And half the time the victim wasn't sure if the items were stolen or lost. No crime committed around the hospital could be considered organized or, for that matter, planned. And God knows there was no crime committed against the hospital itself.

He arrived home and everyone was asleep. Nick looked in on his daughter. Lilly was thirteen, on the cusp of teenage-hood. At school she was fast-talking and popular among the girls. But she lay under a pink blanket, hugging a stuffed unicorn. How long would she stay innocent?

America lost her innocence to the terrorist attacks on September 11, 2001, he kept thinking. This was a different America now, where terror attacks, crime, and violence were now understood, even expected. Nick felt the nation now understood that terror strikes, war, bombings, and shootings didn't only happen in exotic places on the other side of the world, in a country we cannot pronounce or spell. They happened here. Nick often thought of the attack on Pearl Harbor and the bombing of the Alfred P. Murrah Federal Building in Oklahoma City. But after those attacks, we were healed by the fact that we brought the ones responsible to defeat. In Oklahoma City, the homegrown terrorists that perpetrated this act were caught, tried, and the leader Timothy McVeigh executed while his partner Terry Nichols was sentenced to life in prison without the possibility of parole. Hitler? There was a story that ended the right way. Were we oversimplifying? Chalking it up to a few demented individuals who got their punishment? Then 9/11 happened, and nothing made sense. Even when we caught and killed someone, someone else would pop up, crying "Death to America!" What did they have against us?

Nick wondered if his children would even live in a world without that cloud of a threat hanging over it.

He took off his suit and slipped into bed in his boxers. Jen breathed audibly, though you couldn't call it snoring. She curled up on her side with her back to him. He tried to snuggle up to her. She neither welcomed him nor pushed him away. Best he could hope for.

Nick couldn't fall asleep, and his mind wandered. Guardian Angel, along with other trauma centers in New Jersey and the United States for that matter, received grants from the federal government for the purpose of increasing security. The government was sure that another terrorist attack was going to happen; they envisioned another Israel, where everyone is on guard for an attack anywhere at any time. No place was safe. An attack could happen in your office, the restaurant in a crowded downtown area, or even a hospital's maternity ward. This grant money was to ensure that anyone entering the hospital since 9/11 would have seen the "24 hours a day, 7 days a week, 365 days a year" uniformed presence. In addition, a uniformed, armed off-duty Parsippany police officer was stationed 24-7 at the emergency room entrance.

Civilians didn't understand that we were now in a different war, a covert, stealth war. This was a war where the enemy wore regular clothes, spoke English, and detonated bombs secreted on their person. This new war was a war considered by the enemy to be a religious war, where a nonbeliever of Islam should be killed for no other reason than belonging to a different religion. This is a war where there is no negotiation, where the leaders and followers have been fighting wars for thousands of years, and now wanted to bring the war to our shores.

With such a large federal grant infusion of funds into the protection and security department budget, the security director and managers, many of whom are retired law enforcement personnel, began calling and reaching out to their former departments for the newly retired detectives, offering them a position as an independent corporate investigator. These investigators, when hired, are subject to all hospital policies, procedures, and corporate compliances; however, they are not hospital personnel, but rather considered long-term vendors. This was how Nick was selected for the position. This was how he went from an excellent newly retired detective from the Essex County Bureau of Narcotics to a corporate investigator for a healthcare system in Morris County, in Parsippany.

Though the city of Parsippany stood just twenty miles west of the city of Newark, to Nick it was a different world. Born and raised in Newark's North Ward, Nick went to the local schools and attended the local church. He hung out on stoops and storefronts with the rest of the youths from the neighborhood. The only green they saw was in the parks. Before the job at the hospital, he never traveled further west than the mall in Livingston, midway between Newark and Parsippany. Nick was comfortable in Newark with its high-rise projects, multifamily tenements, and two-family duplexes with narrow alleyways separating them. It was what he knew his entire life. It felt normal.

Parsippany, in contrast, was sprawled and spacious and green with lawns, hedges, and trees. Even after eight years at the hospital, Nick was not sure he liked what seemed like too much greenery. In the city there was always action and something to do, entertainment that could be found right next door. In the city, people were always out on the stoops and sitting with friends, talking, playing cards or dominos. Neighbors would stop and talk before entering the house, and kids would always be underfoot playing and laughing. In Parsippany everything was too spread out. The use of space seemed extravagant, and the hedges seemed like a dubiously polite way of drawing the line in the sand. Though he felt safer in Parsippany and the surrounding areas, he was always on his guard and always attuned to his surroundings. He'd been "raised," like most cops, to sense potential threats. Someone could be hiding behind that hedge. A basement door leading outside was an invitation to home invaders. Vigilance was something you couldn't turn off. It led to suspicion and sleeplessness, the price of protecting the peace and keeping the world a safe place for his family.

Nick's life depended on vigilance when he worked undercover, purchasing narcotics from dealers in what FBI reports deemed the worst sections of Essex County, then as the squad leader arresting the drug dealers. The other detectives would relive Nick's jobs as if they had done them, telling other agencies and different detectives how they solved Nick's cases. Nick called this "the playground in their mind." This was where they believed in something they knew was an illusion. This was where fantasy became, to them, reality, and they made stories up in order to bolster up the fabrications of their life. But it made him the stuff of departmental legend.

It was known, for example, that Nick could sense if the suspect was going to sell him the drugs or attempt to take the money and run. In order to avoid this Nick never let them see the money until he saw the drugs. Then there was also the threat that he'd be spotted as a cop and they'd just kill him. He learned to spot their suspicion before they did and soothe it.

Maladaptive. That was the term. The skills he developed to survive on the streets made people uncomfortable with him in normal situations. If someone said something other than what they were thinking, or casually lied, he would tell them what they meant. He was so intuitive, Felicia used to say that he was almost psychic. She liked it. It felt like shorthand in their relationship. But it put the rest of the world on edge. After Felicia died, if he would ask friends out or to come over they would shy away, always make an excuse, or otherwise avoid the invitation. Nick stopped asking. He didn't blame them. Yet he also knew when they had a problem or needed a favor Nick was the go-to guy. They knew if Nick promised something, it was as good as done. And he decided that, if he caught someone in a lie, he would mentally record the information and keep his mouth shut. He stopped pissing people off, but holding the information back made life outside work no different from work. What was the point of having friends?

Nick liked to think his lack of friends left him more time to be a good husband. He loved Jen. And if the fireworks in the bedroom were gone, if he couldn't tell her about work, well, he was lucky to have her anyway.

And his mind drifted to Agent Grazie. He felt he could tell her anything.

Thinking back on his glory days, Nick realized other detectives couldn't survive in the crime-ridden ghettos, where he always felt right at home. He'd actually thrived at narcotics, not just because he understood the city, but because of the everyday action and excitement he found almost intoxicating. Somehow the threat of death cranked him up. If he had fear, he left it in the locker with his gym shoes. He glided on skill and confidence. The swagger made him look, if anything, *more* like a drug dealer. Nick always thought he would have made an excellent actor; he played a long game, passing himself as a dealer while he worked his way up the ladder to the middle-level or upper-level narcotics traffickers, as the other detectives in the unit watched with awe and skepticism. Even the jealous ones couldn't deny his blend of swagger, street smarts, and investigative skill were a winning combination. He would protect his false identity by getting arrested with the dealers, spending time in jail, and then getting bailed out with the others. Nick himself knew he could talk for a year about his career, what he faced, the three times he almost got shot working undercover, and the four to five search warrants he and his squad executed every week when he was squad leader. Then, of course, there were the numerous wiretaps and joint task forces he was on. But Nick did not expound on his exploits to anyone except at the Bureau of Narcotics reunion parties that took place every five years.

Then came 9/11, and swaggering seemed wrong, just wrong.

The next morning, Nick and Al sat in the field office, sorting swipe-in records for the day that security was breached, trying to find anything that might give them a clue as to who the leak was.

So far, they had engaged multiple law enforcement agencies including the CIA, and they had nothing. The facilities guy got his throat cut on a smoking break. A couple had moved through what he realized was lax security—his fault—and made their way to a piece of machinery even he hadn't known existed. This was the kind of ignorance and ineptitude that left the facility vulnerable, the kind that allowed 9/11 in the first place.

Al said, "Look at this, three times last week someone tried to swipe into the entrance of the Emergency Medical Unit, but the access was denied."

Nick replied, "Let's take a ride over and speak to the security officer, maybe there's a reason for it, like trouble with a card or the reader."

They drove over in Al's Ford EcoSport and headed for the door marked Emergency Medical Unit. As Al walked in, Nick heard him yell, "What the—"

Then, following, Nick saw what Al was yelling about. Security Officer Jack Boyle was lying on the floor in the vestibule, dead.

Chapter 9

The two-story redbrick building looked more like a barracks than the scene of a crime. However, inside the building was a command center of unequalled proportions. And the guy guarding it was dead.

Nick gathered the uniformed officers. "You know the area around here better than anybody. Pair up, stay in radio contact both with each other and the command center. Remember, this person or persons are dangerous. Call for help if you spot anything. Also, what you find may be in the form of physical evidence, such as a footprint, clothing caught on a bush, and the like. If you find anything, stay with it, call in, and a forensic team will respond to your location. That's all."

The security officers paired up and fanned out, walking about ten yards apart and checking anything out on the ground, bushes, or structures that looked out of place. A patrol officer, a city cop, approached Nick and Shane.

"I've radioed Central," he said. "We probably shouldn't go inside until they show up."

"Good thinking, soldier," Nick said. "In the meantime, you keep an eye on things and make sure to flag them down when they get here."

The vast lobby inside the command center stood in stark contrast to the brick exterior. The center had the most up-to-date computers, electronics, and communications system. Steel beams rose twenty feet to the ceiling. Metal detectors framed each entrance. A dozen computer stations sat encased in a bulletproof glass enclosure. Swivel chairs lay unassembled in stacked boxes.

Jack Boyle lay faceup on the concrete floor.

A uniformed Latin woman sat at the security desk, the only human in sight, save for Boyle.

Nick said, "Did you make the call?"

She didn't seem to hear him. Of course, she'd called. She was hospital security. She'd called the hospital command center. The city cops would be listening in. Anyone else would have called the city cops or 911 first.

Al said, "I'll sniff around for intruders." He drew his weapon, and Nick almost felt a rush of wind as Al whisked away. Nick and Shane approached the woman. Her name tag said Perez.

"Officer Perez? I'm Nick Moore. I don't think we've met."

She scanned the screen, video feeds from a dozen cameras. Nick pointed to two feeds, about two square inches each. One camera showed the front door from the outside, one from the inside. "That one," he said.

Perez didn't seem to hear him. Then she touched the screen and the two images expanded. She hit rewind. Boyle lay on the floor where he was in real life. Then he snapped up, scuffled with a shadowed figure, and walked backward into the building. The magic of rewind.

She hit play. Boyle responded to a call. Stood inside the front door. Spoke into the intercom.

"Is that recorded?" Nick asked.

Perez said, "Soon. But not yet. The recording program isn't running yet."

For whatever reasons, Boyle opened the door. Then he's scuffling with the dark figure, then he's on the ground. Pause.

Shane said, "It looks like Boyle was physically trying to keep the intruder from gaining access."

They played it again, slower. The intruder appeared to stab Jack in the neck. Jack crumpled to the pavement.

"Follow him," Nick said to Perez. She shrank the screen down, and they could see the intruder enter the building, snapping pictures as he went, of the locks, card swipes, and the entrance itself. He makes his way through the building snapping pictures. Then he exits and makes for the edge of the parking lot, disappearing into the dark.

Al came back, holstering his weapon. "All clear."

"Did he stab him?" Shane asked.

Nick said, "I don't see blood." He turned to Perez. "Do you?"

Responding to another question, one he hadn't asked, Perez said, "I got here right before you. My shift just started."

Within minutes, city cops packed the Emergency Medical Unit The forensic team went to work observing and tagging the minutest pieces of evidence such as hair, fibers, dirt, and grass. The prosecutor's crime scene unit was working in conjunction with the federal team, bagging little pieces of string, hair, and other almost microscopic samples from the hallway and entranceway. The sheriff's office was photographing the body and sketching a diagram of the surroundings and measuring different aspects of the dimensions of the room in relation to the body. Nick was near the body of Security Officer Jack Boyle, attempting to see the laceration or penetration on his neck where he was stabbed, or so it seemed.

Grazie came in, stood next to him, and asked, "What are you looking for?"

Nick felt the warmth radiating from her body. He said, "I was looking for the wound.

Grazie asked, "What do you think? Are Smallwood and I on to something?"

Nick reminded her, "The only photos you guys had were of the outside of the Emergency Medical Unit. Nothing beyond the entrance door. It was a good bet that was the motive behind this attack. They probably didn't know there was a security officer stationed here, and when Jack saw him on the camera and confronted him, the intruder attacked Jack and killed him."

Grazie said, "So they didn't think there was anyone here, but they were ready in case there was."

A flurry of attention greeted the K-9 corps as they arrived. A massive and territorial German shepherd strode toward Boyle, leading a human behind him, and sniffed the area in and around Boyle's body, slowly taking its time sniffing Boyle's clothes. Then the dog began sniffing others in the room to see if they'd been close with him. Then it led the handler out the door, across the parking lot, into the bushes, and apparently lost the scent as Nick and Grazie watch from the edge of the woods, the dog's path turned into a circle, walking the handler around the small wooded area. He'd lost the scent.

Nick said, "Beyond those trees and shrubbery is the PATH train to Newark and New York, and beyond that is the parking area for the train station."

Grazie said, "You think he killed a guy, snapped some pictures, and boarded the train for Penn Station?"

"I don't," Nick said. "But I'll be checking security tapes and talking to conductors. My point is, there are many ways for the assailant to escape."

In rapid succession, all the different emergency and investigative personnel wrapped up their investigations, removed the body to the morgue, and collected what was thought to be useful evidence before disbanding. All stated they would complete the analysis of their investigation and be in touch with Nick and Al. The medical examiner's office removed the body, stating the autopsy would be completed as soon as possible.

Grazie seemed interested in everything Nick had to say including his hypothesis as to why the Emergency Medical Unit was targeted. Nick was explaining different items he would like analyzed and why, such as material on the doorjamb, a thorough sweep and analysis of the space between the shrubbery and the building where it appeared the intruder walked as seen on the camera, and the canvassing of any employees, patients, or vendors that may have observed something.

"The whole thing is crazy," Grazie said. It seemed a very informal comment for the circumstances, from a CIA agent. "Why go to the trouble of killing someone just to scope out a location? It's like they want us to pay attention."

"Maybe they do."

Nick was feeling both excited and confused. Grazie made him feel a way he hadn't felt in a long time. They seemed to understand each other, to click in a way he didn't click with anyone.

She kept talking as she turned to head back to the EMU, but Nick didn't hear a word. He was asking himself if she felt the same way, and these thoughts sent what felt like an electric bolt down to his toes.

Nick shook his head to clear his thoughts and turned to catch up to her.

In the momentary blankness of his mind, something clicked. Plant engineering was renovated. They'd sealed the plant doorway. Harry Barker was murdered outside the sealed doorway.

Suddenly Nick knew why.

Chapter 10

Nick grabbed Grazie by the arm and said, "Let's go to the main hospital. I have to research something."

The hospital was built on a hill, so the front of the hospital was level with the first floor, but the rear of the hospital was level with the D floor, four levels lower than the front. Nick badged them through security, and they walked into the plant engineering manager's office. A mature man with a shaved head and goatee sat at one of three desks behind an unnecessary counter. The other two desks sat empty.

Nick asked, "Otto, do you have any old blueprints around showing the expansion of plant engineering?"

Otto said, "I'm sure they're around here somewhere. When do you need them?"

Nick replied, "Otto, I need them now. We'll wait. If we can help you in any way, we'd be glad to."

Otto took a deep breath as if he were about to launch into a protest, that he was too busy to look now. But he looked at Nick's face and realized it would be useless.

"Okay," he surrendered. "Come with me."

They followed him to a back office and watched him open a door marked "Storage." As Otto opened the door, the smell of old dust and musty papers filled Nick's nostrils. Otto tiptoed in and pulled a chain, illuminating a single light bulb hanging from the ceiling. The room looked like something out of a time capsule, with an old wooden desk, a wooden chair with the slat-back, and two metal cabinets with thin, wide drawers, the kind used for storing anything printed on large paper, like big photos or blueprints. And a bunch of old boxes stuffed with cardboard tubes.

Nick asked, "Otto, is this room always kept unlocked?"

Otto replied, "Well, yeah. Who would want anything in here? It's nothing but old records. Now, let's each take a box and look on the tubes for a label that says 'plant expansion.' Or something like it. No guarantees the labels are accurate."

They sorted through the tubes, found nothing, opened the drawers one by one, laying out the contents and trying to decipher them. Then they started pulling blueprints out of the tubes. Grazie asked, "Otto, could this be it?"

He scanned the blueprint. "Yup. Yes. See, the dotted lines are the old layout of plant engineering, and these are the improvements. These are the new walls, this where the new equipment would go, the boilers, the air handlers...See, the exit door is already shown as sealed and the equipment that would be placed in there. But there should be another set of blueprints that show the area when the door was still operational. These prints you have here are the ones showing how much room would be gained by sealing the door. Do you want to look for the others too?"

They went through the rest of the tubes but didn't find them. Nick knew they wouldn't.

As Nick and Grazie were walking back to security, Grazie asked, "Are you going to tell me what's going on?"

Nick replied, "Working on it. I'll tell you and the director when we get to his office."

Walking through the corridors of the hospital is always tough, with all the people, gurneys, carts, and X-ray machines moving in every direction, but this time, the trip seemed unusually long, Grazie thought as they dodged their way through the maze of hallways. As they entered security, a small woman in the standard-issue baby blue dress that was still the uniform of female cleaning staff, wheeled a FEMA-issued vacuum cleaner out into the hall. Her dress was embroidered with the name Marta. The ID clipped to her uniform labeled her Marta Fuentes.

"Marta?" Nick asked. She hesitated before looking up and turning on a polite smile. She was dark, with thick dark hair. Her smile was empty.

Nick asked, "Isn't Carla usually on this detail?"

"She sick," Marta said, nodding, and wheeled the monstrous vacuum cleaner down the hall. He shook it off. He was just being suspicious.

Nick and Grazie entered the director's office, and Nick spread the blueprint roll onto the table. Nick explained, "Director, I know why Harry Barker was killed."

Chapter 11

Nick began, "Harry Barker was killed because the mole or moles in this organization grabbed the wrong set of blueprints, and though that may seem like a trivial reason to kill someone, to the bad guys it was just collateral damage, the wrong place at the wrong time."

The director asked, "What do you mean?"

Nick said, "What kept bothering me was why a guy like Harry would be murdered. He had no knowledge that wasn't readily available. He wasn't into gambling or drugs. He didn't cheat on his wife. As far as we know, he had nothing to hide. If he did, he did a good job of hiding it. Robbery wasn't a factor since all his money and possessions were on him. But as we saw on the video, the assailant went there for a specific reason, got dropped off, and picked up. Our mole gave blueprints to the enemy showing an entranceway from the outside of the hospital to plant engineering. The intruder went there to check it out. But the door was sealed with a sheet of steel. The intruder saw there was no way into the hospital and left. But poor Harry was smoking there as he did a hundred times before. The intruder couldn't leave a witness. Harry Barker was a victim of circumstance."

Nick continued, "Jack Boyle was killed because the bad guys needed photos of the inside of the EMU. The intruder was willing to break in if need be, snap some photos, and make an exit before anyone responded to the alarm. Unfortunately, the mole did not know or relay the message about a permanent security officer being stationed there, and so when Jack went to see who was at the door, the intruder killed him. Again, so as not to leave a witness."

"But that's crazy!" Director Shane said. "If they got eyeballed, big deal. Someone saw a suspicious guy by the hospital. But now they've got our attention. A week ago, this hospital would have been an easy target. Now we've got it locked down like Fort Knox."

"Maybe that's what they want," Grazie suggested.

The director said, "Maybe. Maybe they're showing how ruthless they are. They're not afraid to kill to get what they want. I'm sending for more staff. I want every position handled in pairs if we can. Put security on high alert. We're under siege!"

As Nick and Grazie were leaving security, Nick spotted another cleaning woman, a familiar face, her light blue dress clearly embroidered with the name Carla.

"Carla!" Nick said. "I thought you were sick!"

"No, I'm fine," she said. "Who said I was sick?"

Nick went rigid for a moment, then began sprinting down the hallway, Grazie on his heels, stopping short at the door that read "Environmental." Seated at the reception desk was coordinator Hanna Sims. She had been an employee for ages.

Hanna asked, "Nick! What brings you to my little slice of heaven?"

Nick answered huffing and puffing, "Hanna, where is your new employee Marta Fuentes right now?"

"Who?"

"Marta Fuentes. She's new?"

Hanna replied, "We have no one by that name."

Nick yelled, "Okay, thanks," as he ran out of the office with Grazie in tow. He ran down the stairs to C level and down to Security Sergeant Vince Towes's office, Identification and Records, where photos of employees were taken and ID badges made.

Winded, they entered the cramped office where they were barely able to move. A dozen assorted new employees waited to have their pictures taken. The desk, photography equipment, backdrop, and lights made it quite claustrophobic.

Towes was about to snap a photo of a slim older black man in green radiology scrubs. Nick asked, "Sergeant, did you recently make a badge for an environmental employee named Marta Fuentes?"

Towes was tall and young, with light hair and lighter skin. "Sure did," the sergeant replied. "Rush job, for the director."

Nick asked, "What do you mean?"

Sergeant Towes said, "Just that. She came with a letter from the director, on his stationery, I might add, to please expedite her ID."

Grazie asked, "May we see the letter?"

"Negative," the sergeant replied. "She said she needed it for occupational medicine so she could be registered immediately. I made a copy, but I can't find it."

Nick asked, "Can we see the photo you took of her?"

"Now?"

"Yes."

Towes apologized to the man waiting for his picture. The crowd grumbled at the delay. "All right, let me look it up on the computer." The sergeant hit a few keys, then yelled, "What the..."

"What is it?" asked Grazie.

"It's not here," replied the sergeant. "It was here, or I wouldn't be able to print the ID, but now it's gone. Wait! When I went over there to retrieve the ID from the machine, Marta was standing by my desk. She must have deleted the photo and records then."

Nick asked, exasperated, "Wouldn't you have seen or heard anything if she did?"

"Look at this place. New employees, renewals. I'm backed up."

Grazie whispered to Nick, "Did someone know that?"

In the hall, Nick called Al and said, "Look at security video and see if you can spot a small dark woman in environmental, light blue, leaving security ten minutes ago. She left the director's office and disappeared. If you find her, hold her."

"Dark?" Al asked. "Like, Latin."

"She's ID'd as Marta Fuentes. But no. I don't think so."

Grazie still held the blueprint in the cardboard tube. Nick said, "Let's run that by Bill Ricks at Parsippany PD, see if he has any ideas." They got into Nick's car and were passing the Emergency

Medical Unit when a silver-haired man in a very nice suit exited the building. Nick pulled up in front of him, stepped out of the car, and said, "Hello, I'm Nick Moore from corporate security. Do you have a moment?"

The fellow replied, "I was just leaving."

Nick said, "I wanted to ask you a couple of questions. It won't take long."

The man replied, "Maybe some other time."

Nick replied, "No, we'll do it now, shall we go into your office? What's your name?"

The man, getting angry, said, "My name is Ted Remo, but I told you already some other time."

Nick knew the name. Remo was administration, high up. Nick replied, "How long have you been working here, Ted?"

Remo answered, "Nine years, but I don't—"

Nick cut in, "Well, I guess in the nine years you worked here at some point you got to read the Guardian Angel Human Resources Handbook?"

Remo responded, "You realize I can have you fired."

Nick explained, "Hospital employees of every department and division are subject to the rules and regulations in that handbook, which lists all behavior and protocol that is both acceptable and unacceptable and the discipline carried for each particular infraction. Investigating these reported infractions are part of the responsibilities of the corporate investigators such as me."

Remo sputtered, "What are we talking about?"

Nick replied, "Your cooperation. You see in order for me to do my job it relies on cooperation of the employee, so my director had the committee that oversees the rules and regulations write a rule that employees must cooperate with an investigation or be terminated. Yes, you can have me fired. And I can have you fired."

Resigned, Remo said, "What can I do for you?"

Nick began, "Earlier today one of our co-employees was murdered in the vestibule of the Emergency Medical Unit, right behind you. Did you see anything out of the ordinary?"

Remo replied, “No, I didn’t see anything. I was at budget hearings all day and just returned.”

Nick, handing him a business card, said, “Thanks, if you think of anything at all, please give me a call.”

Remo showed his teeth in a parody of a smile. “Will do.”

When they got back in the car, Grazie said, “That was very interesting. Remo’s whole demeanor changed when you cited the employee rules.”

Nick replied, “That is one of the most helpful tools we have. We use it all the time to get employees to cooperate. No matter what the investigation, Al and I would collect the information, interview the employee or employees, and determine what if any violation was committed. Investigations is not the department that decided what if any disciplinary action was required. If Remo didn’t cooperate I would report him to human resources who would determine if disciplinary action was required. But usually, they concede to the rules and cooperate.”

“He didn’t seem like he would.”

“He threatens to fire me and expects me to back down. But a blowup over an investigation would make him look worse than it would make me look. Listen, I can run these blueprints over to Ricks later. Would you like to get a bite to eat? I haven’t eaten all day.”

Grazie replied, “Yes, I’m starving. Drop me at my car. I’ll follow you.”

“You could lose me in traffic.”

“I won’t,” she said.

Nick drove to a restaurant in Summit, New Jersey. Sorrento was a dimly lit, rather large place with a circular bar and cozy semicircular booths in the dining room that were made of thick red leather. With the dim lights and lit candles on each table Nick liked the ambiance and also the fact that it was just far enough from Parsippany that he never saw anyone in there he knew. The food was always good and the drinks generous.

Nick waited for Grazie to park, and as they began to walk to the restaurant entrance, Grazie’s hand grazed Nick’s arm. Nick’s heart jumped, and he wondered, *Did she do that on purpose?* As they entered, Nick asked for the booth in the far corner. The waiter led them over. Grazie sat on the right side of the table, leaving Nick the spot he wanted so as to look across the room to the entrance. Nick liked the booth since it was partially blocked by a room divider, yet positioned that he could see who entered. Nick, like many current and former police officers, as well as "wise guys," always tried to position himself with his back against a wall so as to see who is entering the restaurant without someone entering and getting the drop on him. Once you got in the habit of choosing that seat, it was a tough habit to break. Nick had been doing it for decades, for his safety and for the safety of the patrons. He didn't want a stickup to happen behind him. Better to see what's going on.

And he had to admit, better to see someone he knew before they saw him with a woman who wasn't his wife.

The waiter took their drink order, a vodka martini for her and Scotch neat for Nick. The waiter returned with their drinks and said he would be back for their order. When the waiter returned, they each decided on Veal Sorrento, the specialty of the house, and another round of drinks.

Grazie asked, as she sipped her drink, almost like she was thinking out loud, "Why now? What are they doing with the information they're receiving? And more importantly, when do they plan to strike?"

Nick began to answer her, "I think they finally have a mole where they need him. It's got to be soon. They've tipped their hand, maybe on purpose. Maybe not. They realize they're missing some details. They were surprised by the presence of both Harry Barker and Jack Boyle. As far as killing them, they have no conscience. They only see the finished product, and they won't let anything get in their way."

"What's the finished product?" she asked.

"Terror? Anarchy?"

Nick was thinking as he was looking at Grazie that he really enjoyed this, being with her and discussing the case. It was crazy, but he appreciated that she listened to his ideas with interest. Here was a beautiful woman who could talk about work.

As if she could hear his thoughts, Grazie said, "I enjoy working with you. And I like being treated as an equal. Believe it or not, it doesn't happen often."

Drawn together like two magnets, they kissed. Not a long lingering kiss, nor just a peck. But a kiss nonetheless.

Grazie began turning red, backed up, and said, "Nick, I'm sorry but I'm married."

Nick replied, "I'm married too. We can't let this happen."

Grazie replied, "Agreed."

"Good."

"Good." Grazie, regaining her composure, stated, "The scope of this case is wild. Everywhere we turn there is another facet to the investigation."

Nick was thinking of the kiss and knowing it was wrong, still could not help himself and wanted more.

The waiter appeared with their order.

When the waiter left, Grazie said, "I have a confidential informant who can move around freely inside the more militant mosques in Jersey City and Fort Lee. I already told Smallwood that I would help him in his quest for additional information concerning the tapes, but I would feel more comfortable if we all worked with the informant. As a team."

Nick said, "Yes. Of course." He'd worked with CIs before. But not this kind.

Nick was enjoying the dinner and the warm feeling he was getting from the drinks, and from Grazie's proximity. He asked, "Did the informant mention anything about plans or attacks? Or these materials Smallwood found. Do they fit with anything your CI saw? Are these incidents connected to bin Laden's notebooks, or were these some completely new deranged plan for inflicting misery and pain?"

"Big questions," she said.

Nick shrugged. "I think I have a suspect in mind, but I need to check out a few things first. I need to be sure before I label anybody like that."

She said, "You could tell me who it is."

"I could," he said. "But once someone's a suspect, they tend to stay that way."

She nodded. "I like that about you, Investigator."

Nick said, "Let's get out of here."

Nick paid the check, and they left the restaurant. While they were walking to their cars, Nick said, "We should do this again." She didn't answer. Nick waited for her to pull out of the lot before he drove off.

Nick returned to the hospital, but before going inside he drove around the perimeter and checked out the different posts and security patrols. He then parked in the visitor's lot and went to security. Nick checked all the security incident reports for the past twenty-four hours. He then checked the commanding officer's log concerning radio checks and call-in. By the time he finished, he began to realize how tired he was, decided to go home.

On his ride home, Nick felt a strange charge from his gut going up to his chest. He felt, he realized, excited. Like in high school when he realized Mayla Watkins *liked* him. Like a teenager.

Like an idiot, he thought. He thought of his wife Jen and became saddened and guilt ridden. Nothing like this had happened to Nick before. He'd betrayed Jen a hundred times in a hundred ways. Broken promises. Missed appointments. How many times had she reached out to him one way or another, to find him absent, or at least distracted. He'd done everything he could to sabotage his marriage. Except this. He told himself he would put an end to this thing with Grazie, whatever it was. He could never hurt Jen. Not this way. He'd put Grazie out of his head.

When he arrived home he saw a note on the counter.

Kids at your sister's. Gone to Zumba class. Could you…

And then a list of household chores, solidly a week's worth. She was within her rights. If he were home at a reasonable time every night, she'd be asking for one small task a day, practically nothing.

This was perfect, he thought. It gave him time to check his suit for makeup, time to take a shower, in case any perfume was detectable on him, time to unload the dishwasher and fix the drip in the kitchen sink and schedule the spring air-conditioner maintenance, and still have a drink before Jen was due to return home. By the time Jen returned home Nick accomplished all this and was sipping Scotch in front of the news. He woke when she came in and followed her up the stairs. It crossed his mind that they were both home and awake, and freshly showered, and the kids were out of the house, and it might be nice to make love.

"How was Zumba class?" he asked as she dropped her bag by their bed and peeled off her leotard, walking bare-assed into the bathroom as if he wouldn't notice. Were there times when he didn't?

"Sweaty. Hand me a fresh bar of soap."

He dug into the vanity and fished out a new one, struggled with the cellophane, and handed her the bar.

"Are you gonna watch?" she asked.

"Can I?"

She'd disappeared behind the blue plastic shower curtain.

No answer. "Did you do all the things on the list?"

"I did. I was very good. What do I get?"

"A sense of inner satisfaction for showing up for your family."

"There's some things happening at the hospital. You might hear about them on the news, so I just want to—"

She cut off the water and reached for a towel. He snatched it out of her reach. She leaned her head out from behind the curtain, hiding her nudity.

"Seriously?"

He felt the smile drop from his face as he handed over the towel. She was wrapped in it when she emerged from the shower, saying, "I'm tired from the class, I need sleep."

Nick tried again, saying, "You can't believe what's happening at the hospital."

Jen cut him off, saying, "Can it wait till tomorrow?"

Nick felt himself bruise every time Jen refused to hear about work. He knew it was a lot of trauma to bring home. But it was his career, and he wanted to talk about it. But it always seemed she was too busy to listen.

Jen got into bed, and Nick tried again, saying, "The entire hospital is on full alert—"

She cut him off. "What time do you have to get up?"

He shook his head. "Six."

She set the clock. Then under her breath, she said something barely audible about being very tired. Then she rolled away and turned off the light.

Okay, he thought. No sex. And no conversation. What was the point of sharing a bed, or for that matter, a house?

Leave it at work, the guys at the sheriff's office used to say. Don't bring it home; don't tell them about the cases. They think they want to hear about it, but they don't. Well, Jen didn't want to hear about it, not at all. Being home was a time for Nick to share with his wife, son, and daughter. Jen made it quite clear she didn't want to get nervous hearing what he did. So he didn't talk about work at home, or about home at work. The two lives were separate and apart, and that was the way Jen wanted them to stay.

But it meant she didn't know about the life he lived during half his waking hours. More than half.

Nick was thinking of Grazie as he drifted off to sleep.

CHAPTER 12

Before work, Nick stopped at the Parsippany PATH train station and asked to see security footage. No one had boarded the trains going in either direction in the hours after Boyle's murder who looked like a possibility. But what did a murderer look like? Nick phoned the conductors on duty, waking two and getting two voice mails. No, didn't see nothing strange. No one out of breath, no one stinking of murder.

He backtracked to Parsippany PD and talked to Ricks, showing him the blueprint. "So they have an insider, at least one," Ricks said. "And not a genius. Any suspects?"

"Working on it," Nick said.

At the hospital, Nick, Grazie, and Al proceeded to interview everyone in the building that housed the Emergency Medical Unit. Nick utilized an empty office on the second floor for the interviews. The room had two desks, six chairs, and a nonworking telephone. He arranged with the manager of the building to have each employee that worked that day come in for an interview one at a time. After two hours and two dozen interviews, they didn't gather any useful information.

The next person to arrive was a secretary on the second floor of the building directly over the entrance to the EMU. The woman was in her midfifties with dark brown, almost black hair and a round face. She was a plus-size woman who stated her name as Emily Green.

"Hello, Emily. I'm Nick Moore."

Emily replied, "Is this about the dreadful business that happened below my office?"

Nick replied, "It is. One of our security officers, Jack Boyle, was killed by an unknown intruder. We were wondering if you happened to see anything out of the ordinary from your window."

Emily said, "I didn't. My back is to the window, and I normally don't make a habit of staring out the window. You see, we are very busy here and wouldn't be able to accomplish our work if we gazed out the window all day."

Nick stated, "I didn't mean to imply that you stare out the window, but it could have been possible as you got up for something you looked out and saw something unusual."

Emily stated, "Well, now that you mention it, I did see a man walking close to the building in the dirt, behind the bushes. I assumed it was one of the landscapers doing their thing. I only noticed because he didn't have any gardening tools or those infernal blowers that make so much noise."

Nick asked, "That's great, Emily! Did you happen to see what he was wearing?"

Emily responded, "He was wearing one of those hoodies, all his clothing was dark. He kept pulling the hoodie part close to his face, but when he looked back as if he was looking for someone I noticed he had a full beard and he didn't look like the normal gardeners or helpers. He was taller, slim. Not as, you know, as dark as the gardeners I'm used to seeing around here."

"Not Mexican?"

"That's right," she said, relieved. No one here was going to call her a racist. "Not like any Mexican I ever saw."

Nick said, "Very good, Emily. I'm going to ask you to write a statement of what you just told me with this lady, Phyllis Grazie. She'll help you. And thank you for your help."

Grazie said, "Right this way, Emily. This won't take long."

Nick and Al spent the entire morning interviewing employees that were in the EMU or the main hospital but didn't find anything they could use. Grazie helped them until noon, then left for a meeting. Nick and Al decided to break for lunch and headed to the cafeteria.

Over cafeteria burgers and salad, Nick said, "There's so much to do and not enough people to do it."

"The system's growing," Al said. "More yardage to patrol, and more crimes to investigate. The system will hire more investigators. And the crimes are getting smarter, so we have to."

It was true. Nick didn't mention that the director had told him that he'd be heading a team of investigators soon, that Al was good, but Nick was more of a company man. It was nonsense, of course. Al was all company man, down to his socks. What he wasn't was a white man. But the promotion was theoretical. No point in talking about it now.

"We don't want to do what border patrol did," Nick said. "Hiring anyone who's standing nearby."

"Let's lay out the requirements, right now," Al said, an impish sparkle in his eye.

Nick said, "Retired law enforcement professional."

Al added, "With significant time spent in the detective bureau."

Nick said, "Once hired, the individual will be trained and supervised in the ways of corporate procedures, corporate compliance, and the rules and regulations that govern the employees."

"By us!" Al added.

"Right. A retired cop might be able to conduct an investigation, but you have to teach that the employee is not a criminal."

"Not necessarily!" Al kicked in.

Nick said, "What might be justified police behavior on the street is not tolerated in the corporate world."

"And vice versa!"

A laugh burst out of Nick, and he struggled not to spit out his food. "Right, yes." Al was a dead serious investigator, which was what made him so funny. He was the only one who could make Nick laugh.

"What else?" Al asked.

"Well, unlike police investigations, corporate employees are always subjected to an interview and not an interrogation. A good investigator can conduct an interrogation and make the individual think is an interview." Al knew the difference. Though they seemed the same, an interrogation was more accusatory where an interview was ostensibly for fact-finding. Knowing the subtle difference between these two forms of questioning and how to apply them was what made a good investigator. "A good investigator has to have 'the gift.'" He looked at Al. "You have the gift."

Al grinned. "You're not so bad yourself." Al said, "Jesus, you would have thought we'd have collected more information than this from a building full of people. Nick, how did the suspect vanish into thin air? Near as we can tell, the intruder makes a turn around the building and disappears. Somebody should have seen something. The K-9 squad, New Jersey Transit cameras, our cameras, someone in the building."

Nick just shook his head. Then he said, "Unless he didn't go through the bushes towards the train station. What if he went through the bushes and headed the other way towards the residential area across from the hospital. He could have had a car or someone in a car waiting for him."

Ann Stromer came up to Nick and Al in her nurse's whites, holding her cafeteria tray as if hoping to be invited to eat with the cool kids. A big-boned but not fat woman, she wore her hair blonde—almost white—and elaborately coiffured to maximize volume. Also, she wore, to Nick's thinking, entirely too much makeup. "Hey, Nick!" she said, in the tone of a late-night diner waitress. "Hey, allllll!" she added in an entirely different tone. Seductive. Alluring. It didn't work, but Al turned on his FM DJ voice and she almost melted.

"What's the haps, Nurse Stromer!" Al said. "Where you been keeping yourself?"

"A day late and a thousand dollars short."

Nick said, "I thought you drew a good salary."

In the eight years that Nick knew Ann, she'd gone from a woman who never had a hair out of place to a disheveled woman who always looked tired and out of sorts, wearing expensive but worn-out clothes, like she'd raided a theatrical costume shop. Even her nurse's whites had yellowed. To add a little "class" to her life, she drove a new Mercedes. Nick guessed the payments were killing her.

"Expenses," she said. "You know. Never enough. What I need is a good man."

"I thought you had one," Al offered.

"Bums," she said. "All bums. Oh, Officer," she said, leaning her left hip way out to the side. "I'm sure there's a warrant for me somewhere!"

"Got a girlfriend," Al lied. "But I'll keep it in mind."

She turned to Nick. "How about you, slim. You look like third-husband material."

He showed his ring. "Spoken for. But thanks."

Nick liked Ann. She'd worked for the hospital for the past twenty years. She was always in a rush to go somewhere but was never seen at the destination. She would make the rounds at all the hospitals associated with Guardian Angel Hospital System and check on any infectious diseases that had been reported. What's more, she was the liaison with the state of New Jersey and was responsible for reporting any contagious patients to the Centers for Disease Control. She only *seemed* like an idiot.

"What happened to Jack Boyle?" she asked. "Any suspects yet? Are the employees safe at the hospital now that a murderer is running around?"

Al was the first to speak. "We share your concern. We're increasing patrols. If you see something, say something."

Ann asked, "Do you have any leads?" Then she replied to her own question, "I bet not. Have you conducted interviews? What have the police said?"

Nick was paying attention to Ann's body language. The words didn't matter, not hers anyway. Too many people listened for the words. The important thing was to watch for the deception. Nick was good at that.

He'd taught workshops on body language. As a discipline, he found it more helpful than polygraph tests, which could be fooled. Body language, first studied by none other than Charles Darwin, was the nonverbal communication of information by means of subconscious or conscious movement, gestures, facial expressions, eye or head movement, and body movement. Body language is usually subconscious. Nick knew the more one studies and practices, the better they become at noticing even the most subtle clue given by a subject. Subsequently the questions are more difficult as pertaining to the case until the subject either clears himself, or makes himself a prime suspect.

Reading body language was Nick's secret power. Nick knew the answer to questions he asked people before they responded. He knew who was lying, withholding the truth, or giving a half-truth. As far as his career was concerned this was a gift, a blessing, which always gave him the upper hand while interrogating suspects, attempting to solve a crime, or having a suspect eventually tell the truth. At home it made Jen and the kids avoid him. Who wanted to have their mind read?

Ann finally retreated and Nick said, "Let's canvass again, lean harder on everyone with a window facing the lot, anyone who had a chance of seeing the suspect."

Al said, "Maybe they really didn't see anything."

Nick thought to himself how unlikely it was for no one to see anything except Emily. He almost said out loud, "Or maybe they just don't care."

CHAPTER 13

Al and Nick next went to the morgue. As they entered, they were first hit by the formaldehyde fumes, and under that, the smell of the bodies and organs in various stages of decomposition. It was something you never got used to, Nick thought. How did people live with this every day?

The morgue, tiled from floor to ceiling like a public restroom, with two stainless steel drain tables, designed to channel the blood to the drain, bright lights shining on scales, jars, sinks, and instruments like a movie set. The movie was *Frankenstein.* On one of the tables, Jack Boyle's lifeless body was pried open in the typical Y autopsy pattern, following the incision made by the examiner. Jack's face appeared to want to tell Nick what happened. But then raising his gaze ever so slightly, Nick saw that the top of his head was cut off and his brain was sitting in the scale next to him.

They found the chief medical examiner, Dr. Russling, in his office, a bald, bespectacled man with a prominent hunch, likely from spending a long career stooped over corpses.

Nick and Al knocked and walked in, Nick asking, "Hello, Doc. Any results yet?"

Dr. Russling replied, "The preliminary autopsy revealed security officer Jack Boyle was injected with something very strong that stopped both his heart and respiratory system almost instantly. I won't have the results back for a few days, but if you ask me my professional opinion I would say it was fentanyl."

"Fentanyl?" Nick had heard about it, but nothing good.

The doctor continued. "First, we have tests to determine if there are any opiates in the blood. He came back negative. Second, as you know, there is a controversy surrounding the execution of prisoners with drugs because they prove to be unreliable. Therefore, they began using a combination of drugs, one to put the prisoner to sleep, another to stop his heart, and finally one to stop the respiratory system. While they are effective and each has their own purpose, too little or in the wrong sequence and the prisoner appears to have labored breathing or violent movements caused by arrhythmia. However, a large-enough injection of fentanyl causes all three in the victim: unconsciousness, respiratory failure, and heart failure. I'll call you when the official results are in." Nick thanked the doctor as they left.

Nick and Al exited the morgue through the rear exit leading to the refuse and cardboard dumpster areas, then to the parking lot which they could cut through to get to the main hospital. Turning toward the parking lot, Nick caught a glimpse of someone turning in the opposite direction toward the dumpsters.

Nick took off in that direction. Al gave chase.

"Where are we running?" Al asked.

"You remember the fake cleaning woman from Shane's office? Marta Fuentes? I think I just saw her.

Al quickly passed Nick. The female reached the end of the building and turned right, hugging the wall of the children's hospital. Al closed the gap quickly and made the right turn almost at full speed. Nick caught up and made the right turn and there on the ground found Al, sprawled out on his back. Al began shaking his head and was attempting to get up.

Nick asked, "What happened? Are you okay?"

Al replied, "When I turned the corner I spotted the female about ten yards ahead of me, and I knew she was mine. Then a guy jumped out and sucker punched me."

Nick asked, "Did you see who it was?"

"No," Al replied, "I went down for the count as I heard him run off."

Nick was already on his cell phone to the security shift commander. "Get security down to the driveway by the children's hospital. We're looking for a man and woman walking north away from the hospital. Let me know if anyone sees them." Just then, Nick got a text from Shane. Al got the same text. "Come see me. Now."

The director said, "Nick, Al, I have to ask you to go to Atlantic City for a one-day anti-terrorism conference. I know this is a hell of a time to be away from the hospital, but our grant writer said we have a great shot of obtaining grant money if we participate."

"Director," Nick said, "begging your pardon. Are you out of your fucking mind?"

Shane's temples inflated visibly.

Al cut in. "Sir, we'd really rather not attend with all that is going on here. I think we'd be more useful to you working the case."

The director said, "Listen. I hate to bother you two geniuses with the business of paying bills. You're artists. But I went to some lengths to get you into this conference, something set up for active law enforcement, not retirees lucky not to be patrolling a shopping mall."

"Ouch," Al said.

"So go there and be present, sign in, and get the material they will be handing out. Participate. Have a presence. We need the investigations unit to participate to qualify for different programs. This is part of how we get money to hire new investigators. It's also part of how we stay current."

Nick said, "So who's in charge while we're gone?"

"I am," the director said, as if it were obvious. There was no profit in arguing. What could they say? That's great, sir, but aren't you more of a desk jockey? Wouldn't you be more comfortable addressing a budget shortfall?

Shane sighed. "Sorry, men. Obviously, this was planned before Harry Barker and Jack Boyle got killed. You were on the waiting list. Some people canceled out, and you're in. That's how it works. I don't want this any more than you do, but it's a done deal. I want you to go, clear your head, and come back with a new perspective on this investigation. See you when you get back."

As they left the director's office, Nick noticed that Al still seemed out of sorts since being punched. Nick asked, "You want to go to the emergency room?"

Al shrugged it off. "It takes more than a sucker punch to take me down. If they want to stop me, they'll have to kill me."

Chapter 14

Nick arrived at work early, wanting to clean off his desk of any matters that needed attention, make phone calls to the individuals in other cases, and advise them he would be gone for two days. Nick brought an extra suit, but when he got to the convention center where the bus was supposed to leave from, he realized that he had the wrong idea. Nick looked around and recognized managers from the different hospitals, motor pool, emergency departments, the labs, and labor and delivery. In Hawaiian shirts and sundresses. Atlantic City was, in fact, Atlantic City.

The conference was not planned to be a joke, even if people read it that way. Nursing managers were going to give lectures on infectious disease, patient care in a crisis situation, and business continuity after a disaster from a medical perspective. There would be plenary sessions, breakout sessions, a keynote speaker. All expenses were paid, of course, and he'd have free time as well to gamble or whatever else he felt like doing. At any other time, it would have been a welcome break from work. It was not that Nick was opposed to gambling. As a matter of fact, he was gambling in the social clubs in Newark before it was legal for him to drive. Nor was Nick opposed to drinking and dining on someone's tab. It was the timing that Nick was opposed to. He knew something was going to happen at the hospital sooner than later and that the managers and coordinators that were going would all try to "shine their buttons" in front of the director with tall tales and made-up exploits rather than have concern for the hospital and people. Sometimes Nick wondered if the director knew what they were doing and played along, or was he truly interested in these "fables" that they liked to tell, if enjoyed entry into this made-up playground. In either case, Nick was always sitting closed mouth but respectful, listening to someone's bullshit. Today, he couldn't wait for the event to be over.

Nick learned there would be twenty-one people in all attending from Guardian Angel Hospital System. Furthermore, Director Shane had a luxury bus that was going to take them down so no one would have to make the hundred-plus-mile trip in their own vehicle.

Ten minutes before the bus left, a Parsippany detective car pulled up to the bus, and Detective Ricks motioned for Nick and Al to come out.

Detective Ricks said, "Sorry about this, but we're about to begin the interviews of all the neighbors on Smith Street across from the EMU. I called the director, and he said for one of you to stay and conduct the interview with me, and then head down later."

Nick said, "Okay, I'll stay."

Al, however, replied, "Generous of you, Nick, but I'll stay. I can help conduct the interview, but you're better with this crowd." Al said with a wave that included the clowns on the bus and, presumably, anyone in AC who might be attached to funding. "You go and I'll drive down right after the interviews."

Nick nodded, climbed back onto the bus.

When he arrived, check-in went smoothly; each person was handed a credit card with their name on it and were instructed to use this for any expenses except gambling.

Everyone was instructed to be in the lobby at eight forty-five the next morning for the short walk to the convention center. Until then, they had the rest of the afternoon and evening free. The bellboy took Nick's luggage and led him to the room. It was spacious with two double beds, a small kitchenette, and a combination living room and dining room. After he got settled in, Nick decided to go for a walk and check out the place. Getting hungry, Nick stopped for lunch in one of the restaurants that lined the outside perimeter of the cavernous gambling floor.

As Nick was waiting for his food, his phone rang. It was Al Stokes.

Al said, "We canvassed the neighborhood, and the hospital and EMU again. No one was home or looking out their window when the killing took place. No security video we haven't seen. No surprises. I'll wrap up here and head to AC. I'll be there in a few hours."

Nick replied, "Good work." It was good work. That didn't mean it yielded anything.

Al asked, "Why do you think the boss made such a big deal about this conference. What's so special about this one?"

Nick explained, "Damned if I know. Certifications? PR? Funding, I guess. Somebody has to come up with the money to pay for our salaries and all this fancy equipment."

Al said, "Right. And we're just in it for the glory."

Nick finished his hamburger and decided to take a walk through the casino. As he walked down the main aisle, he heard loud laughter and voices coming from one of the roulette tables. Nick spotted Ann Stromer laughing, then gulping clear liquid from a sweaty glass tumbler.

"Another five hundred on black!" she bellowed, as a waiter took her near-empty glass and handed her a fresh one. "Thanks, baby," she said, and laid out five black one-hundred-dollar casino chips on the rectangle marked "BLACK." Black chips stood in stacks in front of her. She'd been winning, it seemed. Or she started with more black chips and she was losing.

"Black on black, baby!" she shouted, to the annoyance of everyone within earshot. "I like 'em dark."

Then in one gulp, she finished her drink, waved for another—they were complimentary, after all—and kissed the man sitting next to her. She continued to kiss his face, then whispered something in his ear, and both began to laugh. The man was much younger than Ann, powerfully built with deep, dark skin and black hair. He was impeccably dressed in a tailored black silk suit (Nick knew custom-made, though he'd never hired a tailor for anything more than cuffs) and, Nick guessed, thousand-dollar loafers. The wheel landed on black, and she prominently thrust the available length of her tongue into the man's mouth. When she turned back to the table, he rubbed circles on her lower back. She reached back and slid his hand down to her buttocks.

Nick suspected the man's drink was water. He sipped sparingly, and he himself did not touch the chips.

Ann spotted Nick and shrieked his name. "*Nick!* Over here, over here!"

She leapt from her barstool and pulled Nick close. He turned at the last second, dodging a gin-soaked wet kiss, but she slobbered on his cheek anyway.

"Look at me!" she said. "What a run of luck! I'm a high roller. Where are my manners. This is my boyfriend Max. Sit with us."

Nick greeted Max with a handshake. "Nice to meet you, Max." The man's hand was smooth and cool. He looked Max in the eyes, and as if seeing the man's soul, or more to the point, his lack of a soul. Nick felt the hairs on his neck go up, as he knew immediately he did not like the man. It was Ann's life. None of his business.

Then turning to Ann, Nick said, "No thanks, Ann. I'm not very lucky at gambling. Don't stay up too late."

Nick walked around the casino, stopped at a bar, and had a few drinks, went back to the hotel room, showered, and dozed in front of the TV for a while. He jolted awake when Al walked in.

"What'd I miss?" Al asked, tossing his overnight bag on the unused bed.

"I gave a seminar on inefficient use of time and resources in law enforcement."

"Put something on. Let's go look at the human spectacle."

As they passed through the casino, Nick noticed people noticing Al. He wore a salmon-colored shirt and baby blue blazer, and he seemed to glide across the casino floor like a fashion model. Nick ambled like a middle-aged cop, which seemed about right. They watched a crap game for a while, a young couple delicately putting down chips they obviously couldn't afford.

"What's that?" Al whispered."

Across the aisle, Ann and her boyfriend were back at the roulette table. Or still there.

Nick said, "The well-dressed guy next to Ann is her boyfriend, Max."

Nick observed that her pile of chips had disappeared. They did not appear to be sitting as close to each other or having as good a time. Nick saw the croupier take Ann's chips off the black rectangle. The air seemed to leave her with a puff. Determined, Ann placed more chips on black, but at this point, Max changed from the charming boyfriend into an evil demon, whispering in her ear with a scowl on his face. Nevertheless, Ann kept placing hundred-dollar chips on the color black. This time Max grabbed her finger and bent it back as though he was going to break it. Ann cringed in pain. The croupier called out, "Zero," and took Ann's money.

Max grabbed Ann by the wrist, twisted it until she got up, and they left. There were no chips in front of Ann as they walked away and left the casino.

Nick was about to go after Max when Al grabbed him under the arm and said, "Stay cool. We know there is something up with this guy. If you crack him now, we may never see him again. Besides Ann is a big girl and can take care of herself. I'm sure this isn't the first time this happened. It's just the first time we saw it. Let's go to the bar and have a drink."

Al then led Nick to the bar, and they ordered drinks.

Later that night, Nick and Al decided to go to the steak house located in the hotel. Al called and made reservations. When they arrived, the host explained it would only be a few moments and he would come and get them at the bar. As they approached the bar they saw Ann sitting alone with her drink. They both said hello to Ann, ordered a drink for themselves and one for her.

Nick asked, "Ann, where's Max?"

She pouted. "He's up in the room and didn't feel like eating. I didn't call for a reservation, and now I have to wait."

Nick asked, "Would you like to join us?"

Ann threw her arms around Nick's neck and seemed to be crying.

Nick walked over to the host and asked, "Could I have another seat added to my table?"

The host replied, "That would be impossible. We're full to capacity."

Nick handed the host a twenty-dollar bill. The host's mouth twisted into a mockery of a smile. "How delightful it must be to live in 1980." Nick handed him another twenty, and suddenly the host said, "A table for three will be ready in just a moment."

The three sat down and ordered their drinks and dinner. While they were waiting for their meals, Nick asked Ann, "How long have you and Max been dating?"

Ann replied, "A year, I guess. But he's been away a lot. I think I finally found Mr. Right!"

Their drinks came. Ann hoisted hers high. "To love!"

"Love," Nick and Al muttered, sipping their drink as Ann tossed back her martini in a single gulp and signaled the waiter for another.

"Max is old-fashioned," she said. "And very religious. These are the things we're working through before we get married."

Al asked her, "Don't you think you're rushing it? Why not take your time and get to know each other first?"

Ann's martini arrived, and she sipped. "We *are* getting to know each other. And his family is getting used to the idea of him dating me. They're very wealthy, you know. His father is a doctor. As a matter of fact, that is how we met. At a medical convention in Orlando, Florida, last year. You remember, Nick, I saw you and your family there! You introduced me to your wife, but I couldn't introduce you to Max since he hadn't arrived yet."

Nick replied, "I remember." He began thinking back to that day. He introduced Ann to Jen and the kids. He remembered the smell of liquor on her breath as she told him how she had to tell these "newbies" to the medical field how much more experienced we, our hospitals, are and how we're prepared for any emergency. During that conversation, Ann said she had given her presentation time and again, and some of her colleagues seem to be bored with the topic, but she tries to change it up and give it new life.

At the time, Nick did not think too much of his Florida conversation with Ann. Nick did not know the players, especially Max, and since he did not know the seriousness of the threat to hospitals at the time he could not have connected the dots. Now Nick was very interested.

He asked Ann, "Is Max in the medical field?"

"No," she replied, "he is in imports and exports to the Middle East but mainly to Egypt."

Al cleared his throat.

Nick asked, "Was Max's father there? Was he a guest speaker? I mean, it was a medical convention and he's a doctor." Ann finished her drink, asked for another, and continued babbling, which normally would have infuriated Nick, but now he didn't want her to stop.

Ann said, "You remember. The convention was for infectious disease and how it pertained to emergency preparedness for natural or man-made emergencies. It was for professionals from throughout the United States. I was just lucky that Max was on vacation and was staying at the same hotel." Her eyes lit up, happy and sad and wet. "By my good fortune, we met in the hotel bar and hit it off almost immediately." Ann continued, "I was a guest speaker, and when we all went for drinks later, Max and I knew it was love at first sight. Max is a good listener, not like my last husband, and he wanted to hear my entire presentation. He was so interested in my career and how I'm the lead nurse of the infectious disease department. What a catch!" she said. "Not only is he loaded, he finds me so interesting and hangs on my every word. And he isn't cheap. He gives me money to gamble. Don't you think he is wonderful, worrying about me and my career?"

Nick locked eyes with Al.

Nick spotted Ann's hotel room key, room 1009. He excused himself and went to the front desk. Nick, no stranger to getting information, slipped the clerk a twenty, and gave him the room number, telling the clerk he wanted to know Max's last name to surprise him at the conference tomorrow by announcing him.

The clerk checked his computer then said, "I am sorry, sir, but the room number you gave me is registered to an Ann Stromer."

Nick said, "Yes, of course. Isn't there a line of credit attached to the room?"

The clerk replied, "If there were, I would not have access to that information."

Nick thanked him and left, frustrated.

Their dinner arrived as well as Ann's hundredth drink. By now though, the hairs on the back of Nick's neck were crawling. Nick wanted to ask her many more questions about her boyfriend but did not want her to get suspicious that he was doing just that. He changed the conversation and let her and Al talk while he was planning the questions he wanted to ask her and more importantly the way he was going to ask them so as not to arouse her suspicions. Nick needed to have Max's last name and his father's name for the purpose of verifying what he had told Ann.

Nick did not like that many coincidences happening all at the same time: Ann met Max at a medical conference when he is not in the field, that Ann met him at a bar since he doesn't seem to drink, and that he was so interested in all Ann had to say about her hospital's emergency preparedness. When Nick processed this in his head, with what he saw earlier in the afternoon, when Max bent her finger and twisted her arm, he got a bad feeling.

Al and Ann were discussing laws of probability as it concerned roulette.

Al continued, "In contrast, when the house pays even money, the odds of that bet coming out are greater. But think of it as flipping a coin. Each time you flip it, the odds of it coming up heads are still 50 percent. So, you can hit heads over and over. Eventually, it'll come up tails. It doesn't mean you're lucky or unlucky."

Ann was gawking at Al and nearly drooling.

Since they were having a good time, Nick did not join their conversation and waited for it to end. Just as the first pause rolled in, Al asked Ann, "What did you say Max's last name was?"

Ann did not answer him but changed the subject, but Al was not sure she heard him.

Nick then asked Ann, "The amount you gamble and win, I bet you get plenty of comps."

Ann replied, "I don't get the comps. Max does. After all, it's his money and line of credit that I play with. He doesn't like to gamble, but he lets me. He only gambles sometimes." Ann continued, "Last year when I came down I lost a bundle, so much, I couldn't pay it back. The casino garnished my wages at the hospital, and it would have taken her forever to pay it off. But thank God for Max! Not long after we started dating I told him of my plight, and he paid off the balance to the casino. What a guy!"

Nick said, "He sounds like a really nice guy. Have you had a chance to meet his family?"

Ann said, "No, we're planning something for next year, and I'm really looking forward to it."

Al then said, "He sounds like a real good catch. And not cheap either."

Nick said, "My nephew is now out of college and working for a freight company in Port Newark. If I can be of any help to Max, let me know. The company's name is Earth Trans and my nephew's name is Greg Moore."

Ann said, "How very nice of you, Nick. I'll let him know. Maybe they can do business together."

"What's Max's last name?" Quickly adding, "In case my nephew gets a phone call, he'll know who it is."

Ann responded without hesitation, "Fouquaan, Max Fouquaan."

Score! Nick thought to himself. Quit while you're ahead. Time to change the subject.

The three had after dinner, drinks, and Al said he was going to try his luck at blackjack when they were finished. He asked Ann if she wanted to tag along, but she replied no, that she has been away from Max too long. Nick said, "I better get some sleep." They left the table, and each went their separate ways. When Nick got to his room, he called his connection in the FBI, Special Agent Dan Camp.

Nick began, "Dan, I need a background check on an Egyptian named Max Fouquaan in the import/export business. His father is a doctor. He is approximately forty-five years old, slim, six feet tall, clean-shaven. Handsome. He's in Atlantic City now. This time last year he was in Orlando."

Dan replied, "Will do."

Nick stated, "I'll try to take his photo and send it to you."

Dan was a good-looking, athletic young man with a complexion of café au lait and a shaved head. Like most of Dan's trusted colleagues, he was ex-military. Nick then asked Dan, "Can you call your state police connections to see how Max registered at the hotel, how much of a credit line he had, and did he give his home address at registration?"

Dan said, "I'll do what I can."

The next day, as they regrouped in the lobby, Nick observed an unusual amount of makeup on Ann's face near her left eye. As he moved closer to her to say hello, almost involuntarily, Ann raised her hand to cover the undeniable bruise around her eye. Knowing she could not cover it and knowing full well Nick noticed it, Ann said, "I got up in the middle of the night and walked into the bathroom door."

Attempting to ease her nervousness, Nick said, "I almost did the same thing!" They both gave a nervous laugh.

The group went to the convention center and suffered through the conference. The day was long, boring, and uneventful. A former prosecutor presented the material in a rote, generic manner, and did not appear to enjoy what he was doing. The mixture was a perfect combination for Nick to lose interest and barely stay awake. Then Nick heard something that caught his attention.

"Jihadists will keep up their quest in order to obtain information about their goal. They are relentless when they set their mind to a goal."

When the seminar was over Nick and Al went for a drink. Nick said, "See if you can photograph Max without him knowing it. Send it to me and Dan Camp." As they were about to order, Ann came by and asked if she could join them.

As their drinks arrived, Ann said to Nick, "I mentioned your nephew to Max. He was very appreciative, but he said no. He has everything in place for his business and your nephew's service would not be required."

Nick said, "No problem," then asked her, "Ann, is that the reason for the bruise?"

Ann replied nervously, “No! What are you talking about? I told you I ran into the bathroom door.”

They had their drinks and ordered another. The mood changed, and they were all laughing and kidding around.

By the time they began to drink their third drink, Ann said to Nick, “You were right. Max hit me. He didn’t like the fact that we were talking about him and snapped when I said I gave you his last name. He didn’t mean to hit me, but it was just that he and his family are private people and like to stay under the radar, that it is safer that way.”

Al asked, “Safer?”

Ann replied with a laugh, “Safer? Did I say that? I meant, easier for them to import since they know the people they’re doing business with for a long time and like them. They’re Muslim, so there is a built-in trust that we could never understand.”

Nick decided not to point out that what she said was complete nonsense.

She then pulled out of her purse what appeared to be one thousand dollars and said, “See! See what he gave me to gamble with! He’s not a bad person, Nick, just a little high-strung and private.”

Nick just nodded in agreement, feeling it was better to not get into it.

Ann stood up from the table, stating, “Well, I’m going gambling.”

Nick replied, “I’m going back to the room and clean up before dinner. The bus leaves at eight.” They could have left in Al’s car anytime, but now Nick had reason to stay. He made reservations at the Italian restaurant located in the hotel.

“I think I’ll take a walk,” Al stated.

Al waited for Ann to leave, figuring he would follow her at a distance to see if she met up with her boyfriend. He didn’t have to wait long. Ann hung up her cell phone and waited a few minutes. When the door opened, her boyfriend stepped out. A suspiciously young, good-looking man, sharply dressed in expensive clothes, took her by the arm and began to walk toward the casino. Al, hiding behind a column, snapped two photos he thought were good and sent them to Nick.

Al was studying the screen to be sure they were sent when behind him the voice of Max spoke in his ear, "I don't like being photographed."

Shaken by the surprise of this action, Al turned toward him. Both were now staring into each other's eyes, tense, dangerous stares.

Al replied, "Don't flatter yourself, I wasn't taking your photo." Al then walked away toward the elevators. As the door closed Max was still standing in the same spot, still staring with a menacing glare.

Chapter 15

As Nick entered their hotel room, he received a cell phone call from FBI Agent Dan Camp.

Dan told Nick, "There is no such person as Max Fouquaan. I checked with Homeland Security and a friend who's stationed in Egypt. No one heard of him. He's not in import/export, not under that name, anyway. He has no Egyptian passport. The entire story appears to be fictitious. It also appears that his entire registration and complimentary services is bogus. What Max did was deposit a large amount of cash on his account to cover any expenses. Max explained he was new in the country and didn't have local accounts. So his father wired him the money to get by. Call me if I can be of any further assistance. By the way, tell Al I got the photos of Max and I'll run them through facial recognition."

Nick replied, "Thanks Dan. Talk to you soon."

Al arrived in the room and said, "I got a photo of Max, but he spotted me and told me he doesn't like being photographed. I told him I wasn't taking his picture and left. I sent them to Dan."

Nick replied, "I got that. Think you pissed him off?"

Al grinned. "I'm sure of it."

Nick said, "Now I know why Max hit Ann. She's talking too much, and he knows we're on to him. None of his story appears to be true, probably not even his name. We need to get his fingerprints without his knowledge."

They stalked the lobby and found Max and Ann as they left the elevator. Al handed them water bottles.

"Water for the bus."

Max appeared harried and said, "I'm not taking the bus," but Al had thrust the bottle into his hand already, and smoothly accepted it back.

As they walked away, Al slipped the bottle into a large envelope. In the car, Nick called the local FBI and told them he was heading over. They took prints off the bottle and issued them to Agent Dan Camp.

Before Nick and Al reached Parsippany, Nick's phone rang. It was Dan Camp.

He said, "The prints were not on file either in the federal database or the Interpol database. Facial recognition was negative."

Who was this man of mystery? Nick wondered, who seemed to have an unending supply of money and a fondness, it seemed, to physically hurt people, especially women. Nick swore he was going to find out.

Chapter 16

Agents John Smallwood and Phyllis Grazie and investigators Al Stokes and Nick Moore gathered in conference room B16 at the CIA field office in downtown Parsippany. The group was considering the best way to use Grazie's confidential informant without compromising him, as he had already proved to be competent at providing information about sleeper cells and future terrorist attacks.

Grazie said, "Ali has proved his worth with the information he supplied, not just here but throughout the country. It is essential that his place remains the same in the eyes of his fellow Muslims. It's taken literally years for him to infiltrate and gain their trust and confidence. I don't want to burn him."

Nick said, "Is there a way we can use him to find out who the mole at Guardian Angel is? I mean, without getting him killed."

Al said, "He has to keep acting the way he always has. If he hasn't been asking questions, but rather gaining his information by listening, then all of a sudden he starts asking questions, he's screwed."

Smallwood said, "What if he says he has information about the hospital he wants to share with them? He learned it from his friend who works there. Naturally it would be information they already know. When they discuss it with him, they may try to compare their notes with his. He could find out if someone is intentionally passing information or is being duped."

Al Stokes interjected, "Maybe he should just start asking questions, the first time about general things then after a few times narrow the questions down to the hospital."

Smallwood stated, "No, not a good idea to be asking questions all of a sudden."

Nick said, "I agree with John. If he starts asking questions, quite possibly about the biggest strike we've seen since 9/11, he will get burned. We'll lose the asset and tip our hand."

Grazie said, "Let's make sure we know what we're doing. Other ideas? Variations?"

Nick was forcing himself to concentrate but found it difficult. Grazie's presence kept distracting him. Every time she shifted her legs, he felt his heart gallop. The team was sitting and sipping their coffee while kicking around ideas. Agent Smallwood added notes to the whiteboard in the front of the room. But they were detectives. It wouldn't be long before they figured him out.

Smallwood, pointing to the board, said, "Here are our options so far. Number one, don't ask any questions, just see if he can overhear something. Number two, ask questions. Number three, go to them with information he received."

Nick didn't hear any new ideas that sounded good or new. He was looking around the conference room, noticing that it was spacious and had all the modern essentials one would expect from the federal government: computers, multiple communication devices, a mahogany table complete with a glass top and twenty chairs around the circumference, an overhead projector that connected to the computer, and a retractable screen in the front of the room. The room also housed two leather couches, on each side of the room, for the unexpected guests invited to attend a conference or briefings. In the front of the room was a podium complete with microphone hookups, recorders, and a backdrop with the seal of the CIA emblazoned on it for press conferences. Though considered a field office, a subsidiary of the Newark office, it had all the bells and whistles of Newark.

Nick said, "I go with number three. The informant should praise them and their efforts, all the while listening for a slip, a name, a position their individual is in, or some other information we can piece together and develop a clue as to the individual's identity. If the informant gives them good information, like the radioactive blood irradiator, even though they know about it, they will know his information is good and maybe drop the mole's name. He's throwing in ideas, they'll throw in ideas. Yeah, it's risky. Either way, they'll tell him to get information from his friend. This friend can't be from security or they won't trust him. I'll ask Director Shane to suggest someone who we can trust. Then we will have them meet and get to know each other."

Grazie said, "So you're setting up a fake mole to find the real mole?"

Nick said, "I'm open to better ideas."

Grazie said, "Remember that Ali is not part of a cell. He is a member of an Islamic mosque that partially turned into a terrorist cell."

"What's the difference?" Nick asked.

Grazie replied, "They know him, like him, and respect him because he was there well before 9/11 when it was only a mosque. He finds out information by listening, not asking, so he hasn't drawn attention. He reads humble. They like that. Furthermore, the true members of the cell aren't known to the members of the mosque, so we can't just raid the mosque and lock up everyone there."

They all agreed with the number three.

Again, Smallwood brought out the photos found in Afghanistan, details now blown up to eight and a half inches by eleven inches so that they were very easy to see even the smallest detail. He had four sets made, one for each of them, and handed them out. Looking at the photos Nick explained the peculiar characteristics of each one. Again, Nick pointed out how the notes on the photos were written first in English then crossed out and written in Arabic, suggesting that the person taking the photos was American. The second photo of the ground plate outside plant engineering was photobombed by a female wearing an expensive shoe. Finally, the last photo was taken in security without the individual being stopped or questioned, indicating the person might have been known to security.

Nick then explained, "The photos don't reveal that all were taken by the same person. But whoever snapped the last photos was a person known and trusted in the security department. I am working on a few leads and will keep you informed of how it progresses."

Grazie said, "I searched the Internet for the type of shoe. I've been talking to the manufacturer, and I'm waiting for the list of stores that sell them. I'll keep you all advised."

Nick stated, "I will be interviewing all personnel that worked that day during that time period to determine if anyone remembers anything."

Al said, "I am meeting with Parsippany PD. I'll see you later."

Nick and Grazie were discussing the case in a general overview kind of way, trying to put the pieces together as to how the different players fit into the case and who were dead ends. As they were talking and moving photos and sheets around as though trying to complete a puzzle, they both reached for the same file when their hands touched. Like sparks flying, with no words needed to be spoken, they moved toward each other and kissed. Nick felt a charge down to his feet. They kissed again, this time deeply, and they didn't stop. Nick realized he was sliding his hands around Grazie and that she wasn't stopping him. He knew they should stop. But he couldn't. He realized they were going to make love right there in the conference room. Nick was thinking how they could get caught at any moment which added an excitement, something he hadn't felt in years. As he started to unbutton Grazie's, blouse, his cell phone buzzed sharply. He picked it up and noticed it was Director Shane.

"Yes, sir." Grazie listened close.

Shane said, "A couple came into the hospital in the ER. As the man was being triaged, the woman disappeared."

"On my way," Nick said and hung up. He turned to Grazie. "I'm going to the hospital. Are you coming?"

Grazie, who was already fixing and straightening out her clothes replied, "Of course."

"Meet me there." Nick then squeezed her arm and left to get into his car. Heading for his car, Nick began to feel guilt, asking himself how he could do this to Jen, and then in the same moment felt a stir in his trousers as he thought of Grazie. It wasn't that his wife Jen didn't turn him on; it was that Grazie was younger, tighter, and, he supposed, new and different. Furthermore, he thought Grazie would be game for anything sexually that Nick had in mind, whereas Jen was old school. He then swore to himself that he would never touch Grazie again.

When Nick arrived at the desk in the emergency department, the shift commander and Al Stokes were waiting for him, with a heavyset nurse whose name tag read "Volts." Nick looked around for Grazie who was walking through the door.

Nick asked Al, "What's going on?"

The shift commander said, "A fellow came in with his wife, and in all appearances, he was very sick. High fever, sweating, coughing. He was quarantined immediately, and the lab was trying to determine what was wrong with him. Meanwhile the woman that arrived with him went missing in the hospital."

Nick turned to Volts. "Were you there?"

Nurse Volts replied, "I was working triage when I saw a couple arrive and walk up to the receptionist. She was dressed in a burka, and the man with her appeared to be very sick. As soon as I saw how sick he was I put on gloves and a mask and told the receptionist I would take him and she could get the information from the female. We walked to the examination room. At this point he was sweating profusely, coughing, had difficulty breathing, and appeared to be turning blue. I laid him down on the bed and called for emergency assistance. The patient had a 104 temperature and began vomiting. All standard procedures were followed for a person admitted that was contaminated with an unknown substance, and he was stabilized for the moment once the oxygen and intravenous were started. I then went to find the woman to get a history and asked the receptionist where she was. The receptionist stated she was in the waiting room, but when I went there she was gone. I thought she could be in the ladies' room, but when I looked she wasn't there. I called security. The patient in the meantime was placed in isolation."

Nick replied, "In addition to the usual precautions, be certain they address the very real possibility that this man may be booby-trapped in order to infect our employees. Have them do a full X-ray, with his clothes on before they proceed to treat him. Take me to him, I want to take a look."

They walked to the isolation room. Nick was asked to put on a surgical mask and gown, as well as gloves. The patient was behind two sets of doors to contain the spread of disease, but they only went through one, far enough to see the patient through the glass. Nick was thinking how easy it would be for a suicide volunteer to infect a great amount of people.

The commanding officer then asked Nick, "What's a burka?"

Nick replied, "Islamic women's clothing, usually black in color, covering her from head to foot."

"Why?"

"Why do we eat turkey on Christmas?"

They arrived at the isolation room, and though Nick was not a medical professional, he knew by looking through the window in the door that the man was gravely ill. A nurse tended him as he bled from his ears, eyes, and nose, with a labored breathing and virtually no sign of consciousness.

Outside, Nick spoke to the chief resident who said, "We know he suffers from poisoning. What type we don't know, but there is nothing we can do for him. We stabilized him, but I think he'll expire before we isolate the contaminant."

Nick turned back to the shift commander and asked, "What is being done to find the woman? Have you reviewed the cameras, alerted the staff, and directed officers to sensitive areas?"

The shift commander said, "Everyone's looking for her. A review of security video revealed she's still somewhere inside the hospital. The K-9 team is on the way, to see if the dog might be able to find her more quickly. Security is stationed at all of the hot areas in the hospital and they have yet to observe her."

Nick said, "They're looking for a woman in a burka. What if the burka's a ruse? She could have ditched it and started walking around in street clothes."

K-9 arrived, and Nick directed them to the shift commander to determine where the individual was and if the dog can pick up the scent.

Grazie stated, "I called in the federal forensic team to help."

Nick ordered, "Commander, execute a red alert. The woman may be carrying any type of hazardous materials, bombs, guns, or God knows what under her clothing. If anyone spots her, have them report to me immediately. Follow her, but do not approach her."

The commander picked up the radio and stated, "This is a red alert. Be on the lookout for a lone female, possibly in a burka, last seen at the emergency department, D level. All security personnel respond to the lab and covert closet and all entry and exits. Report in if observed. Do not approach."

Nick said, "Call in the Parsippany Police and the Morris County Sheriff's Office."

He then took the K-9 officer and his dog to the chair the Islamic woman originally sat in when she arrived. Grazie grabbed Nick by the arm and drew him close to her. Al was standing behind them. Then Grazie went to the other end of the hallway to call Agent Smallwood.

When she left, Al grabbed Nick and said, "I need to talk to you."

Nick replied, "Can it wait?"

Al nodded. "Why not?"

The K-9 German shepherd stopped at the chair, and then began to smell the seat from all different directions. After a few minutes the dog led the officer down a hall that leads to the main building. Nick, Al, and Grazie drew their guns so that they were ready for use. Nick found it odd that the dog made a turn down a corridor that leads away from all the hot spots and toward plant engineering. Walking down the corridor Nick felt the hairs on the back of his neck begin their familiar rise of warning. The K-9 made another left and began to react to a door that was marked "Employees Only." Nick used his master key to gain entry; the dog then led the way down past the main air handlers that push hot air in the winter and cold air in the summer to the entire hospital. As they walked further down the aisle they heard what sounded like repair work being done. A few steps further, they saw an employee, a thick, short man with white hair, dressed in the uniform of plant engineering: dark blue pants with a light blue shirt and "Plant Engineering" emblazoned on it, attempting to remove a plate to the main air shaft. Next to him was an Islamic woman dressed in a burka, holding a gun to his head.

She saw and heard the barking dog first. She fired her pistol while yelling, "Allah Akbar."

Chapter 17

The bullets missed the dog. The woman then began to raise the pistol and take aim at the sheriff's officer. The dog was barking and ready to charge. The familiar smell of burning gunpowder filled the air. Nick was right next to the sheriff's officer with Grazie and Al behind them. Gun drawn, Nick, looking through the smoke from the burnt gunpowder of her shots, thought he would wound her so that she may be questioned later. He fired two shots in rapid succession. But the woman decided to crouch down to make herself a smaller target, instead placing herself exactly where Nick was aiming, low to the left. The bullets hit home. She quickly crumpled to the floor. In an instant the officer was kneeling next to her, securing her gun and feeling for a pulse, but there was none.

The employee from plant engineering warned everyone, "The woman has a bag of chemicals under her clothing that she was going to dump into the air vent. She used a hospital key. She creeped up behind me, pointed a pistol at my head, and told me to remove the air handler service plate."

The sheriff's officer was calling in on his radio. Nick was calling the security command center, and Agent Grazie was calling the forensic team. Nick made sure to call Director Shane and explained what had transpired.

Nick explained to all present that no one was to look for the chemicals.

The director advised, "I am sending a portable X-ray machine to make sure she isn't booby-trapped, and I'm also sending the hazardous material team."

Nick remembered he was still on the force when hazmat teams were just being formed, and thought of the brochure that was handed out looking for recruits to this new unit. As Nick recalled the brochure stated that the new hazmat team would be made up of a group of specially trained task force of police, firemen, and emergency responders who respond to any hazardous material spill or purposely released agent and contain and remove it before it can cause any harm to the population. These teams answer calls from any type of environmental hazard, from an overturned oil truck to a terrorist act. Though initiated before he retired, Nick thought of how this field really took off after the terror attacks of 9/11, and how they were constantly updated on the newest threats being invented to cause harm and mass panic. Wearing protective suits, respirators, and air tanks they are trained for any type of biological, viral, or chemical agent. Nick thought they looked like spacemen.

Director Shane told Nick, "Rope off the area and don't let anyone enter from the beginning of the corridors on each end."

Nick advised the director, "Agent Grazie is on the scene, and the federal forensic team is on their way."

The director said, "Nick, the man that came in with that woman has died. And an autopsy will be performed as soon as they can determine the body is no risk to the medical examiner's staff."

As though on cue, Nick observed all the different first responders appear at once. The hazmat team secured the area, checked air quality, and told Nick to suit up or leave the area. Nick suited up, and after the team X-rayed the body and checked for booby traps with negative results, they began cutting open the woman's burka. Nick was intrigued as he observed that she was wearing a black tactical outfit under the burka and what appeared to be a kind of "utility belt" with a respirator, another handgun, extra clips of bullets, a large knife, a key chain with what appeared to be a hospital master key, and a clear plastic bag about the size of a large watermelon containing a white powder. The powder was quickly secured in a large chest similar to the large coolers families bring to the beach. The guns, knife, key, and ammo were placed in envelopes and secured by the forensic team who quickly moved in after the hazmat leader gave the all clear.

The sheriff's officer, Nick, Al, and Grazie were whisked away to be decontaminated in a room on the same floor. All clothes and other items were placed in plastic bags. The individual then took a shower to remove any contaminants on their skin and was provided with clean clothes and shoes to wear. The officer was then taken to another room where he was questioned by the Morris County Prosecutor's Office. The plant engineering employee was the next to be decontaminated in the same fashion and then questioned. They were decontaminated and questioned separately.

Al called it, "The full Silkwood."

Nick learned they'd removed the body and brought to the morgue for an autopsy and hopefully identification.

Nick hadn't said a word since they were led to decontamination. The four of them—Nick, Al, Grazie, and the K-9 officer (the dog was being treated separately)—sat in an isolation room in hospital scrubs, trying to eat Salisbury steak and Jell-O, waiting for their test results.

Al began to speak, "Everybody thinks it's easy to be responsible for taking someone's life. It's not easy."

Grazie said, "I don't know what it's like. I can only imagine. I never had to shoot someone."

The sheriff's officer replied, "I never did either, but I suppose it does bring out the deep thoughts and sleepless nights."

Al went on, "That is exactly why cops are pulled from active duty after a shooting. There may have been no other choice, like in this instance. But unless you have no soul, you continue to ask yourself if you have the right to stop a person from existing. Who gives us this ultimate power of taking a life? Why, because we're authorized by the state to carry a weapon, this makes us judge, jury, and executioner?"

Grazie replied, "That is the point, Al.

Al asked, "What's the point?"

Grazie continued, "Because of your training, experience, seminars, and schooling, this calling you had to become a police officer, a keeper of the peace, without you and your fellow officers there would be total anarchy where hundreds of innocent people would be hurt, instead of the perpetrator. In my book, as well as society's, that gives you the power, and thank God for that."

Nick just sat there, lost in his own world. In all appearances he looked normal, unaffected by his killing someone moments before. But that was far from the case, whether Nick realized it or not.

The door swung open, and a male nurse came in with a clipboard. "All clear!"

Nick, Al, and Grazie were released from decontamination. Reps from the prosecutor's office, the PD, and a few assorted others met them in the hospital boardroom for further instructions from the FBI, CIA, and the state, county, and municipal authorities.

Director Shane explained, "For the short term, there would be additional security by state and county agencies both inside and outside the facility. Furthermore, there will be undercover operatives placed throughout the hospital in civilian clothes. This extra security personnel will work twelve-hour shifts, and funding for the project would be paid for by the Office of Homeland Security." The director continued, "Preliminary tests by the lab revealed the man that came into the emergency department died of exposure to ricin."

Nick thought how appropriate, that what they were trying to do, expose hundreds of people to ricin, did him in.

No, he realized a moment later. That wasn't fate intervening.

Nick said, "His superiors exposed him to ricin deliberately, or he exposed himself, to distract the staff while she made her way into the hospital's core."

The director stated, "The woman's autopsy determined she, too, had been exposed to ricin. Had the bullets not stopped her, the ricin would have eventually killed her."

Nick began to think. Was she exposed by accident while making or transporting the ricin, or was she infected by her associates to ensure if she was captured she wouldn't talk?

The agent from Homeland Security said a deliberate and massive investigation would now be conducted to determine where the couple was before entering the hospital and where they were infected.

Nick said to Grazie, "The woman used the phrase, 'Allah Akbar.'"

She whispered, "I know."

He said, "It means 'God is greatest.'"

The chilling part about the hospital intruder using this phrase hit both Nick and Grazie. The reason they both were transfixed by this phrase was that it was the same one found on the black box recorders picked up from the wreckage of the planes from 9/11 in the field in Pennsylvania, the last words spoken by the terrorists; this same phrase was used in the attempted bombings of the airliners while the terrorists tried to light the wick of the bombs they carried, and it was the same phrase used by US Army psychiatrist, Major Nidal Hasan, when he began shooting the soldiers at Fort Hood, Texas.

Nick couldn't help but think, *Lock and load.* The enemy is revealing himself.

CHAPTER 18

Nick went to see Peter Rivers, the hospital locksmith, to ask him about the key found on the Islamic woman the night before. Peter sat stooped in his windowless shop on the back of A level. He seldom got company.

Nick showed him the key and asked, "Can you tell where this key came from by the numbers stamped on it?"

Peter looked at it through the reading glass of his bifocals. "It's mine," he said.

"How do you know?"

Peter replied, "See, the numbers represent in code the month, year, and to whom it was assigned, so in the event it was ever lost, we would know who to return it to. If the two numbers in a sequence are stamped '99' it indicates that it was an extra key and never assigned. I do this on occasion if a new wing is going to open or new personnel are about to be hired. This particular key was one left in my desk drawer that I did not restrike with a user code. I didn't know it was missing."

Nick then asked, "Has anyone been in your shop recently that shouldn't have been."

"No."

"You're sure."

Peter replied, "The only one I found in there was the camera guy, Moe Prince. He had the ceiling tiles moved and said he was running cable for a new camera. I can't think of anyone other than Moe."

Nick said, "Okay, thanks, Peter. Keep this conversation under your hat, especially to Moe. If anyone asks about the key, tell them to call me."

Arguably, Moe Prince worked with security, a few lateral steps from Nick and several below. Nick went looking for Moe in video storage, the cafeteria, and the spots where he smoked. When Nick couldn't find him, he told the watch commander, "Find Moe Prince and have him report to me immediately."

Nick saw Al in the corridor. Al asked, "Nick, can I speak with you a minute?"

Nick replied, "Sure, what's on your mind?"

Al said, "Nick, you can tell me this is none of my business and you're right, but listen to me first. You have to end this with Grazie before you get what I call getting Grazie's scent into you."

"Her *scent*?"

Al continued. "My theory is that men who leave their wives, children, and home for a new woman, first they get the scent of the new woman they are fooling around with. Not literally, psychologically, of course. But once it's on him, he can't help himself but to leave his home. Like a snakebite. Once it happens, it's too late and the victim has no choice but succumb. He succumbs to the new girl's scent and then cannot help himself."

Nick said, "Yeah, thanks, I'm fine," and tried to brush by Al, but Al grabbed Nick's arm.

Al said, "This theory of mine…this scent, it isn't instantaneous. It grows over time. The longer the guy is with the new girlfriend, the more her scent takes hold. Once it does, neither the wife nor children can talk the fellow into giving up the girlfriend and staying at home. Nick, I'm telling you like a friend, think about this before Grazie's scent gets into your system and you can't end it."

Nick thought about what Al said and shook his head. "No. No. It's not like that." But he knew Al was right. Now Nick was determined to end this with Grazie before her scent took hold of him. He would end this right now.

If he could.

Nick wasn't at the office ten minutes, barely enough to type up a draft report on the missing key, when he heard a knock on his door. Looking at the video cameras Nick instantly recognized the individual as the hospital's video tech Moe Prince. Nick had often wondered how Moe kept his job. Moe was in charge of keeping the hundreds of cameras working or repairing them until the company that installed them could arrive on the scene and take over. Moe was what people called a character. Physically, Nick thought Moe to be approximately fifty years old, about five feet eight inches tall, average weight, and dyed black hair. But his most distinguishing features were his missing teeth, their absence noticeable every time he talked or smiled. When Nick asked Moe what happened to his teeth he claims they were knocked out while he was in the military. But if that were the case, he could have had the military provide the dental service he needed.

Moe claimed to have done a tour in Afghanistan as a private video contractor. According to Moe, a qualified individual could sign up for a one-year contract for one hundred thousand dollars per annum. If the individual completes the tour, he gets the money tax free and can sign up for another year. The duties include repairing or replacing the many cameras mounted in buildings, airports, and on main streets. He told Nick if he was dispatched to fix a camera, he was taken to the location by a squad of Marines and rode in an armor-plated Humvee. He said he did two tours. He revealed all this information to Nick the first time they met. Nick didn't need to ask anything. Moe just kept talking.

Most people described Moe as rude, crude, and offensive. Moe could get anyone he came in contact with annoyed and ready to report him to security in about two minutes. There had been complaints, formal and otherwise, of Moe "complimenting" women on how well their blouses fit. Moe's crude sexist jokes, his loud voice, perpetual spit spewing out of his mouth, and smelly body odor had prompted Al to describe him as "more camel than human." Moe wore the same clothes for a week before changing even though they were dirty and wrinkled. He had a stink that was a combination of sweat, cigarette smoke, and dirty laundry. It was enough to make one gag. Nick printed out the draft report about the missing key and handed it to Moe.

Nick said, “Read it. Out loud.”

Moe picked up the report and began to stumble over the smallest conjunctions and pronouns.

Nick said, “Okay, stop.”

Everyone at the hospital wondered how Moe got his job. It was evident that he wasn’t very bright. The best Nick could piece together was that years ago, Moe’s brother, who was in the electrical field, knew that the hospital was going to purchase many closed-circuit televisions and digital video recorders. Moe’s brother sent him to the company’s school to learn how to install, fix, or download information. Then when the system was installed, Moe applied for the job and was hired. He possessed the credentials of a company-qualified repairman.

Furthermore, Nick wondered if Moe did, in fact, complete the civilian tours in Afghanistan. Moe was considered a long-term vendor and was paid, as were the investigators, as an independent contractor. It was not that Moe did not know the work. It was just that he was not neat, did not follow through, and was only capable of shoddy work at best. Nonetheless, Nick remembered, during a few high-profile cases at the hospital Moe was able to retrieve and burn a video for the FBI and the state police and therefore was able to hold on to his job.

Moe thought Nick was cool for being former law enforcement, and Moe would buttonhole him when possible to tell some unlikely story of his exploits. Usually Nick would pretend to listen and, every once in a while, would get a piece of useful information from these conversations.

Nick asked, “Did you give a hospital master key to anyone?”

Moe replied, “No. What are you talking about?”

Nick said, “A master key was found on a woman who died in the hospital last night.”

“Died?”

“I shot her,” Nick said. Moe blanched. Nick went on. “She was aiming a gun at a police officer, and I shot her. I spoke to Pete the locksmith. He told me the only one in his office was you. And as a result, she died because you provided the key that gave her access to plant engineering."

Moe sputtered, "Nick, Pete is wrong. I didn't give anybody any key."

Nick pressed. "Peter confirmed you were the last one in his office before the key went missing."

Moe replied, "The day I was in his office running wire, I had just finished and was removing my tools when Ann walked in and said she needed to leave a note for Peter."

Nick excused himself, went into the hallway, took out his cell, and called the hospital switchboard.

"Nick Moore. Patch me through to the locksmith."

When Peter answered, Nick asked, "Okay, that conversation we just had about Moe Prince and the missing key?"

"Yeah?"

Nick asked him, "Did anyone leave you a note that day or the day before?"

Peter replied, "No."

Nick asked, "Are you sure?"

Peter was getting annoyed. "Yes! Yes, I'm sure."

Then Nick asked, "Did you see Ann Stromer that day, near, or in your office?"

He replied, "Oh, wait. Yes, she was talking to Moe." Peter continued, "I was coming back from the bathroom. I spotted her leaving my office, and when she saw me she said she needed to speak with Moe and that's why she was leaving my office. She thought he was in there, but he was in the hallway, packing up his tools. I never gave it a second thought."

Nick asked him, "Peter, are you sure about this? It's extremely important."

Peter said, "I'm sure."

Nick thanked him and reminded him of the confidentiality of their conversation.

Nick returned to Moe and said, "You're free to go. Keep the conversation we had under your hat, because I swear to you, if one word gets out I will have you fired and arrested."

Moe began telling Nick, "You don't have to worry about me, I'm legit. I even tell you what's going on in the hospital. If I hear people are stealing supplies and stuff, remember." Nick remembered the few times Moe did pass along information. It was wrong. Nick wondered if Moe had been passing along information so as to throw the scent off whatever it was he was doing.

Nick said, "Fine. I have an appointment." Moe left.

Nick then went to Al Stokes's office, and he filled Al in on Moe, the key, and Ann Stromer.

Al said, "You see a connection between this and Ann's boyfriend, or whatever he is?"

"There has to be. We just have to figure out what it is without tipping our hand. Meanwhile, I'm going to ask the director to put a blast e-mail to the entire hospital. 'If you see something suspicious, call us.' I'm going to include the cell phone number I have in my desk that I don't use. This way you or I will be able to screen any tips that may come in."

Al replied, "Great idea, Nick. Hey, you never know. That's a lot of eyes that could be helping us. Of course, 90 percent of the calls will be bullshit."

Nick said, "I'm counting on it."

Nick's phone rang; it was Grazie.

She said, "I have the confidential informant. We can meet at 2:00 p.m. There's a warehouse at 55 Morris Street, Parsippany. Smallwood will pick you up at one thirty. Fewer cars, less conspicuous."

Nick hung up, gave Al the address, and said, "Can you get there early and set up surveillance to make sure it wasn't a double cross by the informant? And keep in touch by text?"

Al said, "I'll take care of it."

The front desk sergeant called and told Nick that Agent Smallwood was waiting for him. Nick got him and walked him back to the office.

Nick said, "It's too early to leave for the warehouse yet, so we can kill some time."

John replied, "Like you're doing with Phyllis?"

Nick jolted, recoiled, and answered, "What business is it of yours?"

John replied, "None, but I bet your wife and her husband would like to know about it."

Nick felt his face turn red and he was about to explode, but then asked, "Are you threatening me?"

John said, "Not at all. But there's no bro code. I don't owe it to you to hide your dishonesty. And you know how people talk, especially when a guy just wants to use a woman like Phyllis to just add another notch on his belt." Smallwood leaned forward in his chair. "You know I'm very attracted to Phyllis. I have been since the first time I met her. I know she is married, and I care too much for her to hit on her. I can see you're interested in her, and I just want to tell you don't hurt her. She's a good person, and I think the world of her."

Nick replied, "Not that it's any of your business, but what we do or don't do together is between us. And, just to let you know, Agent Grazie and I are just friends. So, don't let your imagination take over for reality, and don't bring it up again, ever. Another piece of advice. Don't ever threaten me again, or I'll put my foot so far up your ass, you'll taste it!" Nick stood up and straightened his tie. "Now let's go to that warehouse."

Nick's phone buzzed. It was a text from Al. "All set."

On the ride over Nick and Smallwood switched the conversation to business.

Smallwood asked, "Where do you think she got the key from?"

Nick said, "I'm following a lead. I'll let you know."

Smallwood said, "The man who died, the woman in the burka, their fingerprints weren't in the database for federal or Interpol for known terrorists or people of interest or anything else. It appears that Al-Qaeda or ISIS are purposely recruiting new members who are unknown to law enforcement. They can fly under the radar. And this 'Max' you've been chasing, Ann Stromer's boyfriend, was using an alias or is in the country illegally."

Nick and Smallwood were the first to arrive at the warehouse, it seemed. Al was nowhere in sight. Nick pulled his car into a truck bay just as he received a text from Al Stokes stating all was clear both at the warehouse and surrounding area. Agent Grazie pulled into the bay alongside Nick's car, and Smallwood hit a button lowering a garage door, keeping the meeting secret from any passersby. Nick looked around the warehouse office which was dusty and musty but had a table and six chairs. The lights worked, and the temperature in the room was normal. All in all, Nick thought, not a bad choice.

Grazie opened a side door and led in the confidential informant who was dark skinned, about forty years old, approximately five feet seven inches and thinly built, Nick figured 130 pounds at most. He had close-cropped hair, a full black beard, and wore a small brimless cap. Grazie introduced the man as Josef Ali.

After everyone took a seat, Grazie began speaking. "Josef's cover is the most important issue today, and I want to make sure all agree that we would scrap the project rather than expose him."

All agreed and Ali then spoke. "What is it you think I could do for you?"

Agent Smallwood stated, "It appears that some Muslim extremists want to do physical harm to the Guardian Angel Hospital, and this group seems to possess inside information that is not readily accessible to the general public. We were hoping you might be able to acquire information on who the person was that was providing the information."

Nick was pretty sure the leak sat somewhere between Ann Stromer and Moe Prince, but there could be others. He suggested, "Mention that you met someone who works at the hospital named Bob and that he told you the hospital has the necessary components on-site for the construction of a dirty bomb. This friend of yours was drinking too much and told you this information. Your colleagues already have this information, but it is not known to the public. They'll know you're providing good information and may take you into their confidence. They may also ask who the person is that you know. His full name is Robert Gilson and he works for plant engineering. He should be here shortly so you can meet him and feel comfortable with each other."

Nick went on, "Bob was handpicked by Thomas Shane, the director of security, and he was beyond reproach. If this is agreeable to you, we'll bring in Bob. However, if there's anything about this you're not sure of or you'd like to approach it a different way, tell us and we'll make it happen."

Bob was a widower and lost his only son on 9/11 when the terrorists flew the jets into the World Trade Center. But there was no point in telling Ali that.

Ali replied, "I don't know. Perhaps it will be the end of me."

Nick answered, "We are only supplying a name so that when they check, they'll see it's a real person who works at the hospital."

Grazie then said, "Naturally you will be compensated more for this."

Ali said, "I am fine with plan, but remember there are no promises to be made as to whether or not I would be able to find the name of the person providing them with the information."

"We get it. No guarantees."

Ali said, "I am afraid to start asking questions as I never have in the past. However, I am going to approach it as a good Muslim who received information and plan to pass it along. This is all I would do, and if you don't like it I would leave now."

Grazie reassured him, saying, "Do it the way you said, and see what happens. Do what you feel is right and don't worry. I trust you. I'm sure I can get you more money."

Ali replied, "Ms. Phyllis, it is not about the money. These bastards pervert Islam to meet their needs. I want them caught, but I fear them, not for my life but what they would do to my family. If they kill me, who will take care of my family?"

"I will," Grazie said.

"What?"

"I will. Nothing's going to happen to you. But if something does, we'll scoop up your wife and kids and relocate them."

"You would do that for me?" Ali asked.

"Look what you've done for us. But it won't come to that. Don't let it. Try it the way you said, and if there is the least bit of resistance, stop."

Ali responded, "Okay, I will try."

Nick got on his cell phone and made a call to Bob. He then hung up and texted Al that a white male would be arriving shortly. Approximately five minutes later, a short stocky man with a bald head walked through the door. Nick was just reading the text from Al Stokes that the individual had arrived. Bob approached Nick and gave a warm handshake. Nick then introduced him to all in attendance, and they sat down.

Grazie said, "The first thing they should discuss is how they know each other."

Nick suggested, "How about they stop each day for coffee at the same diner and started talking and after a while became friends."

Ali said, "I do not eat in American restaurants, restaurants that are not halal."

"Okay," Smallwood said. "Gym? Supermarket?"

Ali said, "Kabob Paradise in Lake Hiawatha. I eat there. Many white people eat there."

Grazie said, "So it is."

They exchanged cell phone numbers, and Ali said he was going to leave. As Agent Grazie got up to take him, Ali said he would rather walk, that he had noticed the train station down the road, was familiar with it, and would take the train to Jersey City. Before Ali left Nick saw Grazie hand him money which he quickly deposited in his trouser pocket. Grazie and Nick led him to the front of the building, and after Nick checked it out, opened the front door, and Ali, in a brisk walk, blended in with the other pedestrians. Bob left right after through the rear door near the bay doors from which he had entered. At this point Nick texted Al to let him know Bob was exiting. Nick waited a few minutes, but Al didn't answer.

Nick opened the bay door to let Grazie out then closed it immediately after she pulled out, and tried to text Al again. When he didn't respond, Nick dialed Al's number, but it went straight to voice mail.

Nick said to John Smallwood, "I don't like this. Al is one of the most reliable people I know. He answered the texts I sent him all day, and now he stopped answering them. Something is up. Look. The front door leads right to the train station, and it's the busiest part of town. When we arrived we entered through the truck bay entrance on the back, totally set off from the street. You go out the front. I'll go out the back. Maybe there are people around and he can't answer."

Smallwood opened the garage door. Nick pulled out and Smallwood shut the door. Nick drove around looking for Al's car. Nick was asking himself where he would set up surveillance. Almost as if his car was on autopilot, Nick drove to a street that had a steep hill and a clear view of the warehouse. As he approached the top of the hill, Nick spotted Al's car parked under a tree. Nick pulled up to the car and began to smile when he saw Al who appeared to be asleep with his head tilted to the right. Nick got out of his car and approached Al. The driver-side window was rolled down. Then Nick saw a hole in Al's temple, the blood coagulating near the bullet hole.

Al Stokes was dead.

CHAPTER 19

Nick noticed the phone on the seat displaying his unread texts. Nick called 911, gently let the seat down to a lying position, and began cardiopulmonary resuscitation. He was still frantically working on Al when the emergency medical technicians arrived, moved him out of the way, and took over.

The ambulance with Al Stokes's lifeless body pulled away, and Nick thought, *Just like that, it's over, and life moves on.*

His thoughts were interrupted by a Parsippany police officer stating, "Mr. Moore, would you drive over to police headquarters for a chat with Detective Ricks."

"Okay," Nick replied. "I'll be right over."

Nick walked into the detective bureau and took a seat in front of Ricks, who was on the phone. The detective bureau seemed busier than usual to Nick. He looked around and waved hello to the other detectives that were at their desks, some on the phone, some talking to individuals, and others on their computers, typing. The room was old, the green paint was old, the furniture was old, and looking around, Nick began to feel old.

Ricks hung up and said, "Nick, I'm so sorry about Al. He was a great guy and a real gentleman. Please accept my condolences."

Nick replied, "I don't think it hit me yet. I expect him to walk in the room any minute."

"I know," Ricks responded. "Anything you can tell me about it?"

"Not really," Nick replied. "He was my outside cover for a meeting we were having at the new warehouse. When he didn't respond to my texts, I went looking for him, and the rest you know."

Ricks didn't know anything, of course.

Ricks replied, "We'll canvass the neighborhood, and I'll let you know what ballistics turns up. Meantime, go get some rest. You look like shit."

Nick said, "Thanks." He left the police station, got into his car where he began punching the steering wheel. What was left to say? He'd lost his best friend, his only friend. His brother in blue. When he caught his breath, he drove back to the hospital, parked in the hospital parking lot, and called Grazie.

Grazie replied, "Oh God, Nick, I'm so sorry. I know how close you were with Al."

He ended the call and closed his eyes for a few minutes, fighting back the tears. Then, starting his car, he pulled out of the parking area and was going to make a left turn onto the main road for the drive home when something caught his eye. Nick spotted Ann Stromer's Mercedes in the right lane, at a red light. Nick would not have given it a second thought until he saw who was driving her car. It was Moe Prince, with Ann sitting in the passenger seat. Since there was a car separating him, Nick decided to follow them and see where they were going. It was a strange combination, Moe and Ann, with Moe driving her car. At first Nick doubted himself, but as the car turned he saw both of them and knew what it meant.

Nick followed them a few blocks then saw the Mercedes turn into a driveway. A two-car garage door opened automatically, and the car pulled in. However, as it was pulling in, Nick caught a glimpse of a second car in the two-car garage. It was the older black Honda Civic. Nick was stunned. He copied down the address, 92 Prospect Avenue, and left the area before he was seen.

CHAPTER 20

Video Tech Moe Prince was having a bad time at work. He was working under a new supervisor who had no patience for undisciplined individuals who did not take pride in their work. The supervisor, Mike Carter, was hired by Director Shane to oversee the entire video, radio, infant alarms, door access, and panic button system in the Guardian Angel Hospital network. All of these protective systems were growing at an exponential rate. All the systems in each hospital acquired needed to be compatible with the Guardian Angel Hospital System. Carter was a retired career military officer specializing in these areas. Almost immediately, Carter realized that Moe was not the person for this highly skilled job.

Carter told Moe, "Get me lists of all the closed-circuit television cameras in Guardian Angel Hospital in Parsippany."

Moe replied, "Mr. Carter, I don't have a list like that. I'm not sure they ever had a list of all camera locations."

"Then make one. Next, report to all the other facilities and off-site locations and make a report for each. I want this in Excel format and sent to me electronically. Then I want three hard copies in binders for each hospital, one for Director Shane, one for the command center for each hospital, and one for myself."

Carter warned Moe, "I need this as soon as possible. Secondly, I want the location and type of each panic alarm for each hospital along with a current test. I want you to perform the tests to ensure the alarms were working properly."

Moe left Carter and, returning to his office, called Nick on his cell phone and asked, "Nick, can you come to my office I need your help. It's an emergency."

As Nick entered the office, he heard Moe talking to himself out loud, "The panic alarms haven't gone off in years. They want panic alarms, like the silent alarms in banks." Then he yelled, "Banks get held up! Hospitals don't!"

Nick walked in and said, "Am I interrupting?"

Moe explained to Nick what Carter wanted. Moe knew the reason the hospital had them installed. "I get it. I'm not stupid. They collect cash, they stash drugs. Sometimes they get nutcases in the ER or the loony ward. You need security for shit like that."

Everything Moe said was offensive. Even when he said something right, he said it wrong.

"I had some of it on paper somewhere," Moe said. "Here?"

Frantically, Moe began searching for a list. Not an easy task since Moe kept his office in worse shape than his personal hygiene. Papers were stacked and scattered everywhere. The garbage was overflowing with uneaten food, and fruit flies circled above. Coffee cups, soda cans, broken cameras, tools, and candy wrappers littered his desk. Each wall had outdated articles, memos, and procedures tacked up in a haphazard fashion. Moe finally found some list and placed it on the floor near the entrance.

Nick asked, "Can you explain to me what I'm doing here?"

Next, Moe said to himself, "Where did I put the radio sheet?"

The security radio system was state of the art, courtesy of a federal government grant. Each of the fifty radios and the base station required weekly checks to ensure proper operation. Not able to find it, Moe moved on to the door access system. This gave access employees access to the area of the hospital they worked in as well as to parking lots. This system registered who entered, at what location, and when, along with their photo displayed on a perpetual report on a dedicated computer. Moe could not seem to find anything in his mess, but that didn't stop him from trying.

"Baby alarm," Moe muttered. An infant alarm was attached to each newborn. Nick knew an instrument was attached to the remaining stem of each newborn's umbilical cord and could not be removed except by the medical staff. Doors automatically lock, alarms sound, and elevators cease working if an infant is brought out of the nursery floor without being "cleared" in the computer first. This system prevents babies from being taken from the hospital by kidnappers. Moe found the baby alarm folder and placed it by the door. Moe seemed to shift into a panic. "I can't do this. I can't do this," he repeated. "I wish I'd never took this job. I wish this was over."

Nick said, "Wish what was over, Moe?"

Moe jolted, seeming to notice Nick for the first time. He said, "Nick, you gotta help me. The new boss wants a list of surveillance equipment, cameras, and all, like, in an Excel spreadsheet by yesterday. I managed to find some, but I can't find the others that he wants. I'm afraid he'll figure out—"

Nick cut in. "That you're a fraud?"

Moe seemed to choke on a chunk of air.

Nick said, "I just lost my partner Al. I don't know if I can help you."

Moe didn't seem to register what Nick had said. He was getting excited and started raising his voice. "Nick, come on, don't break my balls. This is serious. If I don't get this job done, Carter will have me fired. I can tell he don't like me. He's just looking for an excuse to get rid of me."

Nick asked, "Moe, didn't you go see the director? Wasn't it the director that hired you?"

Moe replied, "The director told me Carter is my boss now. I report to him directly. I gotta do what he says."

Nick saw an opening and said, "Why don't you ask Ann to help you. From what I hear, she's great at this kind of thing."

"Don't believe everything you hear. She's all smoke and mirrors. She's falling apart."

Nick said, "Really? I thought she was finally getting it together since she has her boyfriend Max."

Moe said, "Again, all smoke and mirrors. He's probably the worst thing to ever happen to her. But forget about her. Are you going to help me or not?"

Nick replied, "Of course, Moe."

Moe smiled, a broad, open-mouth smile. Nick felt repulsed at the expanse of toothless gum.

Nick instructed, "Follow me over to my office."

Nick sat at his desk, typed in his password, copied a few files, and e-mailed them to Moe.

"They're in your inbox," Nick said. "Your *e-mail* inbox." Nick explained, "I'd made a list of all the cameras connected to each digital video recorder. This helps me when I need to track an incident at the hospital. Someone had compiled a handwritten list before I got here. I had it typed up, and I've been adding to it through the years. It includes the new cameras installed since I was hired. This is not complete, and I don't have anything else. Ask the shift commander if he can help."

"Thanks, Nick. I owe you one."

"No. You owe me more than that. Remember this, Moe. When I come to you with questions, I want answers, no double talk. And if you don't know the answer I want you to find it."

"You got it, Nick. I can't thank you enough. We'll be friends forever."

As Moe was leaving he said to Nick, "Here's a little payback for helping me. Watch out for Ann. She's poison. Keep your eyes on her. But you didn't hear it from me. And don't beat yourself up too much for not being able to find Harry Barker's or Jack Boyle's killer. They was in the wrong place at the wrong time, is all."

Before Nick could ask what he meant by that, Moe had left Nick's office.

Nick began to think about Al. He had already called the Orange Police Department and advised the chief what had happened. Al was a private person and didn't talk too much about his private life. However, the current chief was Al's old partner and knew who should be called, visited, and consoled. Nick advised him if there was anything he could do he would be available. Then he wiped his eyes and got back to work.

Nick was going over the checklist in his head. The Candor report, background reports, and service reports he ordered were due tomorrow, and that should clarify some of the points Nick could not figure out. He was especially anxious to see the Candor reports or drug dispensing record on Ann and the military and Afghanistan reports Nick had ordered on Moe from FBI Special Agent Dan Camp. Nick asked Agent Camp to become part of the investigation, thus opening up all the resources the FBI had at its disposal to Nick and the rest of the team who were working on the investigation.

Nick received a call on his cell phone from the director who informed him, "The blast e-mail went out, Nick. Let's hope it proves fruitful."

Nick replied, "Thanks, Director, I hope so. I'll let you know."

Next, Nick called Grazie, stating, "I got the reports. Let's meet at your office."

Grazie said, "Okay, I'll see you there," and hung up.

Nick was hoping they could get through the reports and have something for Agent Smallwood when they met next. Nick decided he was going to make a move on Grazie. What exactly he was going to do, he wasn't sure, but he felt he couldn't go on like this. One thing Nick knew: tomorrow was the day. The reports should fill in the blanks that were missing. Tomorrow, something would happen.

CHAPTER 21

Grazie tended to keep her informant on a long leash. She'd given Ali a big assignment. But it was fifty-fifty his people were the ones who killed Al Stokes. If so, Ali was already dead, or they were following him.

If not, who killed Stokes?

The next morning, Agent Grazie called Ali. Grazie asked him if he had anything to report, paying close attention to what he said and how he said it.

Ali stated, "I found this assignment extremely difficult. I mentioned Bob, and I told them about the dirty bomb. They were thankful, I think. I did find out that it was multiple people providing them with information from the hospital, and that at least one of them was a female, a female of color, a convert."

"Do we know which color?" Grazie asked.

"We do not. They told me they have everything they need, that they are getting extremely useful information, and will be carrying out a mission in the future that will have America on its knees and prove to the world that Islam is the great and one true religion. And, with the help of Allah we pray to bring this mission to a successful conclusion, but not without much preparation, reconnaissance, and information."

"Time frame?"

"Not that I am aware of."

Grazie said, "Did they mention another of the hospital's staff was killed?"

Ali replied, "No. Why would they? Do you think it was my people that killed this person?"

Grazie replied wearily, "We'll see. Ali, do you know if you were followed?"

He was silent for a moment. "I thought that I was not."

"Okay." If Ali wasn't followed, that meant someone on her team was.

"Ms. Phyllis. If I was followed, you know what this means."

"It doesn't necessarily mean anything, Joseph."

"You will remember your promise? About my wife and children?"

Nick went to the morgue to see Dr. Russling as the toxicology reports taken from the body of Al Stokes were in but showed nothing lethal in his blood.

Dr. Russling said, "Nick, Al died from a single gunshot wound to the left side of his head. The bullet used was a hollow point and ripped through everything that it came in contact with."

Nick asked, "Doc, do we know the caliber of the bullet yet?"

Dr. Russling replied, "We do. It was a nine-millimeter. The bullet entered the left temple, shattered the sphenoid bone, sending it and the surrounding tissue through his brain. In this case," the medical examiner continued, "there were no defensive marks or wounds on Al's body."

Nick figured it had to be someone Al knew because there were no signs of a struggle or defensive marks on Al's hands or arms, meaning, he did not feel threatened by the individual. The window on Al's car was also opened.

Or they sneaked up on him.

At the meeting, Nick was surprised to hear that Ali mentioned one of the spies in the hospital was a woman of color, a convert, involved in providing classified information. Nick would have bet that Ann, a white woman, was the person providing them with information. Or Moe. Or both. Nick needed time to figure this out. When he saw the black Honda in Ann's garage, he thought he was certain. Nick went to his connection in the police department and did a lookup on the address he had written down. He was not surprised to see the house was owned by Ann Stromer. If the Honda in her garage was the one spotted at the hospital, it would answer a lot of questions. Like, why the car seemed to vanish after it picked up the couple who ran from the maternity ward. Or where the killers of Harry Barker and Jack Boyle hid. Nick thought this must be how the suspects seemed to vanish. How Ann was involved or why was still part of the mystery, but Nick knew her boyfriend Max had something to do with it. But now Nick was wondering if a third individual was involved in providing information, this woman of color, and convert to Islam.

Nick dealt with enough women of color, converts, to know that meant she was probably born in the United States and, at some point, converted, and probably changed her name from an American to a Muslim one. Cassius Clay became Muhammed Ali. There were probably other examples, but he couldn't think of any. Furthermore, what role was Moe Prince playing in this? Nick felt it was too naive to think Ann and Moe were lovers. Nick remembered the few times that he saw them in the same room. Ann was repulsed by the sight of him. She did not find him amusing, good-looking, a smart dresser, or witty. If fact, Nick remembered she told him she thought Moe was repulsive. Now he was driving her car and pulling into her garage with a car in the next garage that was involved in a crime.

Agent Smallwood said, "My team is going to bug Ann's house and the apartment Moe Prince is staying at tonight or tomorrow morning. I'll be with them directing what I want done."

Nick reported, "The drug report I ordered will let us know what drugs are missing and the quantity. I'll review it and see if Ann Stromer is involved with any discrepancies."

Grazie asked if that was standard protocol.

Nick said, "It's become an epidemic in the medical field. Nurses, doctors, pharmacy techs, and others who have access to these drugs, at some point, get addicted for various reasons and begin diverting the drugs for their own use. Or steal them and sell them to cover their habits."

Grazie asked, "What is the percentage of diverters in the country?

Nick replied, "Most studies place the figure at 11 to 13 percent."

Nick explained how the system evolved from years ago when paper records were kept and drugs stored in cabinets, to now when each hospital has drug machines on each floor that are locked and can only be opened by a security code typed into a keypad.

He continued, "Because of the number of patients needing medicine and the number of nurses handling these medicines, some of which are very strong narcotics and painkillers with the potential for abuse, they have to be tracked. Each nurse now types her unique code provided by the pharmacy into the keypad, then requests the drug needed. A door opens containing that particular drug. The nurse is required to count the drugs before she takes what is needed to ensure the previous count is right and count again after she removes the drug. The machine keeps track electronically of when drugs are added by a pharmacy tech and when they are removed by a nurse. The resulting cumulative report is called a Candor report. It's quite accurate and can't be changed or altered by the staff."

Nick explained, "The Candor report would allow us to see what drugs were pulled by Stromer over the course of time specified."

Nick left the meeting and was returning to security when his burner cell phone rang.

"Investigator Nick Moore," he said.

A male voice responded, "Yes. Sir. I'm calling because of a mass e-mail that was sent out to all the employees."

Nick replied, "Yes, please continue."

The male replied, "Yeah, well, my name is Edwin, and I drive one of the shuttle buses that take the hospital employees to different locations."

Edwin continued, "Lately a young light-skinned brother has been getting on my bus and asking all sorts of questions like where all the locations are, which are opened late, something about security. But when I asked him why he needed to know this stuff, he clammed up. He must work in the kitchen somewhere cause he had their uniform on, and also an ID, but I couldn't get the name."

Nick replied, "Hey, great job, Edwin. Listen, we're going to have to get together and see if you can pick this guy out of photos or call me if he gets on the shuttle."

Edwin replied, "Okay. I get off at eight PM. I'll call you then or text you if he gets on before."

Nick answered, "Okay, Edwin. Talk to you then."

Nick's thoughts were interrupted by his own cell phone ringing. He saw it was Agent Smallwood.

Smallwood, said, "Nick, we're on our way to bug Ann's house. Did you want to come?"

Nick replied, "Sure. I'll meet you there."

Nick parked around the corner and approached Ann's house, where a power company van had parked. He walked around the back, and as he approached the back door, it swung open. Smallwood ushered him in, saying, "The techs are going to install a bug in an electrical outlet in each room. The bug is installed behind the plate and tapped into the electric. Each phone will be cloned and monitored at headquarters."

Nick asked if they could also install one in the garage, with a camera. Smallwood instructed his tech to make the installation.

"The garage is empty just now," Smallwood said, "in case you were wondering."

Agent Smallwood then added, "The same procedure is going on at Moe's apartment and should be wrapped up in both places in the next couple of minutes."

Nick asked, "When does the monitoring begin?"

Smallwood replied, "We're already on the phones, and the house electronic surveillance will begin as soon as we clear out of both locations. Our agents already went in dressed as power company employees with one of their vans as well. We don't want the neighbors getting suspicious. We already received a good test signal from each of the installed units. We'll get a full report every morning unless it's important, in which case I will be notified immediately."

Nick left Smallwood and was going to the information technology department to order the Candor reports on Ann Stromer. Since Ann traveled throughout the Guardian Angel Health System, Nick knew he would need a report for each hospital and was going to request one year of her pulls for drugs. Rather than have a report that was too excessive and unmanageable, Nick decided he would request only Schedule II drugs for the report. This information Nick learned in the New Jersey Police Academy Basic Narcotics Course. The schedule of drugs was devised by the federal Controlled Substance Act and ranks drugs by their strength, abuse potential, and other factors. Schedule I drugs are any drugs that do not have a medical purpose, and are either highly addictive psychologically, physically, or both, such as heroin and LSD. Schedule II are any drugs that have a medical use and have a high potential for abuse such as fentanyl, cocaine, and oxycodone. Schedule III are the milder forms of tranquilizers, such as hydrocodone, codeine, and ketamine. Schedule IV are any drugs that normally have a low potential for abuse or dependence relative to other drugs such as alprazolam, diazepam, or zolpidem. Schedule V substances are any substances with a lower potential for abuse and limited quantity of drug such as cough medicine with codeine, diphenoxylate/atropine, or pregabalin. Since Nick knew that a Schedule II drug was used, he would concentrate on that for the reports.

Second, Nick wanted to review a full background check on both RN Ann Stromer and Video Tech Moe Prince. He wanted to do a full assessment on who Ann was to see if she was in trouble financially and how much trouble she was in. Nick ordered one for Moe because now he was curious about the stories Moe had told him: his service record, his time in Afghanistan, whether he, too, was in debt, and if so, to whom. Nick was almost certain he had two big pieces to the puzzle but did not want to reveal any of it on the outside chance he was wrong. He did not want Ann and Moe to be permanently connected to terrorism if they were innocent. That type of stigma would be very hard to shed, even if they were clean. Nick figured he would have answers by the next meeting, and if it did tie them to any form of espionage, he would then need help for round-the-clock surveillance. This was not something he was ready to commit to now and needed the reports to justify the surveillance. Knowing they were part of the game, but not sure where they fit in, Nick had Moe and Ann pegged as small cogs, maybe witless ones, in a big machine.

Third, Nick wanted to go to human resources and check the records to determine how many American Muslims were working at the hospital that were woman of color and begin to investigate them to determine who might be the third person supplying the information. It stank of racial profile, and it twisted in his guts. But a tip was a tip.

When Nick got back to the hospital, Grazie was sitting in his office.

"Nick, what's on your mind."

"My best friend got shot, and I'm trying to save the world. And you?"

It was a wisecrack worthy of Al, and Nick felt secretly satisfied over it.

Grazie said, "I think I know you well enough now to know when you are troubled."

Nick responded, "I am troubled. Once I have the reports and we go over them, I'll have a better feeling of where this investigation is going. The informant telling you the female was a convert and a woman of color made me feel like we've been spinning our wheels this whole time. Also, I got a tip on the hotline. I'm meeting an employee at eight if you're interested. But now I was hoping you would help me look through the records for the female the informant told you was a convert to Islam and a woman of color."

Grazie replied, "Of course. Let's go."

At human resources, Nick asked the coordinator, Molly, "Can you print a list of all female Muslims born in the United States that are women of color that worked at the Parsippany facility?"

Molly replied, "I can list the women of color. I'm pretty sure we're not allowed to ask for their religion. It might be a matter of conjecture."

Of course, Nick thought. Maybe names would help, or photos. "Can you include ID photos?"

"No problem. If you want to go for coffee, the reports should be ready when you return." Nick thanked Molly, and they went to the cafeteria for coffee.

After they sat down, Nick said, "Tell me about your husband."

Grazie replied, "There's not much to tell. We love each other. He's older than I am, but you'd never know it by looking at him. Like most couples, we have our good and bad days. We have no children to worry about or put a strain on our relationship. What about your wife? Tell me about her."

Nick recoiled for a moment, then realized it was a fair question. He replied, "Jen and I have been together for a long time. She's a fantastic mother to our two kids. An excellent manager of the house and the affairs that go with it. She truly excels on the home front. We are comfortable with each other, and I guess that's what counts."

"But…"

Nick sipped. "But the spark has gone out."

Nick was staring into space when Grazie asked, "What are you thinking about?"

Nick replied, "One of the last things that Al and I discussed."

"What," she asked, "about the case?"

"No," he replied, "about you and me."

"What about us?"

Nick replied, "Al was worried I had gotten your scent."

"My scent! What are you talking about?"

Nick answered, "Not your scent in the true sense of the word, but rather falling for someone. It was a theory of Al's, and one he felt a man could not control once the scent, or should I say, feelings, took over."

"And what," she asked, "this is what he felt happened to you?"

Nick, with a smile on his face, nodded in the affirmative.

"Men!" Grazie said as she picked up her purse, retrieved her lipstick, and began applying it.

They finished their coffee and returned to human resources where Molly handed them an envelope containing personnel profiles of 118 American-born women of color. They eliminated anyone wearing a cross, anyone with hair exposed. They added back to the list anyone with a name that might be Arabic in origin. That left twelve. Of the twelve, Nick read eight were patient sitters, who go to the patient's house and care for them, never coming to the hospital. The other four worked at the corporate office building and would not have access to the hospital or sensitive areas. Their ID cards weren't programed to work on the hospital card readers to give them access. Also, if they did try to use them, it would tip off the lieutenant that gets the exception report every week of any employee attempting to gain access to an area they shouldn't enter. Dead end, he thought. Nick couldn't help wondering if he was missing something and hoping he could think of it fast.

Nick and Grazie picked up the Candor reports from the IT department at the hospital. Next, they met Agent Dan Camp for both Moe's military report and his Afghanistan civilian service report. They picked up the financial reports from a service recommended by Director Thomas Shane. Nick then informed the director he'd received the reports and would let him know as soon as he found anything out. Then they went to federal offices and the conference room, where they began to review the reports.

Nick asked Grazie, "Will you get the reports out of their folders and get the pads and laptops ready for work while I separate the Candor reports by monthly usage. I suggest we start with the Candor reports for Ann Stromer. They're in color and display a red mark for any narcotics taken that were above the mean average for the floor she was on at the time. This average is calculated internally by the machine and combined the number of patients, the drugs prescribed, and the number of times the medication could be given."

Grazie said, "Am I supposed to understand all that?"

Nick continued, "In Ann's position, she wasn't pulling drugs the way a regular registered nurse would, who has six to eight patients in her care. So if we see any red flags we would have enough probable cause to call her in and question her. Because of Ann's long-standing position, loyalty to the hospital, notoriety in the niche she carved out for herself in the field nationally and her reputation throughout the system, we have to have her cold, or this could blow up in our faces.

The good news if she appears to be an outlier, the director will take our back and ensure she explains the narcotic pulls."

The analysis of the report did yield a few surprises. First, Ann was pulling prepacked syringes of two-milliliter morphine at an exorbitant rate. Nick had requested the report to go back a full year, but it was evident that Ann began pulling the syringes of morphine only about four months ago.

Nick pointed this out to Grazie. "It appears that four months ago something happened, since that's when Ann started pulling the morphine. This report obviously indicates that something is wrong. Prior to the four-month mark, she had not pulled any morphine back to the beginning of the report. Then, about four months ago she began pulling a combined total of fifteen syringes a month. Make notes to see what reports I need to look up."

Grazie asked, "What reports? Don't we have them here?"

Nick said, "Yes, but there's a program in my computer that will tell us what patient she pulled it for, and whether there was a physician's order report to tell us the doctor ordered the medication for the patient. The next report would be the MAR or medication administration record for the patient. It tells when and how much medicine is given to a particular patient, including date, time, and nurse's initials. IT put the program on my laptop. It's called Chart-It. Basically," Nick said, "it's a file of each patient's medical record scanned into electronic form. Each log-in is internally recorded and must be explained, or the person accessing the file can be terminated and prosecuted for violating the patient's privacy rights." Nick was one of only a few in security and the only investigator Director Shane allowed to have the program.

Nick and Grazie continued to examine the report. Nick was convinced Ann had something to do with Al Stokes's death. If she wasn't the triggerwoman, at least she was an accomplice, luring Al to be comfortable in the situation. Morphine was a powerful narcotic that when abused could make someone do something out of the ordinary. Now Nick needed to prove that the drug was not pulled for a particular patient, but rather diverted for a sinister use. He marked down the date, time, and the name of the patient the morphine was pulled for and would check later in the Chart-It medical records program. They went through the entire report and made careful notes of what had to be checked. Then they decided to jump into the background checks report.

As they were getting them out and placing them on the table, Nick asked her, "How did you meet Ali?"

Grazie said, "He was passed down to me from an old partner who retired a few months ago. He proved himself time and again for reliability. All of the information he has passed along was important. He's been a gold mine."

Nick replied, almost thinking out loud, "I wonder what makes an individual perform this kind of work almost against his religion."

Grazie said, "It's not against his religion. His father was killed by radical Muslim extremists. He feels they betray the Koran when they kill innocent people in the name of Islam. He doesn't do it for the money."

Nick asked, "Then why do you keep paying him?"

Grazie replied, "To keep him coming back."

When Nick was on the job, his informants were providing information to have their criminal charges reduced, knock out the competition, or for the money. Whatever their reason, they were not doing it for something they believed in but rather something they could obtain. Therefore, though they were reliable and would come up with good jobs, they would always leave details out or give a half story because they really didn't care.

Nick asked Grazie, "See what you can find in Ann's background and financial check while I use the laptop to connect to Check-It."

Nick used the program to call up patient's records and look up the questions he'd written down. Nick turned to the final page of the report and noticed a woman expired at 1405 hours. When he went back to the medication administration record, he observed that her nurse had given her the morphine at 1020 hours, which was all correct. The next shot given by Ann was 1420 hours, fifteen minutes after the patient expired. The next patient was discharged from the hospital at 1120 hours and received her morphine at 0920 hours.

The next dose was given by Ann at 1320 hours, two hours after the patient was discharged.

Bingo.

Nick kept finding this with every patient Ann had supposedly administered drugs to. Part of Ann's duties was to check on the patients with reportable diseases, and while visiting the patient she could administer the drug at the appropriate time. This was like a quality-of-life issue where Ann could help the patient by dispensing the drug while questioning them about their illness. Naturally Ann was required, like every other nurse, to keep impeccable records and follow doctor's orders.

Nick said to Grazie, "This program is amazing. See how it recorded everything Ann did for the patient."

Grazie replied, "I do. Ingenious to use a real patient, the correct dosage, and the correct amount. She'd be nurse of the year if her patients weren't already dead."

It now appeared to both Nick and Grazie that Ann was charting the drugs for a patient but taking the drugs for her use or someone other than the patient's use. Nick wanted the opinion of the nursing forensics unit. It appeared to him and Grazie that Ann was manipulating the system by dispensing the drugs at the correct intervals, hoping to avoid notice that the patient had just died or been discharged. It appeared that Ann's plan worked, almost.

Grazie said, "Nick, look at this financial report. Ann is a financial mess. Her house is in foreclosure. Retail establishments are suing her for payment. One department store garnished her wages. It looks like others are lining up to do the same. In other words, she is financially broke and loaded with debt. Yet she owns her car outright, a new Mercedes, takes trips frequently, and eats out regularly, according to her charge receipts."

Nick explained to Grazie, "I met Ann's boyfriend in Atlantic City. She told me he's Egyptian and his name is Max Fouquaan, and that he's in the import-export business, and his father is a doctor in Egypt. He gave her an extraordinary amount of money to gamble with. I had him checked both nationally through the Interpol databases, but they came back negative. I have a photo of Max taken by Al. I'm sending it to you now."

Grazie said, "I'll see what I can find."

Nick continued looking in Chart-It. Ann was dispensing morphine, fentanyl, and Percocet from ten minutes to almost three hours after some patients died. Another anomaly Nick noticed on the report was the large amount of Percocet reported missing whenever Ann was in the hospital. It did not show up as being dispensed incorrectly. It just went missing.

Nick pointed this out to Grazie, stating, "When this happens both the pharmacy and nurse manager of the floor have to do a complete inventory to determine if, in fact, the pills were missing or it was a clerical error. These inquiries take time, and different machines throughout the hospital were registering a loss."

Grazie asked, "Why wasn't this discovered before?"

Nick replied, "It appears pharmacy was becoming aware of the loss but had yet to solve it or attribute it to anyone. It's highly unusual to have such a loss, since a nurse can only open a machine on the floor she is assigned and not on different floors, except Ann. Again, Ann was always in the machine with the discrepancy."

Nick finished looking up the medical records as Grazie finished the financial analysis and excused herself to answer her phone. When Grazie hung up, as if choreographed, they each put the reports down at the same time and went to the coffee machine. Nick knew they still had to finish the Moe Prince analysis but took one look at her and began to lose focus on the job at hand. He forced himself to concentrate on the reports, but Grazie sat next to him and she was leaning on him, reading a report.

Nick repressed his thoughts and urges, and they both got to work on Moe's background, military records, and financial records. Though hard to believe, it turned out Moe was in the Army and was honorably discharged after serving two tours in Kuwait. He was having financial troubles until he came to work at Guardian Angel Health System. His financial record was too good to be true, considering the relative humble size of his biweekly paycheck, as he went from near foreclosure to paying off his home with no known source of cash influx. The more records they looked at, the bleaker Moe's financial status looked. All his major credit cards were maxed out, then paid off approximately four months ago, with no recorded income other than that from the hospital.

Furthermore, from information received from John Smallwood and the agency, it did appear that Moe served as a civilian in Afghanistan and Iraq for a large security company. However, the records indicated he only completed one year. He received the money he was promised, tax free, and thus saved his house from foreclosure. Though Moe arrived in Iraq to begin a second tour, he advised his boss he was quitting and returning to the United States. But they lost track of him, and he did not return for six months, his whereabouts unknown for that time period. All his bills still remained unpaid until four months ago when Moe began making large payments on his accounts. As though Moe hit the lottery, all his past debt was erased under mysterious circumstances.

Nick called Ricks at Parsippany PD. "Quick question," Nick said. "I know you're not in narcotics, but what are the big drugs on the street nowadays. I mean, locally."

"Heroin, always," Ricks said. "But lately? There's been an uptick in pharmaceuticals. I'm gonna say Percocet, mostly."

"And fentanyl?"

"Yeah. How'd you know?"

They wrapped up their work, left the federal building, and headed to the hospital command center, waiting for Edwin the shuttle driver to call back. Nick was convinced that Ann was diverting drugs. Now they needed to find out why. Nick wondered, were Ann and Moe partners in dealing drugs? Was the missing fentanyl used to kill Jack? Nick wanted answers, and he knew he could sweat it out of Moe or Ann if he caught them with their hands in the cookie jar. Nick had a feeling that Al's death was connected, and he was going to find out how.

At 8:05 p.m. Edwin called and said he would be right there. The shift commander escorted an older black male to Nick's office. Edwin had salt-and-pepper hair, medium height and weight with a thin mustache. After the introductions and handshakes, they sat down.

Nick began by saying, "Edwin, can you go over what you told me earlier today on the phone?"

"Sure," Edwin replied. "As I told you, this light-skinned brother gets on the shuttle and began asking all these questions. I been driving the shuttle for five years, and no one ever asked the questions he does."

Grazie asked, "Like what?"

He replied, "Like what are the locations of all the off-sites, warehouses, labs, what are their hours, is there security at each one."

Grazie said, "Did you ask him why?"

Edwin answered, "Of course. Even without the blast e-mail from the director, anybody asking those questions needs to be asked why."

Nick asked, "When was the last time you saw him?"

He replied, "Earlier today. That's why I called you. He was asking about the schedule for different shuttles, so I told him I only know mine, then he stopped. I figure he works in the kitchen 'cause he wears that type of clothing."

Nick then asked, "Edwin, I'd like you to look at the photos on the computer and see if you can pick him out. Keep scrolling until you get to the end."

Edwin looked at the photos scrolling and looking. After approximately five minutes he stopped.

He then said, "That's him. Ben El Karem, kitchen help."

Nick clicked on the photo and printed four copies. Turning toward Edwin, Nick extended his hand and thanked him for his help. With that, Edwin left. Grazie then left. It was for the best.

Nick drove to the federal lab annex. When he arrived, he was escorted to the lab and introduced to the lab manager, Felix Chu.

Nick asked, "Any results from the bullet retrieved from Al Stokes's murder?"

Chu replied, "It was a nine-millimeter copper jacket supercharged hollow point. Most likely fired from a gun with a silencer on it. The spiral cylinder marks changed as the bullet progressed through the barrel. Furthermore, the bullet was drilled and the center fitted with an extra charge of gun powder to ensure whatever it hit would sustain maximum damage."

Nick asked, "Why?

Chu replied, "It would seem these bullets then were custom-made for this person."

Nick left the lab and returned to the hospital security office, checking all reports on access to the hospital in the hopes he would see an anomaly and could check it with the cameras. It was a long shot, but Al deserved nothing less, and Nick was more determined than ever to catch the bastard who killed his best friend.

But who the hell hated Stokes enough to kill him? To make a special bullet, follow him, and kill him?

Who hated anybody that much?

CHAPTER 22

Nick was the first to arrive at the meeting the next day. Pouring himself a cup of coffee he walked over and was staring out the window. FBI Special Agent Dan Camp was at the meeting early. He grabbed a cup of coffee and took a seat in the conference room, spreading out notes and photos from the folder he brought with him. Grazie arrived a few minutes later and sat next to him. Both acknowledged Nick with greetings. Nick turned and sat at the table to wait for the meeting to start.

Glancing at the photo of Ann's boyfriend, Grazie asked, "Have your boys been able to identify him?"

Dan replied, "Yes. Based on our overseas and Jersey City informant information sources, his name is Farqua, and he attends services regularly at the mosque in Jersey City. This intelligence reports he's some kind of enforcer. Whenever he's on the radar there are squads dispatched to different assignments, people mysteriously disappear, bodies are found. And the next time he arrives for a service, he is congratulated and held in esteem. Check with your informant the next time you see him to confirm this intelligence."

Grazie replied, "I will, but how was this information obtained?"

Dan answered, "Several sources, both here and abroad. Also confirmed by different means of surveillance, both physical and electronic."

Grazie stated, "Good job. I'll talk to my informant and see what he can confirm."

Grazie went into the hall and called Ali on the phone she had given him. If he didn't answer on the third ring, it meant he couldn't talk and would call her back. Ali always left the phone on vibrate so no one would hear it ring. He answered on the second ring.

"Hello, Ms. Phyllis," Ali said. "How can I help you?"

Grazie said, "Are you somewhere where you can talk?"

Ali replied, "Of course, or I would not have answered."

Grazie continued, "Joseph, do you know someone from the mosque named Farqua? He also goes by Max Fouquaan. I'm sending you a photo."

Ali replied, "I am thinking he is a new member that has been coming around. I don't know him well, but I will see what I can find out and would then be in touch. But, I also have other information. I found out that one of the informants working in the hospital is a 'brother.'"

Grazie asked, "Who's brother?"

"He is a brother Muslim in a position that he is able to not only provide information but also keep an eye on the female informant that was working there."

Grazie said, "Joseph, find out what you can about Farqua and the others and call me."

This was the first meeting for Special Agent Dan Camp whom Nick had invited to join their investigation. Agent Camp said, "With all due respect, aside from our databases, informants, and other sources of information, I can also furnish a team if, as Nick said, around-the-clock surveillance becomes necessary. This includes not only manpower, but vehicles, radios, and cell phones that are all encrypted and therefore not penetrable by our suspects."

Grazie gave the nod of approval. Nick got a suspicion that she resented Camp as an intrusion, and that she'd only share anything important with Nick. Nick shared the reports he and Grazie had reviewed with the group.

Nick stated, "After a review of the reports for narcotic dispensing, medical records, and patient charts, both Agent Grazie and I agree that Ann Stromer is diverting drugs. Furthermore, Moe Prince is in this up to his eyeballs, but we're not sure how it all ties in. We've seen them together in her new Mercedes. We're seen a black Honda in her garage, though we can't be sure if it's the one used as a getaway car from the murders."

Grazie then reported, "The two of them are in a financial mess, and a huge amount of drugs appear to be missing from the hospital inventory in the last few months."

Nick said, "We have to assume there's some sort of attack being planned."

Dan Camp and John Smallwood spoke almost in unison.

"Whoa, easy there!" said Camp.

"Wait a minute," said Smallwood.

"For what?" Nick asked. "How much more evidence do you need. Two dead. Multiple violations of our perimeters. Reconnaissance missions into the hospital…"

Camp said, "Nick, we can't go crying terrorist every time someone sneaks past security. We have to have proof."

Smallwood nodded.

Nick said, "Are you fucking kidding me? How much proof do you need?"

"More than this," Camp said, "before we call in the cavalry. We have parameters."

Nick considered asking if someone would please shoot him. There had been many attacks. Of course, the CIA and FBI had guidelines as to what constituted imminent threat. But what kind of guidelines?

Would Nick face the terrorists alone?

The meeting broke up, and Nick walked over to Grazie. She spoke before he could.

"Nick, I need time alone with my husband. I'm confused and need time to figure out what it is I want."

Nick shifted his feet. Was she wondering if she wanted to run off with him? Was she just trying to decide whether she was still in love with her husband, and to see if he still was in love with her? Obviously, her husband had priority. What was Nick to her? Nothing.

And yet he wondered what she was thinking about him.

She leaned close to Nick, whispering, "Don't call me tonight."

Dan Camp was saying something to him as they all left the building. But Nick didn't hear a word. He was still thinking about Grazie's announcement. As he got in his car and began to pull away, his phone rang. It was Grazie.

She said, "I hope my announcement didn't shock you. But I need this tonight, this time alone with just me and Tony."

Who was he to ask her for anything? Nick said, "Do what you have to do."

There was no way for Grazie to realize that her pending dinner hit Nick like a sucker punch. He had to pull over and clear his thoughts. This was the point he realized that Grazie was getting to him. He had gotten her scent, as Al told him. He didn't know when it had sunk into him, but it had. Why was she telling him this? Yes, they were working a lot, and no one was getting much home time. He had a wife and kids he wasn't spending time with. But for Grazie to make such a big deal about it, it didn't make sense. Why tell him about having dinner with her husband? It was almost like asking for permission.

He headed back to the office. He'd immerse himself in his work.

There was going to be an attack on the hospital. The clock was ticking. They had to find what Moe and Ann were up to. And where did Farqua fit in?

And could they figure out what was going on in time to stop it?

Chapter 23

Nurse Volts was making her 9:00 p.m. rounds, already thinking about the break that she would soon be taking and putting her aching feet up on a chair for a half hour. She walked down the corridor, checking on each patient and marking her chart that all was in order. That is, until she came to the last room and noticed the patient wasn't in his bed. She checked the bathroom, then checked with the nurse's station to verify he wasn't sent for tests, and then called security.

Nick followed up with Smallwood and found out that surveillance had heard nothing of note from Moe Prince's place or Ann Stromer's. He followed up with Ricks and learned they were still tracking ballistics on the bullet that killed Al Stokes. He wanted to follow up with Grazie, though not for any good reason. Though he tried not to think about it, he was torturing himself wondering what Grazie and her husband were discussing. Was she going to dump Tony, or was this a get-back-together dinner? Nick was starting to feel melancholy, thinking of her in the arms of her husband. It was none of his business. He was married. What did he care? He was considering calling Grazie when his phone rang.

It was the hospital security shift commander calling. "Hi, Nick. I wanted to let you know that a male patient was found outside the hospital doubled over yesterday with severe stomach pains. He was admitted and was on the fourth floor. The reason I'm calling, he was discovered missing on the nurse's last patient check a few minutes ago. He hasn't been seen leaving the hospital. He removed his IV and port, disconnected his monitor. Found his own clothes in the closet and left."

"Can you tell me what he was wearing?"

"We'd have to look at the security video. Sorry. All security officers were placed on high alert. The lab and covert closet are being manned with extra personnel. And I had Video Tech Moe Prince check out the video from the elevators and stairs on the fourth floor as a starting point from fifty minutes ago."

"No, no," Nick blurted. "Moe doesn't touch the videos. He just sets up the cameras."

"Is that the rule?"

"No, it's just…Never mind. Where are they now?"

"They think he's on the second floor, by stairwell D."

"Tell them not to touch him. I'll be right there." Nick realized that if something was going down, Moe Prince might cover for any intruders.

Running down the hall, Nick was hoping the security officers wouldn't overreact. Leaving the hospital without notice, against medical advice or AMA—eloping, it was called—was not a crime. They weren't prisoners. Unless the person was high on drugs or alcohol, or was a threat to themselves or others, there really wasn't much that could be done other than talking to them and trying to convince them it was in their best interest to return. Handle it right, and the patient could wind up safely in bed. Handle it wrong, and you were looking at a lawsuit.

Nick arrived at stairwell D and observed three security officers approaching a dark-skinned individual.

Nick approached them and asked, "What's going on?"

One of the security officers stated, "We just found him."

Nick asked, "Is he here because he is a threat to himself or others? Did he do anything besides elope?"

To which they replied no, almost in unison.

Nick approached the man, saying, "For your health and well-being, we suggest you return with us to your room."

The individual said, "My stomach does not hurt any longer, and I want to leave."

"Where are you headed?"

"Spring Street," the man said.

"Can I give you a lift? It would be a real black eye for the hospital if you collapsed in the street."

"No."

Nick went to security to speak with the watch commander and was surprised to see Director Shane in the command center.

Director Shane stated, "The man was a legitimate limousine driver. He lives in town."

"My men didn't overreact," the shift commander said.

"They were about to," Nick said. "Look, I get it. We're all on high alert. But we can't go in guns blazing every time someone with a tan coughs."

"So, what should we do?"

"Report possible threats, sure. Then we'll determine if the threat is real."

Nick was heading for his car when his extra cell phone, the phone number he'd put on the e-mail blast, began to ring. A woman rambled on about a young Muslim male preaching radical ideas throughout the hospital and instructing anyone who would listen, mainly young people, to go online and read the sites that he says preach the truth.

The woman continued, "He also wants anyone that will listen to attend a rally they are having at a mosque in Dover, NJ, every Wednesday night."

Nick said, "Thank you for calling, I'm going to ask you questions. Let's start with your name."

The woman replied, "No, no names. But I saw him speaking outside the cafeteria this morning around ten." She hung up. The display on Nick's phone read, "Unknown caller."

The woman's voice sounded so odd. Nick wondered if she'd been disguising it. Something about the voice sounded familiar. Not the tones. The rhythms?

Ann? Was it Ann Stromer?

He had no way to prove it, but he heard her voice enough over the years to recognize it. Strange, Nick thought.

He kept thinking of the call on his ride home and about his career at Guardian Angel Hospital, Director Thomas Shane, and the trust that he had placed in Nick from day one. In particular, Nick remembered how the director explained to him that he wanted Nick to run the new Red Cell program and gave him authority to run it as he saw fit. The director explained that the Red Cell program was based on a United States Army exercise. Two teams, blue and red, compete against each other. The blue team attempts to capture the red team's flag. However, in the hospital setting, Nick and his team, without wearing identification, would attempt to gain entry into sensitive areas of the hospital. If the blue team succeeded, the department would be trained on where the security breach took place. If they failed, the red team would go on offense and the blue on defense. Nick remembered how Director Shane insisted he continue to attempt to gain entry into the lab where, Nick realized now, the irradiator was kept. This program was now five years old and had become so successful that Director Shane hired different police personnel to attempt entry to create greater challenges for the team. Nick would captain one team, Al the other.

Al. Al was gone.

Sure, the hospital had made improvements since he was hired. Was it enough? Obviously, it wasn't. This was evidenced by three deaths in a week. Nick had to get smarter, and fast.

Nick arrived early the next day and was typing his reports while having coffee. He wanted to get as much of his tedious but necessary work out of the way beforehand, so he decided to come in early and work late.

About 8:30 a.m., Nick answered his phone and listened while the security watch commander stated, "The roving security detail, post four, observed a woman in a hijab on the parking deck across the street, taking photographs of the hospital. By the time the security officer drove to the location, she was gone. About fifteen minutes later, he observed her near the Emergency Medical Unit building, but he was patrolling the upper decks of the visitor's lot, and by the time he arrived at the Emergency Medical Unit, she had once again eluded him. He called in on the radio about five minutes ago and is in the process of looking for her, but he is not having any luck. That's why I called you."

Nick replied, "I'll be right over."

After parking his car on the top floor of the visitor's lot, Nick exited his car, walked over to the wall, and began looking for the female wearing the traditional Muslim head covering. Looking in a left-to-right pattern, Nick was thankful daylight gave him a better opportunity to spot the woman. He was thinking this could be totally innocent. The woman could be taking photos of the place where she was going to have her baby, in order to send them to relatives both in the United States and abroad. It had happened before. On the other hand, he wondered if this individual was connected to a group of terrorists getting ready to act and making sure none of the hospital entrances and exits had changed. Or, if they were trying to spot the helipad located on a smaller building, tucked out of sight.

Nick didn't spot anything out of the ordinary. He was about to call the command center and tell them he was returning to his office, that she must have left the area, when he noticed her across the street, on the top deck of a parking garage of a private office building. Without drawing attention to himself, Nick returned to his car and made his way down the winding five-floor driveway, all the while hoping she did not leave. When he emerged from the parking garage he caught the traffic light at the entrance to the hospital. When the light turned green Nick drove across the street and into the garage of the private office building, badged past the guard, and made his way to the next-to-top floor and called the command center, stating he was across the street and was exiting his car.

Nick spotted the woman where he'd seen her, perched at the railing, snapping pictures with a digital camera, appropriately, a Canon. He walked toward the woman, looking around the area to make sure there were no vehicles waiting for her. Nick approached her, and in his most pleasant voice said, "Excuse me, madam, I work for the hospital security, and taking photos of the hospital is not allowed."

The woman turned around and, while speaking in Arabic, began to wave her hand into the air. Her eyes were black as onyx stones, narrowing as she continued to rant. Noticing he could not see her other hand under her clothes, Nick turned sideways toward her in order to make himself a smaller target. Then, getting that familiar feeling of the hair on his neck beginning to rise, Nick knew something was about to happen. He reached for his gun but remembered it was in his ankle holster and he couldn't get it.

Nick was about to ask her if she spoke English when he heard her say, in a loud voice, almost screaming, "Allah Akbar."

Almost instantaneously, her hand came out from under her garment and Nick saw what appeared to be a toy gun. Then realizing it was a Taser, Nick tried to dive behind a parked car, but it was too late. He felt the sting of the two needlelike prongs at the tip end of the wires as they penetrated his thigh. He saw the colors and felt pain of the fifty thousand volts the Taser produced. Nick saw all green in front of his eyes. The pain consumed him. Nick was already off his center of balance when the prongs hit him, as he was in the process of jumping out of the way. He'd hit the parking deck with a thud. Nick observed out of the corner of his eye, the woman making a dash for the stairs. Normally he would have been aggravated that the woman took off and had gotten away. But this time he was happy to see her leave, because if she wanted to finish him off, he was lying on the ground twitching like a fish out of water, a perfect target. The only reason Nick could guess the collective enemy's sudden concern with human life was that whoever was behind the attacks did not want another dead body turning up yet. The stun gun was efficient, quiet, and effective.

Nick was sitting with his back against the wall when the ambulance arrived. The EMTs checked his vital signs and then placed him in the ambulance for the short ride to the hospital. Nick kept insisting he felt fine, but they would not be deterred.

When the ambulance arrived at the emergency department, Nick was wheeled into a room, and the nurses again took his vital signs while also preparing him for an EKG. When all the preliminaries were complete, a Dr. Kim came in and told Nick he appeared to be in good shape except for some bruising on his left side and two burn marks on his right side. His EKG as well as his blood pressure were normal, and as soon as the paperwork was complete they would let him go. Nick thanked the doctor, and she left the room. After signing a mountain of papers, Nick was walking out of the emergency department and back to the security command center. Then remembering the phone call, he changed directions and headed for the cafeteria. Though Ann—if it was Ann—had said the preacher was at the cafeteria much earlier, Nick figured it was worth a shot.

Right outside the cafeteria entrance, Nick found the suspect. Nick identified himself and said, "Your identification card, please."

The man hesitated, then thrust his ID into Nick's hand. Nick read the man's name aloud. "Akbar Sharif? Is that correct?"

Sharif replied, "Yes. Is there a problem?"

Nick replied, "The hospital has rules prohibiting any form of preaching, soliciting, or advertising anything by anyone within the hospital or the grounds. So, I'm asking you to please stop what you are doing now and in the future. Failure to do so could lead to termination. Do you understand?"

He answered, "Yes," realizing from Nick's demeanor there was no room for discussion.

Nick then asked, "Now please show me your driver's license."

Sharif produced a driver's license. Nick copied down the information and returned it, noticing that Sharif appeared to be angry.

Nick asked, feeling achy and angry himself, "Is there a problem?"

"No," Sharif replied. "No problem." The man seemed to be mentally photographing Nick for future reference.

When he arrived at the command center, the first thing Nick wanted to know was if post four was able to find the woman who shot him with the stun gun. Then he wanted to do a background check and HR check on Akbar Sharif. The shift commander said they hadn't found the woman, nor was she seen in the area afterward. They assigned an additional patrol vehicle, but so far, the results were negative.

Nick said, "Do me a favor. Pull the HR file on this guy." He gave the commander the scrap of paper with Sharif's name and license number on it.

Director Shane arrived and said, "Nick, take a day off. You deserve it."

Nick was about to argue but realized his hands were shaking, had been shaking since the Taser shock, and said, "Call me if anything comes up."

Post four took Nick to his car. "We can drive you home, sir."

"I'm fine," he lied. Still shaken, he took his time on the drive home, cautious to ensure no one was following him. He had been doing this since his earliest days on the job with the sheriff. If someone wanted to follow him home to do harm to him, his house, or his family, Nick would make it difficult. It meant extra turns, with one eye on the rearview mirror. As far as Nick was concerned, when he was working he was fair game, as were the people he was investigating. But he'd do anything to keep people from following him home.

Once home, after all the hellos and kisses, Nick wanted to tell Jen of the incident. But she kept changing the subject so Nick began telling her he was fine.

The next day was beautiful, with bright sunshine and low humidity. Still, Nick felt terrible, and after breakfast Jen suggested they go down the shore, sit on the beach, and relax.

Jen asked, "How do you feel, Nick?"

Again, Nick lied, "I feel good."

Nick couldn't wait to get back to the investigation and the thought that he would be seeing Grazie the next day. He wanted to open up to her, tell her all that was going on, like the conversations he had with Grazie. He wished he could share these feelings with Jen. But he knew her well enough to know that if he brought it up, she would just change the subject so that her little world was never rocked. Nick figured she thought he was tough and could handle his work, while she handled the home front. Most times this made sense. But that was before this investigation of an impending terror attack and, more importantly, he felt, before he met Grazie. Nick insisted they head home before lunch. He spent the day reading, watching television, and pacing.

In the early evening, Grazie called. "Can I meet you tonight?" she asked. "I want to touch base on a few things before I meet with Ali again."

"No. Yes."

"Meet me at the federal building in the parking lot, in half an hour."

Nick turned to his Jen and said, "I have to go to the hospital for a while. I shouldn't be that late."

Nick ran downstairs to his man cave, had two fingers of Scotch, and headed to the federal building. He had to admit that he really missed Grazie and now could not wait to see her. Imagine, he thought, twenty-four hours without seeing her, and he missed her terribly.

Nick pulled into the parking garage and saw her already there.

Grazie said, "Let's go up to my office, and you can tell me what I missed."

When they got to her office, they sat at a small circular table.

Nick said, "There was a scare they had with a patient elopement that turned out to be nothing, though Camp and Smallwood were checking the patient's background to be sure. We should find out more at the meeting tomorrow."

Nick then briefed her on the woman taking photos, how he was called in to help find her, and ended up in the emergency department after getting shot with a stun gun. Grazie leaned in and kissed Nick.

Nick caught his breath, pretended nothing had happened, and said, "I need Dan to also check an employee named Akbar Sharif who has been preaching Islam around the hospital. Then we can call him in for an interview."

They continued to kiss, with Grazie asking, "Nick, are you sure you're all right?"

Nick replied while still kissing her, "I'm fine, there were no side effects."

Grazie pulled away and picked up the folder in front of her. They pooled information, considered scenarios, made plans. Wiretaps, electronic bugs, car GPS systems were all discussed and schedules drawn up for information retrieval.

Just before they departed, Nick asked, "So, how was your dinner date with your husband?"

Grazie's demeanor darkened. "It was good."

Nick knew it was a mistake to push it, but said, "Good, only good?"

Grazie walked away while talking over her shoulder as she left, "Yeah. Good!"

Chapter 24

Agent Grazie arrived at the field office the next morning where the wiretaps on both Ann's and Moe's phones had been up and running. There were two techs at each panel, headphones on, digital recorders on pause, and each tech making sure the volume and other levels were set and ready. On the far end of the room an exact setup was at the ready for Moe's phone. The phones included both house and cell phone, and thus two techs were required for each house. She was curious to see if any new information had been captured as a result of the wiretaps. Looking over the logs, she observed no incoming or outgoing calls on any of the phones.

Great, Grazie thought, *all set up and no calls.*

She was about to leave when Moe called Ann from his cell phone.

Moe said, "I don't have specifics, but there is sure a major operation is in the works. It involves the hospital, and they're planning to cover their tracks by any means necessary. Not immediately, but soon. I'll call if I hear anything else."

Ann said, "I knew something was up because he hasn't been paying attention to me. It must be something important because he always told me he would rather be with me."

Moe answered, "Yeah, yeah. Let me know if you hear anything."

When Nick arrived at the federal building for the morning meeting, Grazie filled them in on Moe and Ann's phone call.

"So, they're in the middle of this," Nick said. "Now we have proof."

"In the middle or on the periphery. It's probably better to keep eyes and ears on them than to bring them in. I'm not sure they know anything. I showed Ali the picture of Ann's boyfriend Max Fouquaan, and yes, that's Farqua. Apparently, he handles the girl providing the information—I guess that's Ann—and also the Muslim male who is also providing information."

Nick asked, "Moe?"

"You tell me. Ali said that Farqua has gone back to Afghanistan for something. I'm guessing instructions, additional jihadists, financial backing, and their escape route if they make it out alive."

Nick said, "So do we stop him from entering the country again, or do we follow him so as not to tip our hand?"

Dan Camp said, "When he comes back, it means they're ready to strike."

Smallwood said, "If we pick him up, they break up the team and strike again. Yeah, we've prevented this attack, but we've really just rescheduled it for an unknown time and place."

Nick said, "So we watch Farqua when he comes back. We know where the attack is supposed to happen, and we're ready for him. Do we catch more people that way? Is it worth the risk?"

There was a pause in the meeting for everyone to digest what was said.

With that, the meeting ended, and Nick rushed to his appointment with Director Shane to inform him of the progress of the case. Nick told Grazie he would call her later.

Nick's meeting with the director began right on time. Nick explained what Agent Grazie learned from the confidential informant, and the question about how to proceed.

Nick explained, "It appeared it was Moe Prince and Ann Stromer supplying information. Since the main suspect has returned to the Middle East, the investigation team would like to have their end wrapped up by the time he returns, which as far as we know could be anytime."

As Nick left the director's office, his phone rang. It was Grazie. She said, "I'll meet you at your office."

Nick felt giddy thinking he was going to see her in a few minutes. When he got to his office, she was standing in the hall. As soon as the door closed, they began to kiss. Nick pulled away and said, "Someone will walk in." Grazie wasn't fazed. Again, Nick pulled away and asked, "Is this what you want, because I do and we either stop now or we won't be able to."

"Shut up," she said, and unbuckled his pants.

CHAPTER 25

As Nick entered the building, he peered down the cavernous hallway of Guardian Angel Hospital, noticing the uncharacteristic absence of the uniformed security officer stationed at the main entrance.

Dusk was falling, and the change of shift had already occurred. Nick felt the hairs on the back of his neck start to rise, not a good feeling, but one he relied on his entire twenty-six-year career. *It* was an instinct that never failed him, that kept him safe, and warned him of unexpected dangers about to happen or that had already occurred.

The high-top desk and chair utilized by the security officer appeared conspicuously out of place now with no uniform presence, giving the sense of emptiness rather than that of protection and security. They appeared to be desolate relics of a previous chapter in the hospital's existence. Nick approached the security desk and, using the phone there, called the security command center.

Nick asked, "Who's working the main entrance post?"

The command center officer responded, "Security Officer Joe Turro."

Nick asked, "Why isn't he at his post?"

The command center officer responded, "He must be on a 10-11. A bathroom break."

"I know what a 10-11 is. He's supposed to call that in. Someone should be covering for him. Send up post four."

Post four was the outside roving patrol. Security Officer Jim Adamson arrived as Nick placed the phone down. Jim assumed the post as Nick went to look for Officer Joe Turro in the men's room.

Nick walked the hundred feet to the men's room at a quick pace. The daytime employees had left for the day, and a noticeable quiet settled over the corridor. Though he could not explain why, he felt that something was terribly wrong. Then upon swinging open the door he observed Officer Joe Turro on the floor in front of the urinal, unconscious.

Nick turned his phone on speaker and pressed the speed dial number for the command center. Then, checking Joe and not feeling a pulse, began cardiopulmonary resuscitation. As he began the compressions on the officer's chest, the command center answered.

Nick shouted, "I'm in the first-floor men's room. Security Officer Turro is on the floor, unresponsive. I began CPR. Send backup and the cardio trauma team."

As the trauma team arrived and took over the care of the officer, Nick noticed an ice pick not quite disposed of in the trash, but rather caught between the lid and the rim. In an evident attempt to exit hastily, whoever dumped the ice pick did not push it fully into the garbage. Nick quickly retrieved it with his handkerchief and wrapped it in paper towels, careful not to leave his fingerprints on it.

The trauma team revived Joe by using the defibrillator. They hooked him up to oxygen and an IV drip and were beginning to wheel him out on a stretcher when Joe opened his eyes, saw Nick, and waved for the team to stop.

Nick leaned over and Joe said in a breathless whisper, "White guy. Patchy beard. I thought he was headed for the other urinal. Sticks me. Yelling some crazy shit."

"Then what?"

"Then I saw you," Joe said. "Get my radio and key ring."

Nick replied, "Okay, Joe."

As Officer Turro was being wheeled away, he grabbed Nick's hand and squeezed it. Nick looked for the keys and radio and realized they were gone.

Nick again called the command center and instructed the shift commander, "Call Parsippany Police. Call in Director Shane and the security manager for a briefing, and consider this to be a high priority."

Furthermore, Nick instructed the command center, "Place a security officer outside of Officer Turro's room. His keys and radio are missing." Nick finished his instructions by telling the dispatcher to have the armed Parsippany Police officer report to the covert storeroom located in the subterranean level D of the hospital and to instruct him to be on alert for armed intruders. It appeared it was open season on the hospital's security officers. But then again, Nick thought, they were always out front, guarding the important areas of the hospital. They were sitting ducks.

Nick handed the ice pick wrapped in paper towels to the security commander and explained, "Be very careful with it. Tell the lab the police will want to dust it for fingerprints."

Nick began to walk down the corridor at a fast pace, reaching for his phone to call the director. He headed for the blood lab on D level. Instead of waiting for elevators that were notoriously slow, he ran down the stairs and removed his revolver from its ankle holster to put it in his jacket pocket. When the director answered, Nick didn't give him a chance to talk, instead describing exactly what happened and where he had directed the security team.

Nick stated, "I'm on my way to the lab."

Nick was running to the blood lab as quickly as he could. He turned the corner that led directly there when, from the opposite direction, he heard the unmistakable sound of gunfire. Nick counted two shots that sounded as though they were from the same gun, fired in rapid succession.

CHAPTER 26

Calling the command center from his cell, Nick asked, "What the hell is going on?" They replied they did not know. Nick instructed the officer, "Send someone to respond to the blood lab. I'm going to the covert closet. Send backup units. Call Parsippany Police and also advise Director Shane to respond."

Nick had not yet reached the corridor that housed the covert stash of antidotes and reagents when he smelled the unique unmistakable acid, earthy-like smell of fired gunpowder. He turned the corner and found a Parsippany Police officer, Ken Gross, identified by his nameplate, lying on the floor. Nick called the command center again and explained what he had found, telling the desk officer to notify Parsippany Police that an officer was down and to assist the officer.

"*Code green!*" Nick shouted. "Active shooter."

Nick leaned over Officer Gross, looking for the injuries sustained by the gunfire. Upon closer inspection, he was thrilled to observe the officer's body armor—his bulletproof vest—had stopped the bullets from inflicting serious bodily harm. Instead, they'd knocked the officer over, causing him to hit his head on the tile floor. The officer was knocked out from the fall, not the bullets. As the emergency crews arrived, Nick explained what had happened and, giving the description he had gotten earlier from Security Officer Joe Turro, instructed the police and security to begin an immediate search both in and outside the hospital.

When the medical crew and additional security arrived, Nick briefed them. "Officer Gross's body armor stopped the shooter's bullets. There are two bullets lodged in the bulletproof vest. Do not handle them as agents Smallwood and Grazie would be interested to learn if they had any fingerprints on them."

Instructions were given for twenty-four-hour protection on both Officer Gross and Security Officer Turro. At this point, Director Thomas Shane arrived. Nick briefed him on what had transpired and that they were attempting to find the shooter who might still be in the hospital.

The director stated, "I called the Morris County sheriff for reinforcements and the K-9 unit in order to determine if the dogs would be able to pick up the intruder's scent."

Nick was already on the phone with Grazie, explaining, "A security officer was stabbed and a Parsippany cop shot, both in the hospital. We think the shooter is still here."

Grazie replied, "I'll send the forensic unit to collect any evidence that might have remained."

Nick explained, "I have an ice pick used in the stabbing and two bullets removed from the officer's body armor. Make sure your team takes them for analysis. I'll be searching for the suspect."

Grazie said, "I'll instruct the forensic unit to pick them up."

Nick then began his search for the scruffy-looking ice pick wielder, down the corridor and out to the loading dock. Nothing. Nick retraced his steps. This part of the hospital was a remote area used for shipping, receiving, and distribution. He then froze when he saw a white scruffy-looking male climbing out of a soiled laundry basket parked in the hallway.

Nick yelled, "Security! Lie down on the floor with your hands on your head."

The suspect fired at Nick, the bullets whizzing by him as the deafening sound of the shots echoed in the corridor. Nick took cover in an alcove for protection, not taking his eyes off the perp. At that second, a nurse exited the door closest to the shooter. He grabbed her, placing her in front of him and holding her around the waist. She screeched.

Nick yelled, "Let her go."

Nick had his handgun pointed at the suspect. The suspect faced Nick head on, raised his gun, pointed it toward Nick, and fired.

Nick waited for his moment. The nurse was squirming to get free, and she bent over. Nick saw this as his only opportunity, knowing full well the man would kill the nurse.

Nick fired two shots, hitting the suspect with both bullets. The man crumbled to the floor, still holding on to his gun.

Nick yelled to the nurse, "Run!" She took off down the hallway and didn't look back. Nick cautiously walked over to the perp and kicked the gun out of his reach. The suspect attempted to get up but collapsed, his blood creating a crimson pool on the floor.

Chapter 27

The Parsippany Police detectives and two patrol officers arrived first. The Morris County Prosecutor's mobile unit and Sheriff's Office arrived, followed by the FBI forensic team. The Parsippany detectives performed their necessary investigation on the body of the suspect. The county sheriff's office was collecting evidence, securing casings from the bullets in the corridor, and photographing all evidence. Nick was questioned by the prosecutor's office, and the sheriff's office took possession of the gun.

A security officer led the forensic team to the covert storeroom on D level that had been taped off. The team was briefed by Nick on what had transpired. They went down to the emergency department to debrief Parsippany Police Officer Ken Gross.

The emergency room was a zoo as usual. Various patients sat holding towels to their bleeding parts, kids screamed, and older folks sat with their eyes closed. All were waiting for their turn to see a doctor. Officer Gross was already in a room after being examined by the emergency room doctor.

Police Officer Ken Gross stated, "I was working part-time at the emergency room entrance when I was instructed to report to the level-D closet. A white male with a crazy look in his eyes, about five feet nine inches, thin with a scruffy beard, came into the hallway as if he knew where he was going. He was surprised to see a police presence. He pulled a semiautomatic pistol and, without warning, fired what I thought was two shots while shouting 'Allah Akbar.' The force of the shots knocked me over, and I hit my head on the floor, became semiconscious, and I did not have a chance to draw my weapon and lost track of the intruder."

He was sure the individual did not approach him as he was forcing himself to remain as conscious as he could possibly remain. At the time, Officer Gross thought he'd been wounded fatally.

Nick knew this was the same battle cry the Middle Eastern woman shouted in plant engineering before shooting at the K-9 officer, as well as the woman taking photos of the hospital shouted just before she shot him with the Taser, jolting him with fifty thousand volts. There would be more questions for Officer Gross by the prosecutor's office, but Nick wasn't going to wait for that.

Instead he and Grazie went to the covert closet to examine the closet and the corridor for any clues. No clues developed, and Nick was getting frustrated. Everything appeared to be in order in the closet, and they were discussing their debriefing of Parsippany Police Officer Ken Gross. When Agent Grazie saw the forensic team, she exchanged greetings, explained what happened, and had them examine the covert corridor. Agent Grazie then went back to Nick and began reviewing what Gross had told them.

When the forensic team had completed their sweep of the covert hallway, they were ready to take possession of the ice pick found in the bathroom and the bullets retrieved from the vest of Officer Gross. After Nick led them to the security department where the evidence was, the team bagged and marked it and then left the hospital, stating they would have the results as soon as possible. Nick and Grazie returned to the command center to view the security video in order to determine where the intruder went after firing at Officer Gross. Simultaneously, the Morris County Sheriff's K-9 unit was trying to pick up the intruder's scent from the hallway. Additional sheriff's personnel were stationed outside the hospital around the perimeter, along with New Jersey State Police, who responded when the "officer down" call went out.

The security officer on duty had already made room for Nick at the computer. Now Nick called up the segment of tape he needed. Nick saw the intruder walking into the covert hallway. Just as Officer Gross said, he seemed to be shocked that there was a police officer in the corridor. Then without missing a beat, the intruder pulled his weapon from his waistband and fired two shots, which Nick determined by the two distinct flashes visible on the tape. He then turned around and entered a door to the boiler room, and a new segment of tape observed him going down the metal spiral stairs. Another camera observed him going to a metal hatch in the floor and disappearing from sight. Nick only pulled the hallway tape to this point.

Suddenly all the fire alarms went off and the command center phones lit up. The shift commander answered the phone and stood there mesmerized.

Nick asked, "What happened?"

The commander snapped out of his daze, shouted, "Sending help," then dialed the police, yelling, "There was an explosion in the emergency room, assessing casualties, injuries, and damage, please send help."

Nick said, "Call the bomb squad and the state police. I'll call you from the scene."

With that Nick ran to the emergency department. The explosion had caused minor damage to the inside of the department, but the outside looked like moderate damage. Unless you counted the human damage, which was severe.

Security Officer Mike Gerard reported to Nick. "So far three dead. One of the dead has been ID'd as a security officer. Seven people were injured and are being triaged at children's center emergency room. No other deaths were reported yet, and it appeared the explosive was secreted in a garbage receptacle outside the hospital emergency room door."

Nick asked, "Where did they take the bodies?"

Officer Gerard responded, "Nowhere yet. They're behind the yellow tape. You can see the white sheets from here."

Nick turned and saw them. He replied, "Radio the command center and make sure that they and Director Shane know one of the casualties was a security officer."

Officer Gerard replied, "Will do."

Nick then went over and lifted the first sheet. The individual was a male who Nick thought to be about fifty years old. He replaced the sheet and walked to the next body. This was a female Nick thought to be about thirty years old. He covered her gently and walked over to the last body, lifting the sheet.

Nick exclaimed, "Oh God, no!"

Lying on the ground, covered in blood, glass, shrapnel, and debris that had rained down on him was Security Officer Jim Adamson, his eyes still open with the blank stare of death. Nick bent over and closed Adamson's eyes, careful not to touch anything else for fear of contaminating the crime scene.

Nick then called the command center and reported what he had found. Fighting back tears, he vowed to get the bastards that did this. Nick was fond of Adamson. Adamson would have made a great Parsippany police officer, the next step for a young security officer who excels.

Nick observed as extra personnel arrived and cordoned off the area, both inside and outside of the emergency room. Traffic was diverted past the emergency entrance to the children's emergency department. The bomb squad arrived as well as the K-9 unit's bomb-sniffing dogs. The federal forensic unit began combing over every scrap they could find and eventually sounded the all clear. Morris County Prosecutor's investigators photographed and ID'd the casualties, and they were placed on gurneys and removed to the morgue. Plant engineering, hospital electricians, and carpenters began boarding up exposed areas and wires and cleaning the grounds. The count of the number of dead did not increase, and five of the seven injured were treated and released. The remaining two were to be kept overnight for observation. The police were waiting for family members to arrive to identify the dead.

Nick went back to security and began reviewing the tapes outside of the emergency department. It didn't take long for Nick to see the suspect place what appeared to be a backpack into the trash receptacle outside the entrance, then enter the hospital at a quick pace. The suspect, a thin male wearing a hoodie and jeans was the best description Nick could get.

Nick then switched back to the first incident and resumed where he had left off before the explosion, replaying the scene several times, when he realized the man in plant engineering was not the scruffy suspect but a different individual. Nick then pulled the tape from outside plant engineering, and sure enough, the plate on the ground opened and the man emerged, closed the metal hatch, and entered the same black Honda that was waiting for him, the same one Nick had seen when Harry was killed and the Middle Eastern couple drove away in on Easter Sunday. The camera shot picked up the rear of the vehicle, and it was evident the license plates on the car had been removed.

Nick played the tape again and this time observed the scruffy suspect pat the other intruder on the back and then veer off down the corridor and climb into the laundry cart.

The K-9 unit was called off and was returning to the outside perimeter of the hospital when the dog began to bark and pull his officer in the opposite direction.

The officer called Nick at the command center and said, "Nick, I don't know what's going on with my K-9 partner Brutus here. I heard your radio message that there were two suspects, one DOA and the other suspect fled the hospital through the rear plant entrance ground hatch plate, but I can't get Brutus to leave. He keeps on pulling me towards the children's wing."

Nick replied, "I'll be right there."

When Nick and Grazie arrived, sheriff's Officer Stewart was attempting to get Brutus to heel. Officer Stewart said, "I haven't seen him act like this since he was working with explosives. As he got older, the lead trainer thought he was better suited to tracking people, less stressful and less urgent, but now I can barely hold him."

Nick got a bad feeling as he said to Officer Stewart, "Let's see where he wants to lead you."

Then Nick called the director and said, "Boss, I got a bad feeling that the intruders left something else behind. Call the county bomb squad back and have them respond to the children's wing. The dog didn't find anything yet, but I'll be willing to bet that it is just a matter of time."

The dog appeared to be walking in circles, then just as quickly, turned and ran to a utility closet where he started barking. Nick tried to open the door, but it was locked. Using his master key, Nick opened the door, and after removing a garbage cart and a few empty boxes, Nick saw a bomb with the red LED ticking down the seconds with nine minutes remaining.

Chapter 28

Nick called Director Shane. "Sir, we found a bomb in the utility closet in the children's hospital, ground floor behind the reception desk. More importantly, the timer is showing nine minutes."

The bomb looked like off-white blocks wrapped with electrical tape. There were at least twenty blocks banded together with wires on the end attached to an LED timer that was ticking down the seconds. The wires went into the timer box: red, green, white, and black.

Director Shane replied, "I'll call and see how far the bomb squad is and ask them to return." Director Shane got back on the phone and said, "They just arrived. I'll be right down with extra security to remove as many people as possible. There isn't enough time to evacuate the entire wing. We'll just begin moving them into the main hospital immediately and continue as best we can."

Nick was in the process of directing the security officers to tape off that section. Next, he instructed the sheriff's officer to call the Office of Emergency Management and sent a security officer to the door to meet the bomb squad.

When Nick saw the members of the bomb squad arrive he said, "Six minutes on the clock, fellas."

The bomb squad commander replied, "We'll take it from here. Everyone else outside the building. Now!"

As Nick was walking out he asked Officer Stewart to get the rest of the K-9 team here to check the rest of the complex.

Officer Stewart responded, "Nick, I already called in, and they should be here momentarily. But I gotta tell you, I have been leading Brutus around near the other corridors, and if the suspect had carried explosives around we would have gotten a positive reaction from Brutus already."

Nick replied, "Okay, let's check just to make sure."

Nick doubled back to where the bomb squad was working. The sergeant who was working on it stated, "Typical of the bombs we were trained on in New York and at military headquarters in Fort Dix. The terrorists who made this reversed the wiring and also connected a booby trap if it's messed with." More talking out loud to himself than to anyone else, the sergeant continued, "They make the hot wire appear to be the red, when it's really the green, then they booby-trap the green wire so that if it isn't removed first, boom. Now comes the part like in the movies where I cut the wire...Ha ha, will he cut the right one?" With steady hands the sergeant, with wire cutters in hand, moved in toward the wires. Then double-checking his decision on which wire to cut, his hand moved in, and *snip*. The sergeant snipped the wires, leaned back, and sighed. The LED timer froze at two minutes, ten seconds.

The bomb squad carried the bomb out to a specially designed trailer that was able to contain the blast should it happen in transit.

Nick called the director on his cell phone and advised him. "Director, the bomb is deactivated, the bomb squad removed it from the hospital, and the K-9 team were dispatched to sweep the complex to ensure there was only one bomb. I will let you know how they make out."

The director replied, "Great job, Nick. As soon as the K-9 team gives the all clear, report to the conference room for a meeting."

An hour later, the K-9 teams reported to Nick that the hospital was all clear.

Director Shane called a meeting to review what had transpired and to give everyone present an update.

The director began, "As you know, there have been a series of systematic attacks on this hospital. A bomb placed outside the emergency department exploded, killing three. One of the casualties was our own officer, Jim Adamson. There were also seven injured. Security Officer Joe Turro was attacked and is going to be all right. Police Officer Gross was shot, but survived the assault as a direct result of his body armor, and should be discharged this evening. Nick Moore thwarted a hostage situation when one of the intruders took a nurse hostage in his attempt to make a getaway. Nick killed the intruder, but his partner did get away and was picked up by a waiting auto. The K-9 unit found another bomb in the children's wing that was disarmed by the bomb squad. Parsippany Police and the surrounding towns are actively looking for the black Honda, and security will be tightened up outside of the hospital by the sheriff's office and the state police at least for the rest of the week. I want to thank Nick for addressing the situation and calling all the right moves that were deployed."

As he was about to thank the remainder of the people present, Registered Nurse and Director of Infectious Disease Ann Stromer entered the conference room and took a seat in the back. The meeting ended, and Ann apologized to those around her for being late but said she was stuck in traffic on route 24 returning from another hospital. She managed to say hello to the director, then Nick, and was waiting for an introduction to Agent Grazie. The director made the introductions and explained Grazie was working with Nick on an assignment. While all were getting ready to depart, Ann cornered Nick and was asking what the assignment he was working on, using the pretext of inquiring whether it had to do with any contagious patients.

Nick said, "No, they were helping with the murder cases the director asked them to assist with." Lying to her, Nick continued, "I'm only working with Agent Grazie because the director had asked me."

Ann seemed okay with the explanation for the moment.

After the incident with Security Officer Turro, Police Officer Gross, the shooting of one suspect and the escape of the other, bomb explosions and threats, and the meeting with the director, Nick realized he was exhausted and said to Grazie, "I'll walk you to your car."

Grazie said, "Fine, and then I'll drive you around the hospital to your car."

The air was hot with a slightly sticky wind blowing as Nick walked Grazie to her car, parked on the emergency department side of the hospital. Grazie grabbed his arm and moved close to him. As they walked, they began to talk about the events that had transpired.

Nick asked, "Do you remember the slide presentation from Agent Smallwood?"

She responded, "Yes, and I noticed the hallways and corridors were the same as the photos taken by the unknown intruder."

Nick asked Grazie if she remembered anything else, and she replied no. Nick reminded her of the trapdoor outside plant engineering where the intruder had made his getaway from, and almost as if one could see a light bulb go off, Grazie was stunned at how she could have not connected the security video they had seen with the slide taken by the unknown intruder.

Nick then stated, "The Parsippany Police never stopped a vehicle called into them, in particular the black Honda with no license plates. If they immediately radioed in on the statewide emergency police radio, other municipalities, the state police and the town next door would all be looking for the Honda, and it should have been spotted by now." Nick felt he didn't need to explain to her about seeing a lookalike car or about the SPEN radio system, but Nick continued, "SPEN is an acronym for Statewide Police Emergency Network, which each police car has as part of their radio system and can be utilized with the flip of a switch. This allows all police in the state to receive the emergency notice. Even if the car was found abandoned somewhere, the forensic team would be able to get good information and evidence from it."

Grazie then asked Nick, "What do you think of Ann?"

Nick replied, "I think she's full of herself, that she thought she was better than everyone, that no one could be as good as her in her field. I think she always appeared to be chasing the bosses in the hospital as if she were looking for a husband and thinks she thinks she found him in Farqua, not for any other reason than his money. When he first saw her, he must have realized he had a sucker, ripe for the picking. But the fact that she's a dupe doesn't keep her from also being a felon."

Nick reminded her of the Chart-It reports and the fact that she was up to her neck in drug diversion, with or without Moe Prince as a partner.

Grazie told Nick, "Something made me feel very uncomfortable when I met Ann earlier. At first, I thought it was because I was working with you and that she maybe had a thing for you. Then I knew it was something else. I can't explain it but felt something sinister in her demeanor."

Nick said, "I think Ann has changed, from a prim and proper nurse to a has-been, like an old actress or a burlesque queen. Her clothes are expensive but worn-out, and probably no one notices, but I observed fraying at the cuffs of her sleeves and on the hem of her pants or skirts. I knew something had changed, but I was never that interested enough to give it a second thought. I saw her gamble and figured she had a habit, but again I wasn't interested. Now I wonder why she's still wearing crappy clothes. She gets money from Farqua, *and* she steals drugs."

As they continued down the corridor that led out to the parking area, Nick called the security command center and asked if a BOLO had been issued on the suspects.

"About fifteen minutes ago," they said.

When they arrived at Grazie's car, she said to Nick, "Get in and I'll drive you back."

Nick told Grazie he would call her in the morning and got into his car. All he thought of was Phyllis Grazie. It wasn't that he didn't enjoy their lovemaking and kissing sessions. He just knew the longer he waited, the more difficult it would be to walk away. The last thing he wanted to do was hurt Jen, and he had to end it before she found out. He did not want to lose his family over this. They would not have another romantic encounter as far as he was concerned. But Nick could feel the electricity in the air when they were together and knew it was just a matter of time.

As Nick headed home, he remembered the black car parked in the garage of Ann's house, and how he was almost sure it was the black Honda. He thought this to be the perfect opportunity to go peek into the window of the garage door and determine what kind of vehicle it was, since he knew both Ann and Moe Prince were at the hospital. Nick parked his car down the street and removed a penlight from his glove box. Walking casually toward Ann's house, he made certain no one was around. He walked up the driveway, peered into the garage door window, and with the penlight, made a sweep. There it was! Nick was sure this was the same black Honda as the one used during the incidents at the hospital.

He turned and walked back to his car, then called Special Agent Dan Camp, explaining, "I'm almost sure the black Honda in Ann's garage was the same vehicle that was used in the getaways at the hospital. I'll tell agents Smallwood and Grazie about the car in the morning."

CHAPTER 29

Around-the-clock surveillance began on Moe Prince and Ann Stromer. Dan Camp had other information as well and met Nick at his office, stating, "Moe Prince converted to Islam during his second trip to Afghanistan. He only completed half his tour with the private security company and then disappeared for six months. Moe joined a radical group and had been indoctrinated and radicalized. To what extent we don't know."

Nick added, "This tied in with what Grazie's confidential informant said about a 'brother' on the inside, working at the hospital."

Camp said, "The informant said the female supplying information was a convert and a woman of color. This proved to be a dead end. It seems that it could only be Ann Stromer. Her boyfriend Max Fouquaan, who the informant knew to be Farqua, and who is in charge of this project, lured her in and returned to Afghanistan for training, instructions, and money."

Dan asked Nick, "How does Moe act when he is with you? These true Jihadists cannot stand to even talk to an infidel. Does he come across like that?"

Nick replied, "No, not at all. I think he resisted their brainwashing the best he could. He was probably trying to scam them. That might have prevented his total indoctrination."

Dan continued, "We know through our informants and operatives abroad that Moe was indeed trained in the radical camps in Afghanistan. He'd undergone six months of intense indoctrination and military training in the desert training camps and in the mountain strongholds that separate Afghanistan from Pakistan. Though

Moe felt he was strong enough both physically and psychologically to withstand the training and come out unscathed, it didn't work that way. Moe thought that he was going to use them for his own benefit. But Al-Qaeda was using him for secret information that he was supplying. No one stands up to that kind of indoctrination."

Nick replied, "No."

"No?" Dan asked. "Why do you say that?"

Nick replied, "No, I don't think so. I'm not saying Moe isn't capable of doing harm. What I am saying is that he doesn't believe. In anything. He's an opportunist. He's selfish, lazy, and stupid. If anything, he thinks he's working the system. In Moe's defense, he's just not bright enough to figure out what they were doing, or he didn't care. He's not a religious zealot. He was after money, plain and simple."

Dan said, "What they were doing was extracting information from him about the security company he worked for, including the types of cameras, the location of the transmitters, the location of the cameras, and the description of the covert camera camouflage. By providing this information, most of which Moe believed to be inconsequential, Al-Qaeda was able to carry out bombings of Afghanistan's arsenals, police stations, and garrisons without getting picked up on any of the cameras set up to prevent such attacks. While this was confounding the military command, which was unable to stop these attacks, no one could figure out how they were obtaining their secret information."

Dan continued, "From what we learned from our confidential informants abroad, Moe was oblivious to their interrogation that was disguised as conversation, and intelligence was expertly extracted from him."

Nick again interjected, "He was probably only interested in the cash they were giving him. He wired it home in an effort to stop the foreclosure on his house."

Dan resumed, "These informants we have tell us that Al-Qaeda does this over and over. In the beginning, they promise a certain amount of money, claiming they'll take care of the individual now because he's a brother. But then they intentionally hold back, giving the money in small amounts, for two reasons. The first is that he's dependent on them for the money and they can keep stringing him along. The second is to continue extracting information out of him until he has nothing left to divulge."

Dan Camp continued. "Furthermore, Moe, in an attempt to show how much he knew concerning the state-of-the-art cameras, digital video recorders, and the general intelligence computer system that controlled them, was giving information about the hospital system that his brother had told him was going to be installed. Not knowing Al-Qaeda's plans to take out hospitals, Moe didn't realize the sensitivity of the information he was passing along to the enemy. In short order, they were ordering the same equipment online and then studying it and breaking it down so they would know the strengths and weaknesses before they even encountered it. Once in possession of this information, they passed it along to whatever operatives needed to know. This information wasn't just something to be used immediately and then disregarded. Quite the contrary. It was information that would be stored for years until the plans turned into action and this information would be given to the individuals that needed it. I would bet that for the past few years they have been eyeballing this hospital from within and skirting the camera system with the knowledge they obtained from Moe."

Dan said, "Moe felt he would be able to withstand their pressure to be Muslim in every way. But he was taught the contents of the Koran, ritual washing, and specific times to pray. Moe was a non-denominational Protestant who never practiced his religion. Now, however, Moe's praying the required five times a day and also performing the ritual washing before prayer called the wudhu. Like it or not, Moe is a practicing Muslim, but, in his limited capacity, does not realize it himself. Maybe it was brainwashing or maybe it was a source of comfort, but Moe continued this second pillar of Islam as the prayers are called, even after returning to the United States. Moe would have also been shocked if he knew then that the money they gave him must be paid back. He was not told that at the time, but it was made clear to him on his return to America and his arranged meeting with his handler Farqua.

"Farqua made it clear if the money was not paid back Moe would have to work the debt off or something bad might happen to his wife and son. He could work the debt off by supplying the information that Farqua wanted. Naturally this involved the Guardian Angel Hospital where Moe worked. As with any organization, the more people working for the team, the better. So Farqua set his sights, charm, and money on Ann Stromer, another pawn in Al-Qaeda's mission to inflict death and destruction on the United States of America. In the beginning, neither Ann nor Moe knew of the other's involvement. Farqua used this to his benefit. He kept tabs on both, checked out the information he wanted with both separately, and then compared what each provided. This was a strategic maneuver to see who was being truthful in the information Farqua requested. Farqua was probably smiling to himself and was pleased that both did his bidding in an honest and truthful manner."

After listening to Dan Camp and digesting the information he supplied, Nick saw the pieces of the puzzle fitting into place. Like it or not, Nick knew Agent Camp was right. The plans and information supplied by Ann and Moe has been going on for years, and the culmination of their surveillance, planning, and patience was, in Nick's mind, rapidly taking shape.

The investigators regularly held their briefing on what, if anything, the surveillance turned up. Nick read the surveillance reports which detailed that, to date, the team had followed Moe on two occasions from Ann's house to the housing projects in Dover, New Jersey. Both times the surveillance team had to break it off or risk being spotted. If they saw a pattern, they would set up at the projects so as not to follow him there from Ann's. Ann was followed to the hospital where she remained all day, then went home, remained in her house for two hours, and then returned to the hospital where she remained inside less than a half hour before emerging with a brown bag. The team observed this behavior on a few occasions. Ann then returned to her house, where she remained the rest of the night.

Grazie reported at the meeting, stating, "Ali has been supplying names of suspects in different cities that are the planned targets of terrorist activities. Because of this information, the FBI, CIA, and Homeland Security had these individuals under surveillance and were determining through their investigation when to arrest them. They have them on wiretaps conspiring to commit terroristic acts. They may take one of these individuals down in hopes of protecting Ali. They'll let it leak out the person they took down was the informant. The exact sequence of events is being drafted now, and the plan, when ready, will be discussed at a future meeting. Nonetheless, Ali has proven to be invaluable. Special protection will be provided for him. However, he doesn't want it until the terrorists are taken down. Most of the individuals Ali named are in the US, in their respective cities, going about their lives."

Grazie continued, "With Farqua still out of the country, the question is, will they attempt their terror attacks individually before he returns, independent of him, or are they waiting for his return and planning to synchronize the attacks? This is a very important question that needs to be answered as quickly as possible."

Agent Grazie added, "Let's hope our wiretaps lead to someone closer to the plan."

Camp said, "One more twist: Moe Prince has been frequenting all the nightclubs in town that cater to the college crowd. He visits them regularly and is always flashing money on the way in and out. This is a different picture than the one we have of someone in dire financial straits. Rather than place an agent the crowd may be suspicious of, I will have an agent from New York in the club to see what Moe's doing. This agent will be young and look like he's attending college. Since he's a New York agent, no one will know him in the club."

With this final point covered the meeting ended and Agent Camp grabbed Nick for the scheduling of the surveillance for the upcoming week. Grazie saw them get together and left for her office.

Agent Camp said while they were at it, he would have a female agent follow Ann around the hospital on a weekend night to see what she has been doing when she makes an after-hours visit and is not scheduled for anything. Camp said, "Once we have some answers we can bring one or both of them in for questioning and inform them the other is opening up, let's see if we can get them to turn on each other."

Chapter 30

The investigation continued. The female agent that Dan Camp was going to assign was reassigned since it was felt security or an employee would get suspicious of an unknown female walking through the corridors at night. Moe continued visiting college nightclubs in the area, and Special Agent Dan Camp placed an agent there who was college age in his appearance.

Special Agent Steve Turn was twenty-six years old but looked eighteen. Steve knew he was going to like this assignment from the beginning. He was the first to volunteer when Agent Camp put out the e-mail for a young-looking agent to make undercover drug buys in a bar full of college-age kids. Then when Camp briefed him and told him he'd be buying from an older dude, he knew this assignment was for him. Sweet, he thought, as he picked out his outfit: jeans, a button-down long-sleeve striped shirt, and sneakers. He left the light beard stubble and with his short hair with a slight upswing in the center, and he figured he'd fit right in.

Steve was already stationed in the bar when Moe arrived on Friday night. Later, Steve said how easy it was to pick Moe out from the description that he was provided with. The agent observed Moe in what appeared to be drug transactions with the college students. Moe was not subtle about counting money and pills right in the crowded bar. Steve thought if Moe knew how out of place he looked, attempting to talk to the girls in the bar and join in the conversations, Moe would be more discreet. But it wasn't his good looks or charming personality that made him popular: the few people talking to him knew why he was there. Most of girls walked away, but the ones who didn't only engaged him in conversation because it was evident they were clients. Steve observed one female taking out money from her jeans and giving it to Moe in return for what Steve figured could only be pills. The agent worked himself closer to the action in an effort to hear or see what was transpiring. Agent Steve Turn was talking to the various patrons, buying drinks, and talking about classes and courses so that he appeared to be a regular.

Moe asked one of his steady customers, Scott, "Who is this guy Steve? Is he all right?

Scott replied, "Yes, he's attending college. He's originally from down the shore, but he's okay. I been in here with him before, and he's cool. He keeps to himself but has a great personality once you get to know him."

Agent Steve Turn, hearing this exchange, walked to the bar for another beer. A few minutes later, Moe came up beside him, ordered a beer, and began to talk to him.

Moe asked, "Hi, how ya doin'? How's school? You adapting to dorm life and the pressure that comes with a full schedule? The name is Moe, I'm good friends with Scott."

Steve said, "Hi, I'm Steve. Scott is a good person."

Moe replied, "Yeah, he said the same about you. Listen, I know that being away from home can get you down. But if you ever want a little something to take the blues away, I can sell you real Percocets for thirty dollars each."

Steve did not want to appear too interested and said, "What is this? A one-time offer? Or is the price going to double the next time?"

Moe assured him that he is there every day and the price has not changed in four months.

Steve asked, "What are the strength of the pills?"

Moe said, "They're tens. Ten milligrams each."

Steve replied, "Okay, give me…four," and handed Moe $120.

Moe handed Steve four Percocets from an amber bottle, then Moe said he had to go and was off talking to others in the crowd. Steve waited a few minutes, finished his beer, and left the bar. As soon as Steve left the area he phoned Agent Camp and explained what had transpired. Agent Camp stated the surveillance team followed Moe to another nightclub in town where he was probably selling more pills. Camp thanked him and said he would call him tomorrow for another purchase on Sunday.

On Sunday night the same scenario repeated itself. Agent Steve Turn was in the bar and purchased four Percocets from Moe for $120.

The next day, Nick was listening as Special Agent Dan Camp explained what had transpired on Friday and Sunday night. Dan asked, "Any suggestions as to where this should go now?"

Nick was the first to speak up, saying, "He should order up from Moe and then arrest him. With that kind of pressure, he may roll and give up everything. We should also do an integrity check at the hospital during the hours that Ann has been seen departing with bags to see if she is the supplier."

Then Nick explained, "An integrity check is a surprise inspection of bags by security at all exits to ascertain if bags being carried out by employees contain any hospital property. This is a common occurrence, and all the employees sign papers allowing the search when then began their employment."

Grazie stated, "If she is the supplier and we find the pills, we may be able to obtain information from her."

All agreed on the plan, and all agreed that Steve would buy twenty-five Percocets tonight, then order one hundred and ask for a price break for Tuesday. In any event, the integrity check would be put off, and Nick stated he would handle the details with Director Shane.

Agent Camp said, "I will take care of the next buy from Moe and make sure Agent Steve Turn orders up for Tuesday. Also, I have our sources checking on Farqua. If we're lucky they'll be able to track him down and see what his movements are."

Nick said, "The black Honda that I thought I spotted the night I got Ann's address, I confirmed it was the car when I went by the house and looked into the garage window. This just confirms what we all know. Ann is a major player in this, and we should continue as planned."

Agent Smallwood reported, "We have now confirmed the successful arrest of terrorist cells in Florida, Chicago, Saint Louis, California, and New York, thanks to the work of Agent Grazie's confidential informant. This included three roommates in Queens who were arrested in their apartment with a homemade aerosol device and instructions on how to make sarin gas and release it in the subway systems. Some of the raids and roundups will be made public, but most will remain out of the media for two reasons. The first is to protect the confidential informant, and the second is the agency's attempt to get new information out of the suspects now in custody."

As he was leaving the meeting, Nick's hotline cell phone rang. A male voice began talking.

"I work in the hospital. There's a young guy from the storeroom, always writing in a notebook he carries, always asking questions, and always writing down the answers of locations, employees, and other things. He gives me the creeps."

Nick answered, "Thanks for calling. Can we meet so I can ask you some questions?"

The male replied, "That's all I know, but you should check him out. Hey, isn't that what this is for, to report things we find strange?"

Nick replied, "Yes, it is, and thanks for the call, I'll check it out."

Nick went to the storeroom and walked into Manager Ben Edwards's office. Nick introduced himself then began. "Ben, I got an anonymous call on the tip hotline today. The person was telling me about a young guy from your department, who asks a lot of questions and is always writing and making diagrams in a notebook. Does this sound like anyone you may know?"

Ben replied, "It does, his name is Gus Bollot, he is Egyptian and has been working here for over a year. He's a good worker, honest, dependable, and a Coptic Christian. I know this because he requests time off near his holidays and explained he volunteers at his church."

Nick asked, "What about the notebook?"

Ben replied, "Gus has been carrying it around with him since he started. He writes down the names of the people in the different departments and sketches how to get there and where to leave the supplies he delivers. He is a great guy and not someone who would do anything wrong."

Nick answered, "Thank you, Ben. I consider this closed, no need to talk to Gus. You do understand that we must follow up on all tips.

Ben said, "I understand. I'll be discreet."

Nick was almost convinced that Gus was not a threat but would look at his HR file and have Agent Dan Camp do a background check.

That night, Special Agent Steve Turn was again in the nightclub waiting for Moe Prince to arrive so that he could purchase Percocet from him. He was going to request twenty-five, and if all went well he would order one hundred for the next day. Moe arrived at approximately 10:30 p.m. and began doing his business with other students in the nightclub.

He then made his way over to Steve and asked, "What's going on, do you need anything?"

Steve answered, "I told some of my friends, and they wanted some too. I'm going to need twenty-five."

Moe said, "I'm not sure if I have that many on me, I'll go into the bathroom to check."

He was gone a few minutes then came back and handed Steve a vial containing twenty-five Percocet.

Steve handed him the $750 and asked, "If I take a hundred tomorrow can I get a price break?"

Moe said, "Yeah. For a hundred I would sell them for $27 each."

Steve asked, "Is that the best you could do?"

Moe replied, "Yeah."

Moe then disappeared into the crowd, and about ten minutes later, Steve watched him leave. Steve then left and called Special Agent Camp and explained what had happened, that he bought twenty-five and ordered one hundred for tomorrow.

Dan Camp said, "Great job, I'll call you tomorrow."

Agent Camp informed the others what had transpired with Moe, and that Steve plans to buy one hundred Percocet tomorrow.

Next, he asked, "If all agree, Moe will be arrested after the sale."

All agreed.

Nick then brought up Ann, and all agreed to keep her under surveillance but put off doing anything until they saw if Moe would crack. They planned to meet at the FBI field office the next day for the takedown of Moe Prince.

Nick said he would take a back seat so he could appear to come in later to help Moe. Nick went to Director Shane's office and explained what was going on with the investigation. Nick explained this is an offshoot of the terrorist investigation, because Farqua was still out of the country and Ali had no information as to when he was returning. But now since they already had buys on Moe, the agent was going to order up and Moe would be arrested. They needed to flip him and get the information before it was too late.

CHAPTER 31

That night, Agent Camp and his team, while conducting video surveillance, saw a well-dressed male driving a black Nissan enter Ann's house. Though the surveillance team was not sure, they thought it was Farqua. When Dan reached Agent Grazie on the phone, she said she would reach out to Ali to see what he knew. Extra agents were called in. Camp wanted Farqua followed when he left the house. An hour later, Moe arrived at the house and entered through the front door.

Agent Grazie called back and said she couldn't reach Ali. With no further information available, they could not afford to lose Farqua now. Information from the past indicated that something was going down when he returned. As other agents set up in the area, Moe left the house and drove away. A surveillance team picked him up and followed him to the flophouse he was sharing with three town drunks on the other side of Parsippany. The agents found a lookout spot and settled in. Back at Ann's house, the lights went out, and for all appearances Farqua, or Max as Ann knew him, was staying for the night. Nick was lying low as he was the only person known to all three players involved. He remained in his office while monitoring the radio as a precaution. In the event something went down, he was much closer coming from the office than he would be coming from home.

Agent Grazie was about a block from Ann's when, at 5:00 a.m., she heard a radio transmission that the subject left the house and was entering the Nissan he arrived in. A check of the license plate revealed that car was a rental. Agent Dan Camp transmitted that his team would begin the surveillance in a leapfrog fashion: one car follows the suspect until he turns, then the first surveillance car turns in the opposite direction or continues straight, and the next car takes over. All other vehicles should parallel the route he was taking, that would be called out over the air. Camp said that he would call in the other units and his team would back away if they felt they would be made.

Camp said, "The lead car calls out the street and direction and the car that turned off, then gets in the back of the five surveillance cars until it is his turn again to be lead car. The lead is always right behind the suspect vehicle and therefore cannot remain in that position for very long. As the lead car breaks away the next agent becomes the lead."

Camp knew the parallel units would be on a completely different street heading in the same direction as the lead team. In this way they remained hidden and unseen by the suspect and would be utilized when needed.

He reminded the agents, "If the suspect gets on a highway, one vehicle will pass him and remain a safe distance ahead until needed or the suspect exits the highway. In that case the agent that passed the suspect car will exit and catch up as best he can."

Agent Camp and his team followed Farqua to the mosque in Jersey City, where he parked his vehicle and entered the mosque. The section of Jersey City was crowded as members of the Muslim community headed to the mosque for early morning prayers.

Agent Dan Camp called all units in the field on the radio and said, "Call off the surveillance and meet me in the Sip Avenue Junior High School parking lot five blocks west of the location on Sip Avenue."

Camp had an agent dressed like a homeless man stagger past the vehicle Farqua was driving and slipped a micro GPS under the body of the car. Since there was no way to hardwire the device to a power source, Camp was estimating they had four hours of service before the batteries would run out of charge. With this device in place, Camp would know when Farqua was on the move without compromising their presence in the close-knit neighborhood.

When the surveillance units arrived, Dan Camp told them, "Find a place to park, not too close to the subject vehicle, and I will let you know when the subject is on the move. The agent in the street, the homeless man, did confirm it was Farqua by the photo we have. Until then, remain in radio contact."

One hour later, word came that Farqua was on the move.

Agent Camp radioed the other units and said, "I will call out the streets that he's taking. Don't get too close. The GPS will advise us of his location."

The agents followed him to Fort Lee, New Jersey, where he entered an apartment building. Agent Camp called on his team and said, "Park in the area, and the other teams can break off surveillance. It appears the suspect arrived here to sleep."

He instructed, "Team two, take up positions and change the GPS after three hours." All responded they understood, and team one was dismissed. Camp was not choosing the Moe investigation over this one, but experience told him Farqua was not ready for the mission he was planning. He was moving slow, being careless, and, most importantly, was alone. As long as surveillance was in place, Camp knew he would have time to complete the Moe investigation.

Camp told the team, "Keep me informed and let me know if and when he leaves."

The hours passed, and when Nick looked at his watch he realized it was 6:30 a.m. As he exited the building, Nick realized the sun was about to come up. He walked to his car and thought how peaceful it was this time of the morning. The day was not yet here, the air still cool, and it was as if the night didn't want to relinquish its grip on the earth. The canopy covering the morning light would soon bring dawn back, and daylight would spread over the landscape. The thought of the long days ahead in this investigation made him weary. He switched his thoughts to Grazie, and his mood began to change. Thinking about holding her, stroking her naked body, and making love to her made him forget his sadness, and he began to smile. Nick could not forget her and the way she made him feel. Grazie made him feel like a man both in regards to his job abilities and capabilities and, Lord knows, physically, since he thought about her every day since their encounter. His drive home seemed very short when he was thinking of her.

All that night on surveillance, Grazie kept thinking about Nick. She realized that whether he knew it or not, she had fallen for him in a big way. Phyllis Grazie was not now nor ever would be thinking about leaving her husband for Nick, she kept telling herself. To her, having an affair was not something she approved of. She wasn't quite sure why she made love to Nick, whether it was his good looks, confidence, intelligence, or a combination of it all. But she didn't regret it. It happened. She wanted it to happen. But making love to Nick was a one-time thing, she thought, uncertain and confused as to whether she really meant it.

Tony Grazie was older than Phyllis. He came from the same town in Indiana, and she was crazy about him from the first time they met. Grazie began to think back. He was a writer for the local paper and would cover the high school games when Phyllis was a cheerleader. She knew who he was and always fantasized about him with his studious good looks and athletic physique.

Phyllis went away to college and, for the most part, dated one fellow—Carl— for her entire four years. Though they were on again and off again, Phyllis knew in her heart that Carl was not the man of her dreams and that it would not last. It was a good-enough relationship to keep her busy and fulfilled while concentrating on her studies. Now, thinking about Carl, she almost laughed out loud, shaking her head and wondering why she ever went with him. When she graduated, she returned to her parents' house and became a moderately pleasant memory. She went home to regroup and decide what career path she was going to take. Phyllis knew she did not want the typical career women seem to choose: teacher, nurse, administrative assistant. She wanted a job with excitement and challenge and would not even think about settling until she found what she wanted. At first, she considered joining the police force, but realizing her town was small with relatively no crime, she felt she would be bored.

Since she was not in a relationship, and wasn't sure she wanted one just yet, she decided to apply for government jobs that had the potential for travel and excitement in different states. Phyllis applied to the Central Intelligence Agency and the Federal Bureau of Investigation, thinking she would take the first one that contacted her. It did not matter which one called as she was researching both and found them to be equally interesting. Both applications stated it could take up to three months for an initial interview and then another three months for background checks if the candidate was successful.

Knowing she had enough money in the bank, Phyllis decided she was going to make the most out of the summer by enjoying herself and relaxing. She reacquainted with past friends and went to dinner parties, barbeques, and get-togethers, having a wonderful time and seeing her old friends. At one party in particular, her friend told her she was going to introduce her to an older, handsome fellow. This friend was sure they would hit it off. Phyllis was not so sure she wanted to meet him, let alone worry about whether they would hit it off. In any event, that evening Phyllis was introduced to Tony Grazie officially, and she felt an immediate attraction and comfort level she had not experienced before. As they began to talk and got to know each other, Phyllis explained how she remembered him from the high school games and had kind of a crush on him. Tony said he was flattered and glad he didn't know or he might have gotten in trouble for kissing a younger girl. With that Tony leaned in and kissed Phyllis, a warm, delightful kiss. With every sense tingling, she knew she wanted more.

They began dating. Tony was a warm and caring lover, and Phyllis was an excited, intense, and creative lover. Between them they were a good match, good company to each other, good friends, and good lovers. All summer their love blossomed, and they grew closer and more deeply in love.

Phyllis felt life couldn't get any better. Now she even had a boyfriend who fulfilled her idle time with dates, walks in the park, and romance. She thought she could not be happier. Then in late August she received a letter from the Central Intelligence Agency stating they were going to hire her and she had to move to Virginia to begin training October 1. Phyllis was enjoying herself so much all summer, she had forgotten she applied. When she did apply, she didn't have anything holding her back. But now Tony was a big part of her life, and she didn't want to lose him. Before she answered the letter, she knew she had to talk to Tony and get his thoughts. If it were up to her she would want both, the career in the CIA and Tony also.

That night, when Tony picked Phyllis up, she asked him to take a ride by the lake. All the way there, they made small talk and laughed at each other's stories.

When Tony parked the car he turned to Phyllis and said, "Okay, what's on your mind? I can see something's troubling you."

Phyllis started by saying, "Tony, you know how much I love you and love being with you. I love our time together. I consider myself lucky to have met you."

"But…"

"I got an acceptance letter from the CIA. If I accept I would have to move by mid-September in order to start training in Virginia on October first. I would rather tell the CIA no than lose you, and that's what I plan on doing."

Tony told Phyllis, "You do know that now I'm a columnist for the regional newspaper."

Phyllis said, "I understand. I couldn't possibly ask you to leave after all the time you worked there."

Tony replied, "You don't understand. I'm a columnist. I can write from anywhere. Indiana, Virginia, it doesn't matter. I submit my work electronically. So ask me to leave and come with you, and I'll say yes."

Phyllis was so excited she began to cry.

Then Tony told her, "I'll only go under one condition, that you marry me, here, where our friends and family are."

Phyllis said yes and they got married. They moved to Virginia, and after a few years, she was transferred to New York, working out of the New Jersey office, where she met Nick.

Grazie was still daydreaming when Dan Camp, calling the surveillance off, told Grazie to go home for a few hours and get some sleep. As she was driving home she began to think about her past again. She and Tony talked about it, and both decided that they did not want children since Grazie would have no time and they didn't want a nanny raising their child. As for Tony, they both knew when he was writing an article, he got so engrossed that he would forget if they even had children, a trait Grazie loved. As she entered her home, she spotted Tony asleep in the recliner, TV remote in his hand, gray hair hanging down partially covering his glasses, and realized all over again how much she loved him.

She had to choose.

CHAPTER 32

That night, Agent Steve Turn was in the nightclub at ten thirty waiting for Moe to arrive and thinking about what was to unfold. Once Moe arrived, Agent Turn would get him to go outside for the deal of one hundred Percocets where the other agents would arrive and arrest both of them. Agent Turn would also get arrested so as to keep Moe confused as to how the police were on to him.

A half hour later Moe arrived and walked up to Agent Turn, asking, "Do we still have a deal?"

Agent Turn replied, "Of course. Let's go outside were we can count without being disturbed."

They left the bar, and Agent Turn suggested they sit in his car which was parked two cars away. It was a nice night out, so nice, some of the patrons were hanging outside smoking electronic cigarettes and conversing. In addition, this part of Parsippany was always busy with pedestrian traffic at any hour, especially on such a beautiful night.

They entered the car, and Moe produced a white bottle labeled Percocet and showed it to Turn, saying, "Now show me the money."

Agent Turn, at this point, stepped on the brakes, causing the lights to go on, and this was the signal to the backup agents to make the arrest. Moe suddenly pulled out an automatic pistol and pointed it at Agent Turn's side.

Moe yelled, "Drive!"

Agent Turn responded, "What's the matter? What's wrong?"

Moe yelled again, "Drive!"

Agent Turn hoped the backup team was near. To stall, he started the car, put it in reverse, and hit the gas. They collided with the car parked behind them. The agents appeared out of nowhere, pulled Moe and Agent Turn out of the car, handcuffed both, and told them they were under arrest. They searched Moe and found the pills for Agent Turn and another two hundred pills on him. Taking the money from Turn, they were led to different cars and were driven away. An agent took Steve Turn's car, finding Moe's gun on the front seat, and another agent took Moe's car. Agent Turn said to the backup agent, "Search him good. He pulled a gun on me."

"Already retrieved," the agent replied.

All went back to the federal field office where the agents produced a search warrant for Moe's car and began to search it. Moe was brought to a desk where he was being processed, and Agent Turn went down to the garage to see what they found in Moe's car.

While all this was transpiring, they heard on the radio that Farqua had left the apartment in Fort Lee and a team was following him to the highway. Agent Camp instructed them not to lose him and to keep him informed. About forty-five minutes later, the surveillance team followed Farqua back to Ann's house, where he parked his car and went inside. Back at the federal field office, Moe kept repeating they weren't his pills, they were this kid named Steve's pills, Steve was the dealer. Agent Camp did not answer but kept processing him. Approximately thirty minutes later, an agent came to call Camp out and sat with Moe. Camp went into the other office where the agents produced the fruits of the search warrant. They found additional pills, marijuana, the loaded nine-millimeter handgun, loaded with hollow-point bullets, various hunting knives, two passports, one from Pakistan and one from Afghanistan in Moe's name, and radical Islamic propaganda pamphlets. The hollow-point bullets were illegal in New Jersey except for police officers that were currently on active duty. These bullets were even illegal for retired officers that were allowed to carry firearms.

Nick was observing from another room with a two-way mirror as Moe was brought into the interrogation room and again began telling the agents, "You got the wrong guy. I want to talk to Nick Moore, the investigator at the Guardian Angel Hospital."

They finally got Moe to sit down. Agent Camp said, "Mr. Prince, my name is Dan Camp, and I am a special agent with the FBI. To begin, I want to explain the charges you are facing for the various contraband that was found both on you and in your car."

Again, Moe denied the contraband was his, stating, "All the stuff in the car belonged to that kid, not me. I am the user, not the seller. That kid was selling the pills to me." Moe continued, "I want to speak with Nick Moore only, and I won't speak to anyone else."

As the questioning continued, simultaneously, agents had fanned out to the flophouse where Moe was staying, and to Ann's house, where the search warrant team was waiting for Farqua to leave before executing the search warrant.

Nick was in the room next to the interrogation room, observing what was transpiring. He was getting bored with Moe's answers and waiting for Camp to bring him in. The interrogation room had a table and four chairs. No other furniture. It was kept purposely sparse. There were no windows, but one wall had a three-foot-by-three-foot two-way mirror that Nick sat behind. This was generally used for law enforcement to observe how the interrogation was going, or to send in suggestions if they thought of something not being asked. The mirror was also there for the safety of all concerned, to protect the suspect from overzealous questioning or physical contact of any kind.

Agent Camp entered the room and indicated for Nick to follow him. Nick entered the interrogation room, took a seat across from Moe, and asked, "I heard you wanted to speak to me."

Moe replied, "Nick, please, don't clown around. Help me."

Nick replied, "Moe, how can I help you? Do you realize the trouble you're in? The only one that can help you now is yourself."

Moe avoided Nick's eyes and stared at the floor. "They think I'm a drug dealer. Tell them Nick. You know me. Tell them they made a mistake, that they got the wrong guy."

Nick replied, "Moe, you keep this up and I'm walking out. Do you really think they believe your bullshit, that it wasn't you?"

Moe didn't answer. Nick said, "We found some bullets in your house."

"Not mine!" Moe protested.

Nick said, "Nine-millimeter. Hollow points. My partner Al Stokes. You know Al. Al was shot point-blank in the temple with a nine-millimeter hollow-point just the other day."

Nick pointed his index finger like a gun at Moe, then held it up to Moe's temple. "Pow. My friend Al."

Moe began to sniffle.

Nick then turned to Dan and said, "Send him in."

Then, turning to Moe, Nick said, "After this, all I want from you are truthful statements. We know a lot more than you think we do, and I promise you I'll walk and let them throw you in a cell until your arraignment. Do you understand me?" Moe was about to reply when the door opened and Agent Steven Turn walked in.

Moe's jaw dropped.

Nick said, "Moe, this is Agent Steve Turn of the FBI. We've been working together for a while, and we've been watching you. Now, do you think you feel like giving us some straight answers?"

Moe lowered his head and began to cry.

CHAPTER 33

A few minutes later when Moe Prince composed himself, had a cup of water, and wiped his face, he looked at Nick and asked, "What do you want to know?"

Nick replied, "First of all, where are you getting the pills from?"

Moe was about to lie again when Agent Camp asked, "Ann?"

Moe looked like he got hit. Then he exhaled and nodded.

"The truth," Agent Camp said. "In return, we'll talk to the prosecutors on your behalf."

Moe began. "While I was on civilian assignment in Afghanistan, I was offered money and women if I would convert to Islam. I was going to just go along with it and convert till I got what I wanted then I'd tell them I decided against it. I found out it wasn't that easy to leave once you say yes. In the beginning it was really good. They were giving me money, and I was wiring it home to my wife. Then when I went through their indoctrination, I was assigned to a guy named Farqua who was going to be my handler when I returned to the United States. After I got hired at Guardian Angel, they told me what they wanted me to do: different photos, blueprints, and other things. Farqua told me do not lie or make things up. He said he had a woman on the inside whose job it will be to corroborate what I told them."

Moe continued, "The money they gave me was also a scam. They wanted it back, and if I couldn't pay, I would have to do more work for him. One day, just before I was supposed to fly back here, Farqua called me in to his office where he had three other jihadists. Farqua told me it was time to settle up my account. He said I owed them the thirty thousand dollars they had given me. The money was supposed to be returned. I told them they never told me I had to repay it and I sent it home, I didn't have it. That's when he told me I would be doing work for him, getting information he needed until the debt was paid. I never gave them anything worthwhile, and the only reason why I did it was for the money."

Nick asked sarcastically, "Oh, really? What about that crap about your supervisor Mike Carter wanting to know all the locations for the security cameras? Did you really expect me to believe he needed the locations of all the cameras? Did you really think I would be fool enough to give you that information?"

Moe, replied flustered and shaken, "Nick, I swear he wanted the reports I asked you for."

Nick stated, "Yes, he did. It was just that you added the locations for all the cameras. Did Farqua pay you for that list too? I hope so, because he's in for a surprise when he tries to avoid cameras and will be staring right into covert cameras that I left out of that report."

Moe needed a few minutes to stop crying and compose himself. Moe asked, "How did you figure it out?"

Nick replied, "No wonder you're in the trouble you're in. I called and asked him. He said he had the locations already."

"Christ!" Moe said.

Nick said, "Continue."

Moe continued, "I figured out Ann was the other mole, so I blackmailed her into supplying me with Percocet so I could sell them and try to recoup some of the money I needed."

Nick asked, "How did you figure out Ann was the other mole?"

Moe replied, "It wasn't as difficult as you would think. She was practically tailing me throughout the hospital, but then when I saw her taking photos in different places I told her I knew she was mole, and she said she was. She said she would keep an eye on me and do what she had to do for her boyfriend Max. When I asked who that was, she replied I would meet him soon enough. Nick, I only did it because I was going to lose my house. You gotta believe me."

Nick replied, "Moe, people died because of your greed. Now tell me, what are you doing with all the hypodermic syringes of morphine and fentanyl that Ann was supplying you with?"

Moe replied, "Nick, I'm telling you, the only meds that Ann supplied me was Percocet. I never got anything else from her. You better ask her, she seems to be more out of it than usual. Maybe the bitch is a user."

Nick asked, "What's your relationship to Farqua?"

Moe replied, "I told you, he was assigned as my handler from the beginning. One of the first days I met him, he showed me a photo of my wife and son outside our house and told me to make sure I did exactly as he told me or he would kill them both. After a while I made believe I was having marital problems and left the house to put distance between me and them. That's why I'm living in that flophouse with three drunks."

Moe then began to tell Nick what he knew of Ann's relationship to Farqua.

Moe stated, "When I first told her I knew she was the other person supplying information, Ann said her relationship with Max was different, because whatever she did was for love. When I asked her about Max she said she was going to set up a meeting. When all this was first going on, I thought they were two different people. But when we finally met at Ann's house, I realized it was the same person. He keeps on handling both of us, but it's Ann that's really doing the bulk of the work for him. She's in love with him. But I don't know how much he loves her. I think he beats her, 'cause she's always bruised. This guy has less and less for me to do, so I guess Ann is doing more."

Nick asked, "What's the story with the black Honda in Ann's garage?"

Moe's eyes went wide, apparently wondering how Nick knew this.

Moe replied, "Nothing, as far as I know. She says it's her son's car and he's away at college so she took the license plates off and keeps it in the garage so she doesn't have to pay insurance on it. But why do you wanna know?"

Nick said, "Never mind." Then he asked, "Moe, what do you know about Harry Barker's murder?"

Moe replied, "Ann's boyfriend and his crew were looking for different entrances and exits to the hospital, you know, off the beaten path. Ann had swiped the blueprints for the hospital, but she didn't realize they were outdated. Her boyfriend sent one of his people to check it out, and the first thing that was wrong was Harry was in the old alley, smoking. So Farqua's guy took him out so he couldn't tell anyone they were casing the place. The second thing that went wrong was the door on the plans no longer existed. This made Ann catch a beating from her boyfriend."

Nick asked, "How do you know all this?"

Moe answered, "I had to meet her the night she got the beating. She was drunk or high on drugs, or both. She asked me to get her ice for her head. After I got the ice she said I was her only friend and rambled on what I just told you."

Nick continued to question Moe. "What about Jack Boyle's murder?"

Moe replied, "Another mistake by the genius Ann. Photos were taken of the EMU from the outside, but that wasn't good enough for them. They wanted photos of the inside. But Ann forgot to tell them there was a security officer stationed in there. Their guy was going to break in and take the pictures, never expecting a security officer to open the door and confront him. That was the reason, Nick. Plain and simple. They were killed for where they were at the wrong time. No other reason."

Nick was sure Farqua was ordering all these different hospital security breaches. Farqua was the source behind of all the murders in and around the hospital and the bombs. Now he was more determined than ever to prove it.

Nick told one of the agents, "Watch him. We'll be right back."

The investigators met in the conference room. Agents Camp, Smallwood, and Nick all thought it was time to execute the warrant at Ann's house under the premise that Moe was a frequent visitor. Now that they knew about Ann and the drugs, they could charge her and see if she would set up Farqua. Agent Phyllis Grazie had returned from the surveillance and thought they would be better off waiting since Farqua was in Ann's house. Grazie expressed that if they reacted too soon they, the terrorists, would just have someone take Farqua's place as lead in the operation. However, if they waited and bust them in the act, they may get his entire cell.

Nick said, "Let's go see if Moe knows anything about their plan."

Nick and Agent Camp walked into the interrogation room together

Moe looked frazzled and tired, but when he saw Nick he sat up straight and said, "Nick, what can I do to help myself? I've been thinking and I'm done with them. They reneged on everything they ever promised me. I don't want to be a Muslim, and all Farqua does is threaten my wife and son. I want protection for them and a deal for me."

Agent Camp was the first to speak to Moe, stating, "You must know some interesting plans to be making demands. The way I see it, without substantial information, and I do mean substantial, what you want is irrelevant."

Moe answered, "All I want is a fair shake. I can't live like this anymore, with drunks in a flophouse and worrying about my wife and son. I got information that you need. You need it to stop this animal and his friends. Listen, I sold drugs, I admit it. But there is no way I want innocent people killed in the name of something I don't believe in."

Nick said to Moe, "Okay, let's hear what you got."

Moe replied, "Nick, what about the deal?"

Nick said, "Moe, Agent Camp is in charge of that, but he can't promise you anything until he hears what information you have."

Agent Camp responded, "I will have a deputy United States attorney come in and verify that depending on the information provided, a deal will be made with you and your family."

With that, Agent Camp left the room and returned with US Deputy Attorney Vince Stratton.

Stratton introduced himself to Moe and said, "Mr. Prince, if the information you possess is what the agents need to prevent the loss of lives and it can be verified, I will do everything in my power to ensure you receive the deal you are looking for. Understand this: nothing is promised, and everything hinges on your cooperation and information. Do you understand?"

Moe nodded.

Stratton continued, "Then, Mr. Prince, I suggest you begin."

Agent Camp turned on the recorder and adjusted the microphones.

He asked Moe, "What do you know about any plans involving the hospital and your handler Farqua, Ann Stromer, or anyone else?"

Moe cleared his throat and said, "About three nights ago, I went to Ann's house to pick up pills. She was high on something as usual and began to talk. She liked when we sat on the couch together, and I held an ice pack on her head. That was when she began to say she made a mistake with her boyfriend Max. That he was not the nice guy she thought he was and was only out for himself. At this point she knew she was being used and he really didn't have feelings for her. Ann kept repeating over and over she wished she never met him, he has no soul, and all he wants to do is hurt people. When I asked her what she meant, she kept repeating over and over in a drunken haze, 'Three prong, three prong, three prong…' Ann fell asleep mumbling these words, and I put a blanket on her and left."

Moe continued, "The next night I was there and I asked her what 'three prong' was all about. Ann got up and got very nervous. She told me never to mention that, if I did they would kill me. They would kill me and anybody else that gets in their way. She said it was going to be an attack on the hospital, very soon. She did not know when, and it would involve three different forms of attack. She told me never to speak of it and that our very lives depend on not mentioning it. She overheard Max talking about it on his cell when he thought she was asleep."

Agent Camp asked, "That's it? That's all you got? What forms of attack? When? Where? In the hospital? Moe, I'm sorry, what you just told us doesn't qualify for any deals. We'll put you back in the cell so you can think if there is anything else."

Moe was yelling over his shoulder as they led him away. "Bust Ann! Get her in here! She'll talk!"

When Nick and Camp returned to the conference room, they heard Agent Smallwood saying, "I'll be the first to praise Ali and other informants that have located and identified almost all of the cells that were mentioned in the notes and CDs found in the different hideouts in Iraq, Pakistan, and Afghanistan. Nonetheless, with Farqua captured and detained I am sure this would place a burden on the groups for leadership and direction. Since we know where he is now, we should take him down. Not taking him down could be disastrous to America's safety in the future."

Nick was being quiet during the discussion. But he voted in favor of moving now. He knew Ann would crack like a rotten egg under interrogation and give up anything she had on Farqua. Furthermore, Nick did not want Farqua to slip through their fingers only to return again with more plots and terror strikes in the future. They discussed whether or not to wait and take Ann down at work, so as not to tip off Farqua. But this was quickly dismissed since no one wanted any evidence to disappear at the house in case there were others involved. As with any execution of a search warrant, the elements of surprise, safety, and coordination were key, along with knowing where the suspect was, and having a chance to question him at the location if the evidence was hidden and couldn't be found. When all had their say at the discussion, they again took a vote and it was decided to execute the warrant immediately.

It was nearly 6:00 a.m. by the time the search warrant team and the SWAT team were in place and had surrounded Ann's house. Since Nick was not allowed to go on the initial securing of the house, he took a radio and sat two blocks away listening to silence. The air outside was already getting hot and sticky at this time of the morning. Grazie was with Agent Camp, and another female agent was with Steven Turn. Agent Camp parked the car at the end of the street, out of sight of Ann's house. Under federal procedure for conducting search warrants, the investigative team would not enter until the search warrant team and SWAT team had declared the premises secure. A house is deemed secure when all rooms are checked for individuals with firearms or who could otherwise pose a danger to the team. Once all rooms are checked, each member giving an all clear for each room, individuals in the house are handcuffed and rounded up to one location such as the living room. Then the search team is called in with an 'all clear and secure' call on the radio. Waiting patiently was not one of Nick's strongest virtues, and he was doing everything possible to remain focused.

In Agent Dan Camp's car, he and Grazie were waiting for the radio transmission that the place was secure. Grazie was studying his features and wondering what he would be like in bed.

Dan turned to her and asked, "Is there something I can do for you, Agent Grazie?"

She blushed and said, "I'm not sure. Maybe."

They broke free from each other's gaze and concentrated on the job at hand. The next moment the radio blared that the premises were secure and Agent Camp should respond immediately. Then the radio called for emergency personnel and the forensic team. All units converged on the house, including Nick who was parked two blocks away. Outside of the residence, the area was already taped off with the yellow police "Caution" tape. Nick went inside, joining the rest of his investigative squad. Nurse Ann Stromer lay on the living room couch, dead.

CHAPTER 34

When Nick entered the room, he saw Ann lying on the couch. Ann's eyes were open and cloudy with the vacant stare of death. Her mouth hung open, drooling saliva mixed with blood, RN Ann Stromer was gray and cold. It was obvious that she had been dead for a while. Nick took a blanket and covered her. He admitted to himself that, though she was a criminal and a pest, in his own way he liked her. Nick was also getting angry that Farqua was killing people all around them—Al, Ann, Harry Barker, Jack Boyle, Jim Adamson, and the ice-picked Security Officer Joe Turro—and still they couldn't catch him. Where did Farqua disappear to? And how? Farqua's Nissan was still in the driveway. He should have been in custody by now. But he was nowhere to be found. Nick asked Dan to send some agents to the house in Fort Lee and the mosque and set up surveillance. Since Farqua hadn't taken his car, they should be checking security tapes at the train station and talking to the car services.

An ambulance arrived, but Ann was pronounced dead at the scene. A thorough search garnered many syringes of morphine and fentanyl, both full and empty. As they were lifting Ann's body onto the stretcher, Nick saw her bare feet. She'd been injecting the drugs into the veins in her feet and between her toes. She had visible new and old tracks from all the drugs she had been shooting. There were no other pills found, nor money or guns. The agents next focused on the car, the black Honda parked in her garage without license plates. The forensic team called for the flatbed truck in order to have the car taken to their facility. While waiting, they carefully checked for booby traps, then did a quick check of the glove box, console, and trunk for any dangerous contraband. A full search would be conducted at their garage.

Nick noticed how all of this was going on at a quick pace: the body was removed; the car placed on the flatbed; evidence boxed, labeled, and listed, and carried out to waiting vans; and the house getting prepped to be secured. A special truck waiting in the driveway contained plywood, studs, and other hardware needed to fix all openings that the entry team had created. A skilled group of agents made short work of securing the physical structure of the house. Nick noticed the attention Camp and Grazie were giving each other and how they were getting cozy with each other. Their actions were far from a prescribed work ethic and more flirtatious than they should be, Nick thought. He felt the green monster of jealousy creeping up inside him, even though he realized he was married. He had no right to feel this way.

The agents gathered and were briefed that they would wait for Ann's autopsy, try to locate Farqua, and complete the search of the vehicle later that day. It was almost 9:00 a.m. Camp radioed the agents looking for Farqua and instructed them to call him immediately upon locating him. Everyone not on duty was departing, and Nick, as he got into his car, observed agents Camp and Grazie get into Camp's car and drive away. Nick watched them pull away as he turned in the opposite direction to go home.

As he was driving, thinking of the events of the night, Nick had a hard time focusing on any one thought. First, there was the arrest of Moe, and his admission of his crimes. Second, there was the death of Ann. Though she wasn't one of Nick's favorite people, he was sad to think that she died. He'd grown to like her in a distant way. Third was the disappearance of Farqua. His car in the driveway, his girlfriend dead, he pulled a Houdini act and disappeared without the surveillance team noticing. Finally, there was the last vision he saw before leaving, Grazie and Dan Camp in Camp's car before they pulled away. This was tugging at him the most. It wasn't that Grazie couldn't do what she wanted, but the fact that she didn't tell him it was over. Had Nick done something wrong? Something to hurt her? They both knew it was this investigation that was keeping them apart. They both were married. Still, Nick had no indication that Grazie was going to break it off with him. But he couldn't bear to picture her with anyone else. The thought of her in another man's arms made him physically ill. He knew he had to keep it out of his mind until he could talk to her, and he knew now was not the time.

Nick began talking out loud to his friend and dead partner Al Stokes.

"Al, I could really use your advice now. You were right when you said I'd gotten Grazie's scent on me. You were right when you said I should have kept my distance. Well, I didn't. I loved being with her, and when we made love I didn't think I could be any happier. And now—get this, Al!—it looks like she's falling for Dan Camp! I know this shouldn't bother me, but it does! I know what you're gonna say. 'Nick, go home to your wife and kids.' I will, my friend. I will."

CHAPTER 35

The next afternoon, Nick went to see Director Shane at his office.

The director stated, "Nick, Ann had a puncture on her neck from a syringe. They're performing the toxicology tests, but it's my bet that she was given a shot of fentanyl in the neck the same way that Jack Boyle got it."

Nick replied, "If that's the case, it was Farqua's group that killed Security Officer Boyle and Ann, as well as slicing Harry Barker's neck, blowing up Jim Adamson in an explosion, ice-picking Security Officer Joe Turro, and putting a bullet in Al Stokes's head."

"Al?"

Nick said, "I just wonder. Farqua's cell would have used Ann to get Al Stokes off guard in his car. He knew Ann, and they controlled her. That's how they got close enough to shoot him in the head."

Nick thought to himself that Al, the poor bastard, probably didn't know what hit him. Nick felt himself getting angry. It was now Nick's personal mission to get Farqua dead or alive, preferably dead.

Nick informed the director, "We haven't located Farqua yet, but Agent Camp has his teams at all the spots they know he goes to."

The director asked, "Has an APB been issued to the various agencies?"

Nick replied, "No. They didn't want to drive him further underground. That's what would happen if it was made public that he was being hunted. If they don't find him in the next few days, then we'll do it."

The director said, "Okay Nick. Keep me informed."

As Nick left the director's office, he called Grazie, but it went right to voice mail. He left a message for her to call him back. Now Nick's mind was running wild. Were she and Dan still together? Should he have offered to leave Jen for her? At that moment Nick's phone rang, and it was Dan. Dan said, "We still haven't found Farqua. We have all our resources on it."

Now Nick felt some relief, knowing Grazie was with her informant and not with Agent Camp. Nick decided to go back to his office until anything happened or until Grazie called. He did not have to wait long as five minutes later Grazie called.

Nick asked, "Any word on the whereabouts of Farqua?"

Grazie replied, "No, nothing."

Nick said, "It's too bad. The surveillance is in place, but now we have to keep a constant vigil until he turns up. Do you want to get a bite to eat?"

Grazie replied, "No, I can't. I have something to do, but I'll meet you in the parking lot of your office in ten minutes. I can only stay a minute, I'll call you when I arrive."

Nick was wondering what she was going to say. Was it about the job? Dan Camp? Him? Grazie called his cell and told him she was in her car at the side entrance. A minute later Nick got into her car, and she drove to the far end of the parking lot and turned off the engine.

Grazie then said, "I can't stay long. There is someplace I have to go."

"Dan's place?" Nick knew the words were a mistake as they slipped from his mouth.

Angry now, Grazie answered, "It's none of your business what I do or who I meet up with. Who the hell do you think you are? Do I question you when you're not seeing me? You got a hell of a nerve. Don't you ever think you've got a claim on me!"

Nick replied, "Listen to me. It's not that. I know you're free to do what you like. I was just wondering…if I had done anything wrong, you know, to upset you, since we always had a good time and, you know, enjoyed each other's company."

Grazie leaned back. "You're right. We did. And no, you did nothing wrong or to upset me. I just want to move on. Not get too close to anyone. That's how I am. We had a good time, and now that time has passed. Don't dwell on this part of it. Remember the good times that we spent together."

"But…"

Grazie said, "Nick, we're getting too close. Think about it. Where were we going? Did you fantasize about us being together as a couple? You know that would never happen. But I'll tell you this, Nick. If it doesn't end, we would both hurt people we don't want to hurt. It's better this way. You think it hurts now. It would be worse if it went on any further. Nick, please don't think badly of me. I'm doing this for both of us, and deep down you know I'm right. I'll see you when the investigation wraps up. Take care of yourself."

Grazie was still talking as Nick leaned over and kissed her. They kept kissing more and more passionately as Grazie, between kisses, murmured, "No. No, Nick, we can't. Please. We have to stop." But stopping was no longer an option. Right there in the car, in daylight, they could not help themselves.

Nick kissed Grazie down her neck, unbuttoned her blouse, and kissed her all over her now exposed breasts. She pulled his pants down. He removed her panties from under her skirt, and she climbed on top of Nick, sliding him inside.

As they straightened up, Grazie spoke first. "Nick that doesn't change anything. Get it. That was goodbye."

Grazie drove him back to the side entrance, watched him exit the car and enter the building without looking back. She then drove away and pulled into a parking space in a strip mall and began crying. She knew both the investigation and the affair were coming to an end. She didn't want any long confrontations with Nick. She loved him too much for that.

But she also knew he was the type of guy who would never hurt his wife. So, she came up with a plan. Grazie did not want Agent Dan Camp. But she realized if Nick thought she did, he would back away. Grazie figured by her making Nick think she was interested in someone else, he would end it with her. But she also knew Nick well enough to know he wasn't strong enough to do it without prompting. She just had to get the ball rolling.

And she was walking a fine line with Dan. If she flirted with him too much, he would think he was going to get into her pants. If she didn't flirt with him enough, she knew Nick would see right through it. Evidently, it worked. Nick brought it up. Now she just had to keep Dan at bay until the investigation was over. She knew it wasn't right, but there was no other way to end it with Nick. Not the right thing to do. Just the best thing.

Grazie thought of the story Nick once told her. Al Stokes had said once if Nick got Grazie's scent on him, there would be no way out for him. No, she knew it was the right thing to do, as difficult as it was. Grazie laughed to herself and thought, *I got hit by Nick's scent.*

Nick did not realize it was after eight o'clock at night. He had gotten so involved writing his reports that time flew by. He was packing up his desk when his phone rang.

It was the hospital watch commander. He yelled, "Nick, every alarm in the place is going off. I called the director, Parsippany Police, and the fire marshal. I sent more guards to the covert storeroom and the lab, and the director told me to call you. You better get over here right away!"

Chapter 36

As he was exiting his car, Nick received another call from the shift commander.

"Nick, the manager of Guardian Angel Ambulance Service called and said an ambulance was carjacked on a run back from the hospital in Elizabeth. The information that was available came from the two EMTs that were left tied and beaten in an old freight shipping yard in Hillside. Though one of the EMTs was badly beaten, both will survive. The one that was conscious said that four men approached them for directions, then jumped them, threw them in the rig, and began to beat them. The next thing he knew he was in an abandoned shipping yard. He managed to get out to the street where he flagged down a motorist who called the police and then the dispatch office."

Nick replied, "Okay thanks."

He then relayed this information to agents Smallwood, Grazie, and Camp. Nick reminded them how easy it would be to move explosives, men or arms in the back of an ambulance.

Agent Camp said the terrorists of the first World Trade Center explosions in 1993 stated they wanted to blow up the tunnels leading to New York.

Agent Camp continued, "They talked about stealing an ambulance or other emergency vehicle, loading it with explosives and detonating it in the Lincoln or Holland tunnels, the busiest traveled roads linking New York and New Jersey."

As Nick was running to the hospital, he remembered how the ambulance center had the finest of security and anti-theft protection installed after 9/11 and was almost impenetrable, with perimeter fencing, camera, motion detectors, and security officers. The terrorists would only have to drive by to know this. Knowing the center had tight security, they went after a weak link: the ambulance after it left the new fortress. Nothing could be done to protect the sixty-five ambulances and crew after they left the building. Adding security to each ambulance team was considered but not acted on because of the amount of security needed. If the terrorists were following the plan mentioned from 1993, it was a chilling, frightening thought. Aside from the deaths, the lasting economic disaster would be felt for years to come. Nick said it was time to put an APB on both the ambulance and Farqua, as something sinister was afoot. All agreed, and it was done.

Nick now turned his attention to the trouble at Guardian Angel Hospital. As he made his way to the security command center, he heard every alarm imaginable going off in unison. When he arrived, the shift commander stated, “We think the alarms are a diversion.

Nick asked him to explain, to which he replied, “A couple entered through the delivery bays with a vendor. The vendor called security. Then four men entered through the morgue area, along with an undertaker and his helper. And finally, we saw a group of what appeared to be Middle Eastern men pass through the main entrance. They’ve now disappeared.”

Nick didn’t like the feeling he was getting. Something major was about to unfold, and they had no clue where the intruders were.

The director immediately called for backup from Parsippany Police Department, the state police, and the Morris County Sheriff’s Office, explaining what was transpiring and asking them to surround the perimeter with half their people and split the rest into two groups, half at the main entrance and half at the emergency department entrance.

The director stated, “I’ll be at the main entrance, and Investigator Nick Moore will be at the emergency department entrance.” Nick called the agents and told them, “Split up with half your men and women at the front door to meet the director and the other half at the emergency department to meet me.”

Nick removed his gun from his ankle holster as he made his way down to the emergency department. As he was running down the hall, he was hoping that Grazie chose his group to respond to because all he wanted to do was see her again. When he arrived, uniforms crowded the area. Nick explained, "The director's group were going to the covert closet, and our group will be heading for the radioactive blood irradiator. There is another target they plan to attack somewhere in the hospital, but we can't wait. We will take care of the two targets we know for sure while security tries to locate the last group on the cameras."

As they were making their way down, Nick had a fleeting thought to himself that he and Grazie were really over. She didn't choose his group. On the way, Nick was dispersing the backup units to hallways and exits the intruders might use.

The director was utilizing the backups in the same way down to the covert closet. The director was concerned for the immediate problem of these intruders in the hospital, but he was also worried about the patients, visitors, and staff in the corridors. By positioning his men at the intersections of the hallways, they would be able to divert the people and keep them away from the corridor that led to the closet and lab.

When Nick's group was approximately two corridors away from the lab, they heard a muffled explosion. It shook the hallway under their feet. As they picked up the pace and turned down the lab hallway, they found the corridor cloudy with fine particles of dust and smelling like a fireworks display on the Fourth of July. In the distance, they saw men pushing and pulling what appeared to be a desk.

Nick realized it was the irradiator and yelled, "Everyone, take cover."

At the same time, the Middle Eastern men opened fire on Nick's group with AK-47 automatic weapons. Bullets buzzed past Nick's ears like hungry mosquitos. Nick's crew fired back. They were close enough now that Nick spotted Farqua shouting, "Allah Akbar," as he was firing an automatic weapon with one hand, and pulling a chain connected to the irradiator with the other.

Nick looked at him and could see the fury in his eyes, a fury to kill everyone there and then kill everyone in America. Nick remembered Al Stokes. Also, Ann Stromer, Jack Boyle, Harry Barker, Jim Adamson, and Joe Turro. Something in Nick was drawn to the surface, and all he could think of was to kill this wild animal before it had the chance to kill anyone else. Assuming Farqua was wearing body armor, Nick took careful aim at Farqua's head, holding his breath, and squeezed off two rounds.

A smoke grenade burst. Smoke clouded the hall. Nick was firing blind. The other four men with Farqua were firing automatic weapons also. This firefight seemed like an eternity to Nick. Bullets whizzing, the sound of tiles cracking, the smoke, and the noise all combined to make for a chaotic scene.

When there was a pause in the salvo, Nick and his team fired with everything they had. There was silence.

Farqua's men were killed. No one on Nick's side was injured. Farqua was dead, in a heap with his men.

On the other side of the hospital, the director's group reached the corridor of the covert closet. Two men and two women were already there and appeared to be rigging the closet with explosives. They were told to stop and get on their knees with their hands on their head, but instead, turned and fired their automatic weapons, while yelling almost in unison, "Allah Akbar."

Bullets were whizzing by, hitting the walls, doors, and columns that the director's team took cover behind. The team fired back, shot in rapid succession, with smoke, dust, and cement particles filling the air and making it difficult to breathe. The covert closet was at a dead-end corridor, giving the director's team an advantage for both their cover and aim for the intruders. As the other team stopped firing their weapons, the director called for a cease-fire. Then looking down the corridor as the dust settled, the director observed the two men and two women lying dead on the floor. The director's group was ready to celebrate when they noticed Grazie in a sitting position against the wall. She had her hand on her neck just above her vest.

The director saw immediately she had been shot. He called for the emergency trauma team and began cardiopulmonary resuscitation. She reached for the director's arm. He leaned over, and she whispered between gurgles, "Get…Nick…Nick…N…" The trauma team arrived and took over from the director and, in a last-ditch effort, used the cardio defibrillator on her, but there was no response.

CHAPTER 37

Nick turned the crime scene over to the police who promptly taped off the area. Forensics began its job, and plant engineering and the various alarm companies began turning off or resetting the alarms. The investigators along with the forensic team took photos and picked up and labeled all evidence.

Nick was about to return to security when one of the agents on the forensic team told him, "Agent Grazie was shot dead in the gunfire at the covert closet."

Nick was paralyzed and felt he couldn't breathe. He asked the agent, "Are you sure? Could there be a mistake?"

The agent replied, "No mistake, Agent Grazie is dead."

Nick told his crew he was going to the covert closet and to get him on the air if they needed him. Now running down the corridors, he felt as if he were moving in slow motion. It seemed like it was taking forever to get there. Once he arrived, he immediately noticed the sheet covering something in the hallway. As he was about to lift it, the director asked, "Nick, are you sure you want to see her that way?"

Nick nodded and moved the sheet off the body. Looking at her, he could not control himself. He fell on his knees weeping and tried to hug her. The director and Dan pulled him up and placed the sheet over her again. The various teams had also arrived at this scene but were on standby until the sheriff's bomb squad gave the all clear.

The closet had been rigged with C-4 plastic explosives. Contrary to popular belief, C-4 was quite stable until fused with a detonation charge. The bomb squad made short work of clearing the area of the explosives and then gave the all clear so the other squads could perform their duties. Grazie's body was lifted onto a gurney and the sheet placed over her body. Nick peeled the sheet back again and kissed her, knowing this was truly their last kiss. As they rolled the gurney down the hall, Nick thought he could hear her saying, "Just remember the good times we had."

His phone going off shook Nick back to his senses. The command center reported they located the last of the intruders on the stairway to the helipad. Nick began to lead the two groups up the stairway that led to the helipad, and as he was climbing the stairs he recalled the director telling him when he started that Guardian Angel Hospital was a class-A trauma center. As such it had a helipad to deliver medical emergencies from the accidents on New Jersey highways from all over the state. The helipad was utilized approximately ten times a week both by the state police helicopters and also by the two owned by the Guardian Angel Hospital System. Nick thought of how much the terrorists knew. They knew of the helipad and the correct staircase that led to it. Any patients arriving by the helipad would have a medical crew on board and a designated elevator that would take them directly to the trauma center. The intruders were secreted on an aluminum platform outside the hospital that connected the hospital to the helipad.

The four men were visible now. They were wearing black pants, black shirts, and black skullcaps. All appeared to be in their early thirties, carrying what appeared to be semiautomatic handguns. Lying on the side of the platform, with their black clothes, they were hard to see against the tar roof under the walkway.

Nick had the command center radio all state police helicopters that the helipad was closed until further notice and to use one of the other designated trauma centers. One floor away the teams could see and hear the men above them just waiting to hijack a helicopter. The elevators were locked by the command center.

Agent Dan Camp was the first to speak. "Attention, this is the FBI, you are surrounded, drop your weapons and show us your hands."

With that, they all turned and began firing. Nick, Dan, and the members of the two groups strategically placed themselves where the intruders, four of them, were sitting ducks. The two groups returned fire, and in minutes it was over with the four suspects dead. Nick radioed the command center and told the different units to report to the helipad stairwell landing where four suspects were dead on arrival. No medical license was needed at this point. Nick had seen enough death in his career to know what it looked like.

Nick, Dan Camp, Smallwood, and the director returned to the security conference room where they went to discuss strategy and press releases. The director stated that, according to the watch commander, very little of what went on was noticed by patients, visitors, or staff not associated with the response to the locations. Therefore, little if any information was needed to be shared with the press. The press that did monitor police radios would be told that this was a drill conducted by the various agencies. For now. Agents were reaching out to Grazie's family. As far as Farqua was concerned, they would check to see what if any identification he had on his person. All the various departments were removing the intruders' bodies and blocking off the hallways and the room where the irradiator was held.

Nick was so devastated by the death of Grazie, he was not paying attention to any of the briefing. He daydreamed through all of it. Every time he came out of the fog his brain was in, he expected to see Grazie seated next to him. Then remembering she was dead, Nick fought to hold the tears back, which led him to daydreaming of her again. He hoped she and Al Stokes were hanging out together. All of a sudden, as if Grazie and Al were reminding him, Nick's head cleared, he blinked his eyes, and in a state of alarm he remembered the missing ambulance.

Nick went to the security command center and asked the shift commander, "Any hit yet from the GPS on the missing ambulance?"

The commander replied, "Not yet, but the signal to it is being transmitted every ten minutes."

Nick then called Dan Camp and explained, "Dan, the GPS on the ambulance is still not working. Send the agents out to physically search for it, especially in Jersey City, Paterson, and Fort Lee."

Dan Camp replied, "Okay. I'll call John Smallwood and see if he can spare some men."

Nick replied, "I'll call the state, county, and locals and make them aware."

Though a very real pressing problem, the missing ambulance had not been given much thought in the past hours. Where was it? And more importantly, what did they plan to do with it?

Chapter 38

Nick was fuming that the GPS installed on all Guardian Angel Hospital ambulances after 9/11 could not be activated on the missing ambulance. Either it was broken, removed, or in a garage not allowing the transmission to get through. Any federal agent along with state, county, and local police were looking for it. Frustrated, Nick continued making phone calls to various police agencies, telling them about the missing ambulance and asking if any officers spotted it to be extremely careful and to call him. His cell phone was ringing incessantly, with calls from the director, Camp, and Smallwood. When it rang again, he answered it and at first he didn't recognize the voice.

Then the male voice stated, "Mr. Nick, this is Josef Ali. I have been trying to get in touch with Ms. Grazie for half the night. She is still not answering her phone. She gave me your number and said if I cannot get in touch with her to call you. She told me to trust you, that you are a good person. I believe her from when we met. That's why I am calling you. I am worried about her."

Nick, still an emotional mess from what happened, gathered all his strength to remain calm and collected. Nick asked him if he was on the secure phone Grazie had given him, to which he replied yes. Nick then began telling him what went down, how the targets were protected, about the death of Farqua, and in the ensuing gun battle, how they were successful in stopping the bad guys. He explained that an ambulance was missing, the markings on it, and the license plate.

Then gulping hard to hide his emotions Nick said, "Ali, I also have some very bad news. Please know that there was nothing that could be done, but Phyllis Grazie was killed in a shoot-out with the jihadists. I'm so sorry. I know you knew her a long time and liked her."

There was silence on the phone, and then Josef Ali spoke, "I know that was very difficult for you to do. You see, I know you loved her as I do but in a different way. She spoke very highly of you, and I knew by the way she talked about you she loved you too. This is a very sad day."

Nick asked Ali, "Is it time for you to be relocated in the Witness Protection Program?"

Ali replied, "No, I am not afraid of death. Now I have a friend in heaven that I miss very much." Ali then hung up.

Nick then called Dan Camp. Nick said he wanted to talk to him, and they agreed to meet at the hospital parking lot in an hour. Nick wanted to talk to him about Grazie. He didn't know how he was going to bring it up but was determined to do so. When Nick arrived, Dan Camp was already there waiting for him. They got out of their cars, and Dan started first saying what a tough night last night was and how he still couldn't believe that Grazie was gone.

Dan said, "It kind of puts a damper on the entire investigation and the fantastic job everyone did."

Nick replied, "I know. I miss her very much. When I think of her in the hallway with the sheet over her, I get sick to my stomach. But I know you guys became very close in the last couple weeks."

Dan replied, "I thought so too. Twice she gave me the idea she was interested in me. Then when I put the move on her, she asked me if I was crazy. She said we're done, your job is over. I'm still trying to figure that one out."

Nick figured it out as Dan was still talking. Grazie didn't want a hard breakup, nor did she want their families broken up. What she did was make Nick think she wanted Dan. Nick would bow out of the picture without any drama or unpleasant scenes. Nick knew this point also. She was also fighting the scent. She'd been hit by it and knew what the future would hold if they stayed together: nothing but heartaches for all concerned. Nick wanted to think she loved him too much for that and hatched her own plan using Dan as a ploy. Now, thinking about this, he missed her more than ever. But he would do what Grazie would wanted him to do: remember the good times.

They were about to walk into the hospital when Nick's cell phone began to ring. It was Smallwood. He was speaking so quickly that Nick could not understand him.

Nick ordered, "John, slow down. I can't understand you."

Agent Smallwood repeated in a slower, calmer tone, "The missing ambulance's GPS is working again. It's showing a location on Kennedy Boulevard in Jersey City, heading towards Route 3."

Nick replied, "Call the state police and advise them. I'm with Dan and I'll fill him in."

All emergency vehicles had GPS units installed after 9/11 for just such an emergency. Nick told Dan what was happening, and Dan immediately called his office, telling them to direct police and federal agents to set up roadblocks on Route 3. The road was the main highway that led into the Lincoln Tunnel. If this was a direct action of the confiscated notebooks and tapes, then the ambulance was packed with explosives that a suicide bomber planned to detonate in the tunnel.

Dan and Nick jumped into Dan's car and with lights and siren blaring. They headed to Route 287, which would take them to Route 46 and then Route 3. Both were trying to listen to the radio while Dan was navigating the highways and Nick was calling the Port Authority Police of New York and New Jersey in an attempt to have them close the tunnel in the event the ambulance got through the barricades. H couldn't get a person on the line.

Then Nick call the director and explained, "The missing ambulance GPS just went on, and it's located in Jersey City heading towards Route 3. We will have to call Weehawken, Hoboken, and Jersey City and have them set up roadblocks. We have to talk to Port Authority police and have them close the Lincoln Tunnel. We will also need the state police. Smallwood is calling them. We need the use of their helicopter along with the various bomb squads from the area."

The director said, "I'll handle the calls. Kill the bastards!"

Kennedy Boulevard, Nick thought, was always a traffic nightmare, and today was no exception. Two federal agents were now tailing the vehicle from a distance and could report back while actually observing the ambulance. Two barricades were set up, one at the beginning of the helix that led to the tunnel and one at the entrance of the tunnel itself. The Port Authority Police moved their heavy-duty tow trucks in front of the entrances and other vehicles behind the trucks. Meanwhile, on the top of the helix, local, state and federal agencies had set up a roadblock that was four cars deep, interlaced with police trucks. Traffic was being diverted off the helix and into the cities of Hoboken and Weehawken. The routes to all other highways were blocked so that the ambulance driver, if he saw the roadblock, would not be able to change routes and possibly reach another target. The hope was that once the occupants of the ambulance realized their plan has been foiled and there was nowhere to go, they would give up.

Nick wondered if that hope was naive.

On the side streets were parked emergency vehicles from eight different cities, ready to help if the terrorists still blew themselves up. All hospitals were on alert, and two medical helicopters were ready at the police parking lots if they needed to be utilized to fly the injured to specialty hospitals.

As Nick and Dan were racing down Route 3, Nick looked out the window and observed two news helicopters flying in the direction of the tunnel.

He said to Dan, "Just what we need. It looks like the media somehow got hold of this and sent news teams via helicopter. I'll look at the news coverage and see what they know."

Nick looked at his phone. "It's worse than I thought," he said. "Not only do they have helicopters, but the live feed they are broadcasting shows two news vans closing in on the ambulance."

Dan asked, "What are they saying?"

Nick replied, "One of the vans is speeding next to the ambulance to get a shot of the in…" Nick didn't finish his sentence but screamed out, "Holy shit! Josef Ali is driving the ambulance!"

Chapter 39

Nick asked Dan, "Is there any way you or Smallwood can patch me in to the ambulance two-way radio. I have to talk to him. Ali would never do this."

Dan was on the phone with his information technology department. He had Nick read numbers off his phone, then told them to call the command center at the hospital for the two-way radio numbers. He then instructed them to call him back when it was set up. In less than three minutes, Dan's phone rang. The tech told Dan it was ready to go, to call 1111# for the connection to the ambulance radio. Nick was listening to the call on the speaker and was already dialing the number.

Trying to control his tone when the connection was made, he said, "Ali, what are you doing?"

Ali replied, "Mr. Nick, I am barely able to talk. They found out I was supplying information. They beat me severely and are forcing me to drive the ambulance to my death. If I do not do as they say, they will kill my family. I don't know what to do."

Nick replied, "Ali, I need you to remain calm. We're going to send agents to your home and get your family. They'll be all right. Who else is in the ambulance?"

Ali replied, "Thank you, thank you for saving my family. There are two of Farqua's men in the back making last-minute adjustments to the bomb. They taped my hand to the wheel. If I attempt to remove my hand from the wheel, the bomb will explode. I do have a plan, though. When I get over the water, where the road bends, I will drive straight through the guardrail. I will remove my hands after I count to three. If there is no explosion, please have your men shoot through the walls. I am fast approaching the turn. Goodbye, Mr. Nick. I will tell Ms. Phyllis you send regards."

Nick and Dan were fast approaching the helix when they saw the ambulance crash through the guardrails. Nick found himself counting one, two, three…then the ambulance exploded into a giant fireball that continued until it hit the cold water of the Hudson River below, where what was left of the ambulance and its flaming parts got extinguished as the vehicle began to sink into the murky water.

CHAPTER 40

Dan called Smallwood and asked him to call NYPD for their recovery and salvage boats and dispatch them to the area of the Hudson River where the ambulance hit the water.

Dan said, "John, the state police helicopters are flying over the spot now so they can use that as a marker. Also, inform the diving teams that they should be aware of the explosives in the event all of them didn't detonate."

Nick was on the phone himself, explaining to the various departments they could return to their commands, and for the Port Authority to send a repair crew for the guardrail that the ambulance crashed through. The spot was now blocked by police patrol cars.

Nick and Dan stopped at the mobile command center set up at the bottom of the helix and began to explain to the incident commander what had happened.

Nick began, "After the trouble we had at the hospital, we began a concerted effort to locate the ambulance. The GPS spotted it and the rest you know."

Agent Dan Camp said, "We want to thank you for your cooperation and professionalism that undoubtedly saved many lives. I will provide you with the handwritten official press release to be given to the media, feel free to call a press conference after the helix is repaired and opened."

The emergency responders returned to their various departments and the helix, tunnel, and on-ramps were reopened.

Dan dropped Nick off at the hospital. Nick met with the director, filled him in on the events of the day, the ambulance and the death of Ali and of the jihadists. Nick then made an appointment with the director for the next afternoon at 1:00 p.m. where an entire review of the case would be discussed, including the responses to each emergency and any mistakes that were made. Nick advised the director he would bring his detailed report, which would include all correspondence with the federal agents, reports, checks, and surveillance logs. Nick included all agencies that participated. He listed the deaths associated with the investigation, and the crimes committed.

The report would account for the recovered keys taken from Security Officer Joe Turro. They were found in the lab door that led to the blood irradiator. Farqua retained possession of them and used them on the night of the attack on the hospital. Nick included in his report that the amount of collateral damage was surprisingly low, considering the scope of the operation and the almost all-out war that was declared on the Guardian Angel Hospital by the jihadists. Nick also would make recommendations for new security procedures, including locking the storage room in plant engineering as well as the proper storage of any blueprints or documents.

As he arrived at his office, Nick decided to call his wife Jen and tell her to plan a trip for both of them to an island where they could relax and forget the world. He telephoned Jen and asked her what she thought of a trip for the both of them now that the job was over. She was good with it, and Nick asked for her to start checking flights. He said he would see her later. Nick then settled down to write reports.

All day, Nick stayed at his office, writing and gathering his reports. Nick placed the complex reports, photos, surveillance footage, and closed-circuit television recording together in one package. This took Nick the entire day, and Nick was surprised it was seven o'clock at night when he finally finished the package for the director.

The next day, Nick arrived at the director's office with two binders which pertained to the investigation. After their review, notes, and suggestions, Nick revised it and handed the director a thumb drive which contained a PowerPoint presentation of the investigation. Nick knew that the director would need this in order to make a presentation to the board of directors who would be anxious to know what exactly happened, what was done, and what was being done to ensure they would be prepared for the next incident. The director thanked Nick, then informed him that the toxicology report revealed that Ann Stromer died of fentanyl poisoning injected into her neck. The only prints on the used syringe taken out of the trash were Farqua's. He was the culprit on all the syringes used, and the ice pick used on Security Officer Joe Turro. The Middle Eastern man they thought died of ricin had actually been injected with fentanyl. Though praise was given to Director Thomas Shane, the hospital, the federal forensic team, and Investigator Nick Moore for their cooperation, support, and dedication of duty for the successful outcome of the investigation, the mood of all concerned was far from celebratory.

The director said, "Nick, the director of Homeland Security for New Jersey praised the effort of all concerned. Furthermore, if anything, it made Washington and this state realize just how vulnerable the United States is to attack and how susceptible our citizens are, for whatever reason, to helping the enemy. Some people are suckers. They'll commit treason for love, money, ideology, or some other reason, giving the people that would do us harm an edge to carry out their plan."

Nick was thankful that the media couldn't lay out every last detail of the attacks for public consumption and possible copycat incidents. The main reason was the use of federal radios communication. The media was unable to clone them so they couldn't listen to what was happening during the investigation, as they did with local departments. Therefore, the car surveillance of Farqua, the visual surveillance at Ann's house, and the locating of the ambulance were all off the radar of the press.

Nick's cell phone rang; it was Dan Camp.

Camp said, "Nick, Tony Grazie is on his way to the funeral director to pick up Grazie. Her body was already released to him, and he planned on having it flown back for burial, to a little town in Indiana where she grew up and still has relatives. The funeral director will take them to the airport and take care of the arrangements for him. He asked if you could meet him at the funeral home. He really wanted to meet you."

Nick replied, "Of course. Give me the address." He hung up and began thinking, *Does Tony know anything? Is he going to deck me?* Nick felt he deserved getting sucker punched if that's what Tony planned on doing. It was better that way, that Tony got closure. Nick thought it was as if she had this planned also. He was smiling to himself, doing what she told him to do: remember the good times.

Nick arrived at the funeral home and spotted a man waiting outside. Nick thought, *That has to be him*. Tony was as Nick had pictured him: all white, straight hair, glasses, slim, medium height, dressed in a blue blazer, denim slacks, and a pressed blue shirt.

Nick got out of his car and walked over to him, extending his hand while saying, "Hi, you must be Tony."

Tony approached Nick, took his hand, then hugged Nick and began crying. Between sobs, Tony said, "I know you took care of Phyllis and looked out for her. She told me. They explained to me how she got killed, and I wanted to tell you not to feel guilty, that somehow it may have been your fault. On the contrary. This was her life, the way she chose to live it. She wouldn't have it any other way. I wanted to meet you and explain how I feel about it." Tony broke away and wiped his face. "I'll take her to her hometown, back to her family and friends. Thank you for looking out for her. I will always remember you as her dear friend."

They shook hands, and Tony walked into the funeral home as Nick got into his car and drove away. What poison Nick was to Tony's marriage, the man would never know.

Chapter 41

While driving home, Nick had many thoughts running around in his head. He was trying to categorize them as to work, family, and his emotional state when his phone rang.

"Nick, John Smallwood here. I need you to sit down or pull over if you're driving. Don't be a macho man and listen to me."

Nick pulled into a parking lot of a paint store and said, "Okay, I'm parked in a space. What the hell is going on?"

Smallwood continued, "I know you're not going to believe what I'm about to tell you, because frankly I can hardly believe it myself."

Nick asked, "What's going on?"

Smallwood said, "I want to let you know we confirmed it by multiple sources including visual surveillance, as well as a cloned cell phone and camera surveillance."

Nick, getting angry, said, "John are you going to tell me what the hell the reason for this call is or do you want me to start guessing."

Smallwood replied, "We at the agency were wrapping up the case, boxing evidence, writing reports, and recording thumb drives. We had the younger agents create a list of all the jihadists involved in the investigation, including Ann and Moe. Each one had their own folder and photo attached."

Nick, getting frustrated, shouted, "*And?*"

Smallwood continued, "When I checked to ensure Farqua's folder contained the photos we had of him alive and postmortem, I didn't find any postmortem folders or even an autopsy report."

Nick replied, "Okay, I'll turn around, go to the morgue, and get you what you need. They probably forgot to send Farqua's folder over with the others."

Smallwood replied, "Nick, you don't understand, Farqua was not among the dead. We went over to the morgue and saw all the bodies and reports. He was not among the dead."

Nick said, "No, something has to be wrong, I saw him. He got shot multiple times and went down."

Smallwood continued, "Based on this information, we employed the facial recognition cameras at all transportation hubs and got a positive hit for Farqua boarding a plane for Nassau, in the Bahamas."

Nick asked, "But…"

Smallwood replied, "I know it's hard to believe, but Farqua, now identified as Akbar al Fasam, is what's known as a mercenary jihadist. A fake. He's only in it for the money. He recruits others and lets them take the fall. He brokers arms deals and always makes money for himself. All indications are he is at the Deluxe Resort in Nassau and has a slip in the marina for his yacht, the *Tub of Salt, Too*."

Smallwood continued, "We're putting together a group of agents to go down and bring him back. Dan Camp will be leading the FBI contingent. I'll be in charge of the CIA contingent along with the agents stationed in Nassau. We asked and got permission for you to come. No need to pack. We have a government jet, and we'll only stay as long as the mission takes. Are you in?"

Nick replied, "Yes, of course, I'm in, but—"

Smallwood interrupted, "Nick, we'll have three hours of flight time to go over this. See you at Newark Airport Terminal B, flight departure floor in an hour. By the way, bring your gun. No check-in the way we go."

Nick arrived at the airport in thirty-five minutes, parked, and walked in to the departure floor. The floor was under construction and almost empty except for construction workers and the occasional Port Authority workers. The dust was heavy, and the construction lights gave everything a glow. Nick was about to ask one of the workers for directions when he saw Agent Smallwood waving to him. Smallwood led the way, and they walked out a door marked "Authorized Personnel Only." They made their way down aluminum flight steps and walked about one hundred yards on the tarmac to a waiting jet. As they boarded, Nick observed about twenty men and four female agents were already there and strapped in. Smallwood directed him to two unoccupied seats, and they, too, buckled in.

Nick was about to start asking Smallwood questions when FBI Agent Dan Camp entered the plane and greeted them.

Camp said, "Hey, guys. Guess you never expected all of us to be working together again this soon."

Nick answered first, saying, "I just found out an hour ago, and I still have a lot of questions."

Smallwood replied, "Ask your questions. Between me and Dan, I'm sure we'll be able to answer them."

Nick said, "Okay, the first question is, I saw Farqua get shot and go down. I even moved down the hall after the shoot-out to remove the gun from where it fell."

Smallwood responded first, "Right! We saw the carnage, and all appeared to be dead. Then we got the call about Grazie and went to the covert corridor. None of us checked to see who was alive or dead before we left."

Dan said, "Here, Nick. Look at this. This is the photo recognition we used at Newark Liberty Airport."

Nick took the photos and was stunned to see Farqua at the security checkpoint looking as if nothing had happened.

Nick said, "I can't believe it, but that's him."

Smallwood said, "After he was identified and we learned his location, the rest was easy to put together."

Camp said, "We went to work on the logistics, got surveillance on him, got permission for you to join us, and here we are."

Smallwood said, "The State Department worked everything out with the Bahama government. They'll be there to assist if we need them."

Nick asked, "So what's the plan?"

Camp replied, "On this plane are the best of the best CIA and FBI agents, trained to secure premises without any collateral damage.

When we arrive, we will be transported to his location and immediately begin the takedown. As usual, we will be waiting outside for the 'all clear, secured' transmission before we enter."

Smallwood said, "Then we sign papers for the government and return to the US."

Camp smiled. "What could go wrong?

The teams were transported over to the villa like clockwork. It was still dark out, and one would think a bit cooler for four o'clock in the morning, but it wasn't. Adding to the unpleasantness, the humidity was unbearable. The local government was told of an action that was going to take place and to keep their distance. Upon arrival, the team surrounded the villa. Nick looked down at the dock and saw a magnificent yacht moored in a slip. He knew it was Farqua's without seeing the name. A transmission came through Nick's earpiece stating they observed a male, fully attired, on the ground floor of the villa. Nick remembered what Agent Smallwood said on the flight over, that Farqua had been a resident of the villa for a long time and it was constantly under construction. In Nick's mind, this guy was capable of anything after somehow surviving the shoot-out at the hospital and escaping to the Bahamas. But a new transmission made Nick forget his thought.

It was Special Agent Dan Camp, in a harsh whisper, saying, "Go!"

The special units kicked in the front and back doors and entered the villa. Armed to the teeth with automatic weapons and complete body armor, the agents secured the residence within minutes. Then a transmission in his earpiece left Nick cold despite the oppressive humidity: "Premises secure, no suspects present."

Nick thought, Farqua would never be trapped in a villa without a secret escape route. Nick looked to the yacht, thinking that's where Farqua was heading, planning to escape by sea.

Nick began running toward the yacht while yelling into the microphone, "Farqua is heading for the yacht."

Just as these words were being spoken, Nick heard the sound of the twin engines starting with their familiar sound. Straining to see who was on the bridge, Nick spotted one solitary person at the helm. All but convinced it was Farqua, Nick removed his gun and was about to jump on the starboard side when Farqua turned the boat and, at full throttle, headed out of the marina. Gone…for now.

CHAPTER 42

Driving home from the airport, Nick was glad he decided to take a few days off and go to an island with Jen. He needed a change of scenery and needed to clear his head. What he did throughout his career was to think about the recent events from the latest investigation: facts, mistakes, good points, bad points. Then like placing old souvenirs in a box for storage, he placed them out of his mind and moved on. This was what he needed to do now, he realized. Think of the recent investigation, the deaths, what was and what could have been. Most of all, he needed to think about Grazie and then release her from his mind and set her free. He owed this to her, he owed this to himself, and most of all he owed it to Jen.

On the way home Nick decided to make a stop at the cemetery and say a prayer at his first wife's grave. He wasn't sure why he stopped, but supposed it was because of the silence, tranquility, the peace he found there, and also because he missed Felicia terribly, all of a sudden. He missed Al worse, but Al hadn't been buried yet. Nick hoped Al would meet Grazie and look after her, that Grazie would look after him.

Nick returned to his car and drove to the town church. He felt he needed to confess his sins before he went home to Jen. Nick wanted to make things right in his mind and needed to unburden himself in order for the process to begin. All of this was from Nick's heart. He wasn't close enough with anyone else to discuss these things. Not with Al gone. He felt it was nobody's business except for his, God's, and the priest's. When he couldn't find the priest, Nick asked the janitor who was sweeping the church if he knew where the priest was. The janitor called on his cell phone, and the priest arrived a few minutes later.

Seeing it was Nick, the priest gave him a hug and asked, "So, Nick, what can I do for you?"

They started walking outside, and Nick explained, "Father, I want you to hear my confession."

They walked around the church while Nick was confessing, and by the time they arrived back where they started, the priest blessed him and sent him on his way. Nick felt this alone was not enough for the betrayal he committed against Jen. But he thought it would help him lead a better life and hopefully keep him away from temptation in the future. He knew what he had done was wrong. But had no intention of telling Jen. It would relieve his conscience while destroying Jen, the one person who had been with him through thick and thin, and the one he loved. This he would never do.

Nick arrived home and was never more excited to be there. Jen met him at the door where he practically swept her off her feet while kissing her in the most romantic way he could think of. He said the investigation was over at the hospital. "Are you ready to go away?"

She said, "Nick, I made the plans. Take me to an island! Marlena said she would look after the kids. I booked tickets for Aruba." She knew Nick well enough to know that after a big job, he wanted nothing more than to sit on a beach and recharge his battery.

The next day, Nick was in the water by 3:00 p.m. Jen knew he was good to stay in there for at least two hours. She opened her book under the hut and began to read. Every once in a while, she would glance into the water to make sure Nick was okay, and there he would was, eyes closed, facing the sun, neck deep in the water with a smile on his face. Jen did not really know what Nick faced at work, but she knew this was the medicine he needed to keep going. Maybe, she thought, she would ask Nick if he still wanted to spice things up in the bedroom. There was no better place to try things out than on vacation.

Thinking about this, she realized that someday she would have to read the book that Nick always said he was going to write.

End

ABOUT THE AUTHOR

Joseph Pasquarosa, born and raised in Newark, New Jersey. He retired as a detective from the Essex County Sheriff's Office headquartered in Newark, New Jersey, after twenty-six years. Working in the streets in the urban cities across the county and assigned to federal task forces throughout his career, the author has a unique and true sense of how to conduct investigations. Arrests, search warrants, phone wiretaps, and court proceedings were all part of daily life. Upon retiring he was hired as lead corporate investigator for a large hospital system. In this capacity, he investigated thefts, drug diversions, workplace violence, and other rules and regulations violations throughout the hospital system. In this novel, the author combined an interwoven story of fictionalized terror with real-life investigative techniques. His storied experience as a detective will give readers accurate insight into the mind of a law enforcement officer, and a unique reading experience given the untapped genre of corporate investigation. The author delights in writing in his spare time and wanted to share with his readers the art of conducting an investigation, along with the twists and turns, and dead ends that can happen when seeking the truth. Furthermore, how seemingly unrelated incidents, like pieces of a puzzle, can become an entire picture.

CPSIA information can be obtained
at www.ICGtesting.com
Printed in the USA
BVHW031334040919
557558BV00001B/20/P

9 781645 448495